A WEDDING
for the
HOME FRONT GIRLS

BOOKS BY SUSANNA BAVIN

The Home Front Girls Series
The Home Front Girls
Courage for the Home Front Girls
Christmas for the Home Front Girls

A WEDDING *for the* HOME FRONT GIRLS

SUSANNA BAVIN

bookouture

Published by Bookouture in 2025

An imprint of Storyfire Ltd.
Carmelite House
50 Victoria Embankment
London EC4Y 0DZ

www.bookouture.com

The authorised representative in the EEA is Hachette Ireland
8 Castlecourt Centre
Dublin 15 D15 XTP3
Ireland
(email: info@hbgi.ie)

Copyright © Susanna Bavin, 2025

Susanna Bavin has asserted her right to be identified
as the author of this work.

All rights reserved. No part of this publication may be reproduced, stored in any retrieval system, or transmitted, in any form or by any means, electronic, mechanical, photocopying, recording or otherwise, without the prior written permission of the publishers.

ISBN: 978-1-83618-376-1
eBook ISBN: 978-1-83618-375-4

This book is a work of fiction. Names, characters, businesses, organizations, places and events other than those clearly in the public domain, are either the product of the author's imagination or are used fictitiously. Any resemblance to actual persons, living or dead, events or locales is entirely coincidental.

*For Elizabeth and Ray,
whose wedding was the first I went to.*

CHAPTER ONE
APRIL 1941

'Are you sure you don't mind?' Andrew asked Sally, a frown creasing his brow.

They were alone in the sitting room at Star House. Spring sunshine poured through the windows between the criss-crossed stripes of anti-blast tape, creating a pattern of diamonds on the carpet. It was a comfortable room with a faded maroon and dark-blue carpet, an upright piano, a pair of armchairs and a matching settee. Sally was glad of the privacy that enabled her darling husband to take her hand, though she had to blink away a couple of unshed tears before she could meet his eyes. She pinned a smile on her face.

'Of course I don't mind,' she assured him in the brightest voice she could manage. She wanted to make this as easy as she could for him. It was essential that he should leave home with memories of how staunch and cheerful she'd been, supporting his decision every step of the way – even though the truth was that she felt churned up with distress and anxiety. In recent weeks she had lain awake at night, dread weighing heavy in her chest, making it hard to breathe.

'Thank you,' said Andrew. 'Thank you for understanding. You always understand.'

'Don't be daft. You don't have to thank me. Now, it's important that you go and say your goodbyes.' She gave him a little push. 'Go on – skedaddle.'

He gave her a swift kiss and, as he moved away from her, it was all she could do to stay put and not take a step after him. She had a smile ready on her face for when he looked back at her from the doorway. He looked back lovingly at her – and then he disappeared. Sally imprinted the moment on her memory, his kind brown eyes, his narrow firm jawline, the boyish smile that added a suggestion of vulnerability to his appearance. Her heart ached at the thought of the loss that lay ahead of her, but she had to be strong, as all the wives and sweethearts of servicemen did.

She imagined Andrew in the hallway, popping on his trilby and patting his jacket pockets to make sure he had his cigarettes. Then she heard the front door open and shut, and she released a soft breath that she hadn't realised she'd been holding. Andrew going off to say his other goodbyes brought them one step closer to the point where they would say goodbye to one another, and she wasn't sure how she was going to bear it – except that this was wartime, and people had to cope with all kinds of things. You just got on with it.

Like when the house they had lived in with Andrew's mother had been bombed. On a night when several dwellings in their road had been hit, the whole of the front of their house had been blown off in the blast, leaving the rooms on show while the smells of soot, rubble and burnt wood mingled with that of cordite. Losing their home had caused all three of them the most awful shock and upset, especially Mrs Henshaw, who had lived there ever since she'd been an eighteen-year-old bride.

But they had coped with the shock, helped immeasurably by dear Mrs Beaumont, the landlady of Star House. Before the war she had been a theatrical landlady – hence the name of the house – but now she accommodated war workers. She had immediately opened up her home to the Henshaw family, able to do so because her three munitions girls had recently departed for a new billet closer to Trafford Park, where the factories were situated.

'It wasn't that we wanted to leave as such,' Stella, one of the munitions girls, had told Sally afterwards. 'Far from it. It was just that we needed to be closer to the factory.' She'd grinned. 'What we really wanted was to carry Star House, complete with dear old Mrs Beaumont, over to the Trafford Park area so that we could all keep on living with her without the hassle of having to travel.'

Sally switched off the wireless. The City of Birmingham Orchestra had been playing in the background while she and Andrew talked. Behind her the door opened, and she turned to find her mother-in-law standing there.

Mrs Henshaw was tall for a woman, with a slim build and blue eyes, her faded brown hair carrying a lot of grey in it. She had an air of capability and efficiency that must be very reassuring to all the people she helped in her capacity as a member of the WVS. Although her features always looked austere in repose, her face softened when she smiled, showing her kind heart. But there hadn't been many smiles recently.

'Has Andrew gone?' she asked softly.

'A minute ago,' Sally answered, sure her mother-in-law was well aware of this.

'I'm surprised you didn't want to go with him.'

There was a suggestion of criticism in that *want to*, and Sally felt it as a little sting. She loved and admired Mrs Henshaw and, until recently, they had got on like a house on fire, but now things were strained. After the Christmas Blitz that had devastated the centre of Manchester, Andrew had announced his intention of joining up, and then Mrs Henshaw had surprised everyone by deciding it was time for her to quit Star House. She had never been truly comfortable there. Oh, she'd been comfortable in the physical sense of its being a clean house, nicely furnished, with tasty meals included; but Mrs Henshaw, a housewife from the age of eighteen, had wanted to assist with the household chores. Mrs Beaumont, however, had put her foot down firmly: she was a professional landlady and she required no help, thank you very much.

Sally and Andrew had tried to persuade Mrs Henshaw to let herself be looked after, telling her she deserved it, but to no avail; and, with Andrew's days at Star House numbered, Mrs Henshaw had arranged to move in with her sister, Andrew's Auntie Vera. Not only that, but she'd wanted – no, more than wanted – she had *expected* Sally to go with her, and she'd been more than a little bit miffed when Sally had wanted to remain at Star House.

Sally knew she had fences to mend with her mother-in-law. She was sure it would be easier after Andrew had gone and the new living arrangements were in place. *After Andrew had gone* – pain clutched at her heart as she replayed the words in her mind. She didn't want to think of it. She wanted to cling to every last second of his presence here.

The front door opened and Lorna, Sally's colleague and friend, called, 'Only me!' A moment later, she entered the sitting room. She was tall and graceful, with glossy hair of darkest brown. Her green eyes and smooth complexion were bright from her brisk walk in the fresh air.

'I've got it,' she announced, smiling.

'Got what?' asked Mrs Henshaw.

'One of the sack-trolleys from the depot,' said Lorna. 'Sally and I are taking Betty's suitcase to the bookshop this afternoon and it's going to be a lot easier to push it than to carry it.'

Betty, who worked alongside Sally and Lorna at the salvage depot, had got married yesterday and was now Mrs Samuel

Atkinson. While the newly-weds were on their honeymoon, Sally and Lorna were going to take Betty's things from Star House to Samuel's bookshop, which had living accommodation in the back and upstairs.

Lorna looked at Sally. 'Shall we go?'

'We shan't be long,' Sally said to Mrs Henshaw and gave her a quick kiss on the cheek. Not so long ago it would have been an affectionate kiss, but now it felt more of a dutiful one. Sally sighed inwardly. Yes, there were definitely fences to be mended.

The two girls headed upstairs. Betty's old bedroom, Marie Lloyd – all Mrs Beaumont's guest rooms were named after the greats of the music hall – was on the first floor at the front, with a view across the old recreation ground, which had now been turned into allotments for the duration of the war.

Behind the privet hedges surrounding the rec were rows of vegetables, some interspersed with glass cold frames. This afternoon, men could be seen making shallow trenches with their hoes and using dibbers to make holes for the seeds. One old boy was busy 'sticking' his young peas, providing twigs to give them support as they grew. Sally knew about that because her dad was very keen on his own veg patch, and loved to talk about it.

Betty's old room had curtains patterned with light-blue and pink flowers with stems of muted green, and a matching pelmet up above. Standing in the corner was the lightweight frame covered in blackout material that had to be fitted over the window every day at dusk. In another corner stood a little washstand with a gingham curtain round its lower half to hide the shelf underneath. As well as a narrow cupboard for hanging things up, there was a set of drawers.

At the foot of the bed was a linen chest and on top of this was Lorna's expensive leather suitcase, which she'd offered to lend to Betty for her move. Lorna's father had made a lot of money and everything Lorna possessed was of the highest quality. The case was already fastened, its straps slotted through the metal buckles, just as Betty had left it before she had set off for her dad's house in Salford, from where she had got married.

'Just a tick,' said Lorna before Sally could grasp the handle. She darted from the room and returned carrying a pretty, royal-blue dress.

'Didn't you lend that to Betty when she took Samuel to meet her dad and Grace?' Sally asked.

'Got it in one.' Lorna dropped the dress on the bed and bent over the case to undo the buckles.

Sally picked up the dress and held it up to admire it. Made of jersey wool, it had a collarless neckline and patch pockets, and the buttoned bodice nipped in at the waist above the skirt's slight flare.

'She looked lovely in it, didn't she?' Sally said admiringly.

Lorna threw open the lid of the case and stood up straight. 'She looked gorgeous.'

'And now you're giving it to her?'

'It looked much better on her than it ever did on me,' Lorna said casually. 'She's got the right colouring for it: blue eyes and golden hair, not to mention having curves in the right places, which is more than I've got. Call it an extra wedding present.'

Sally carefully folded the dress and laid it across the top of the case's contents.

'That's a nice gesture,' she observed with a smile.

She made light of it because Lorna wasn't the sort to do a kindness for the glory of it, but the truth was that this was considerably more than a nice gesture. For Betty, a good dress like this, beautifully made as were all Lorna's clothes, would be a real boon and would last for years.

Sally fastened the suitcase once more and Lorna hefted it from the linen chest.

'Let me help you with that,' Sally offered, but Lorna shook her head with a grin.

'I can manage. It'll pay me back for all the times I swanned about leaving porters and drivers to cope with my luggage.'

Sally picked up the carpet bag containing Betty's emergency running-away things. Most people had one of these, ready to be grabbed at a moment's notice if Hitler's army invaded. *Perish the thought.* They'd had a reprieve from the threat of invasion through the winter months, but once the days had lengthened the thought was back in everyone's minds.

Lorna lugged the bulky suitcase downstairs; she was slender but she was strong. Sally followed with the carpet bag. She put it down in the hallway to put on her hip-length swing-jacket and her felt hat. Then she popped her gas-mask box over her shoulder and grabbed her bag.

The sack-trolley waited on the garden path. Lorna positioned the suitcase and Sally balanced the carpet bag on top. She opened the gate and Lorna tilted back the trolley, paused a moment to ensure nothing was going to fall off, then pushed it onto the pavement.

'You push until halfway, then I'll take over,' said Sally, wanting to be fair.

'It's not heavy,' said Lorna, adding in a teasing voice, 'You're not in charge now, Mrs Salvage Depot Manager.'

Sally responded in kind. 'But that's a salvage depot sack-trolley, so maybe I *should* be.'

Lorna turned her face up to the sun. Though rather cool, it was a pleasant day with a light breeze.

'I hope the weather is as good as this in Southport,' Lorna remarked.

That was where Betty and Samuel had gone for their short honeymoon, lucky them. All Sally and Andrew had had for their own honeymoon had been a single night alone in the Henshaw house while Mrs Henshaw tactfully went to stay elsewhere. Not that Sally begrudged her friends their special holiday. They were a dear couple and they deserved every single piece of happiness that came their way.

'Yesterday was just perfect, wasn't it?' said Lorna. 'Betty didn't stop smiling all day.'

'And Sergeant Hughes looked so proud to be the father of the bride that I thought he might burst,' Sally added with a grin.

'He certainly gave her a wonderful wedding,' said Lorna. 'The deputy chief constable's Daimler, the police choir in the church and the police guard of honour outside, all holding their truncheons aloft.'

Sally smiled, recalling the happy couple walking beneath the archway of truncheons. Betty had looked beautiful in an ivory satin gown with tiny pearls edging the wide scooped neckline, and a semi-fitted bodice that fell to her hips and then flared to floor-length, with a short train. With it she had worn a full-length veil that had floated mistily behind her. Betty hadn't been sure about the veil to start with, worrying that it would look extravagant, as if wartime shortages meant nothing to her, but her friends had been happy to persuade her that it was the perfect veil for her. Mrs Beaumont, with her theatrical connections, had borrowed both the gown and the veil from a wardrobe mistress she was friendly with.

'What about you?' Lorna asked suddenly.

Sally's heart gave a thump. 'How d'you mean?'

'I'm talking about Andrew joining up. Tell me to shove off if you want to, but we're chums and I care about you. If you want to talk about it, I'm here.'

After a moment Sally admitted, 'It's rather a strain. It feels a lot closer all of a sudden.'

'Now that Betty's wedding is out of the way,' said Lorna, understanding.

'It was good having that to concentrate on,' said Sally. 'I don't mean to sound as if it was nothing more than a diversion from the thought of Andrew leaving. I cared terribly about the wedding, for Betty's sake.'

'Of course you did.'

'But at the same time,' Sally said frankly, 'it was a great distraction. There's nothing like a wedding for taking over everyone's thoughts.'

'And now it's over,' said Lorna. 'It's going to be hard for you to say goodbye. I understand how you feel – up to a point. I know it's different for George and me. He's only down in London, whereas goodness only knows where Andrew will end up. All of which means I know my situation is different from yours, but I still understand.'

'It isn't a competition for who has it the hardest,' said Sally, her sensible nature coming to the fore. 'It'll be tough for both of us, in different ways.'

'Tough on the boys too,' said Lorna. 'Sorry. I wanted to make you feel better, but I don't think I've done a good job.'

'Shall I tell you how today feels?' Sally asked in a burst of honesty. Mostly she tried to keep her anguish about Andrew's impending departure under wraps because she didn't want to make a fuss, but now her feelings came bubbling up. 'Today is Sunday the thirteenth but, honestly, with Andrew on the verge of going, it feels more like Friday the thirteenth.'

CHAPTER TWO

Tuesday was a funny sort of day. Betty and Samuel were due home from their honeymoon later and it would be lovely to have Betty back; but at the same time, Sally's skin felt prickly with the awareness that this was Andrew's last day at home before he joined up. And tomorrow, she would be seeing him off. It was deeply unsettling. She knew she could have shared her feelings with Lorna, but just now she thought it better to keep them to herself. Otherwise, she wouldn't be able to prevent the tears.

Although she and Betty were now close friends with Lorna, it hadn't always been that way. To start with, there had been just Sally and Betty working at the salvage depot; then Lorna was brought in to join them. At first, it had seemed like the worst possible thing that could have happened. Lorna hadn't wanted to work there, and had made her feelings only too clear, which had put Sally and Betty's backs up no end. But as they all got to know one another, they had shaken down together and ended up becoming real chums.

At the end of the day, Sally and Lorna followed the usual routine of locking up. As well as securing the building, they had to lock the yard's large front gates before they left via a door in the wooden fence. The yard gates would remain locked only until the fire-watchers arrived for duty late that evening, after which they would stand open all night in case help was required in an emergency should the depot building or the contents of the yard catch fire. The gates weren't open just for the benefit of the depot, either. It worked both ways. The fire-watchers up on the depot roof might have to dash down to help when incendiaries landed on Beech Road, too.

Sally and Lorna walked home together, but they had hardly got through the garden gate before the front door opened and their landlady appeared. Her fashionably waved hair was black, which couldn't possibly be natural, but none of the girls had ever glimpsed even a hint of a root of another shade, let alone a bottle of dye. Mrs Beaumont's blue eyes, which were often quick and assessing, were now bright with pleasure.

'Come on in, girls,' she said. 'We've got visitors.'

Her excitement was infectious. Exchanging glances, Sally and Lorna slid their gas-mask boxes off their shoulders and shrugged out of their jackets.

'I'll hang it all up,' said Mrs Beaumont, gathering everything and shooing them onwards. 'You go into the sitting room.'

Sally stood back to let Lorna go first and heard her exclamation of delight just before she too walked in and found Betty and Samuel sitting together on the sofa. As Samuel politely came to his feet, Betty jumped up and crossed the room in a flash to hug her chums.

'It's so lovely to see you,' she cried, her cheek dimpling for all it was worth.

Behind them, Mrs Beaumont chuckled. She squeezed past, saying, 'I knew you'd be pleased.'

Lorna shook hands warmly with Samuel and kissed his cheek. 'Welcome home.'

'Betty, you do realise that your home is now above the bookshop, don't you?' Sally teased. 'You haven't dragged Samuel here out of habit?'

'Daft ha'porth, of course not,' Betty said as she and Samuel resumed their seats. 'As if I'd forget that.' She gave her new husband an adoring look.

'W-we've already been home to unpack,' said Samuel.

'And then we wanted to come here to say goodbye to Andrew and wish him the best of British luck,' Betty added.

Sally locked her smile in place. She was delighted that their friends had come to say their farewells; she wouldn't have it any other way; but all the same, the reference to Andrew's departure hit her hard for a moment.

Andrew was leaning against the armchair where his mother was seated. He moved his arm and Sally went to him and slid her hand round his waist, leaning into him as his arm gently tightened, holding her close. He kissed the top of her head. It probably looked like a casual gesture, but it made Sally want to cling to him for ever.

'Have you got an early st-start in the morning?' Samuel asked.

Andrew nodded. 'Sally's coming to see me off at the station.'

'Take as long as you need,' Lorna told Sally. 'Betty and I can hold the fort.'

No amount of time could possibly be sufficient for this most painful of farewells, but Sally smiled and said, 'Thanks.'

'How was Southport?' Mrs Beaumont asked Samuel and Betty. 'I haven't been there since before the war. I used to love shopping on Lord Street. It must all be very different now.'

Mrs Henshaw was also familiar with the place, and the two ladies and the newly-weds compared notes. Sally let the conversation wash over her. It was strange to listen to details of sandbags on Lord Street and the damage caused by parachute mines near Alexandra Road, when tomorrow she faced her own heartbreak.

. . .

After the evening meal, Sally and Andrew waited for what might just about be deemed a reasonable amount of time before, holding hands, they went upstairs to their room, and Sally didn't care that Mrs Henshaw, Mrs Beaumont and Lorna must be well aware of what they were going to do when they got there.

They made love with exquisite tenderness. Tears poured down Sally's face, though she didn't realise it until Andrew kissed them away. Afterwards he dozed off and she lay snuggled in his strong, warm arms. How on earth was she supposed to live without him?

In a moment of weakness, she had asked her mother that question and Mum had replied, 'You'll manage exactly as you did before you met him, Sally. You haven't even known him a year yet.'

Sally had felt slapped down but, honestly, what had she expected? Much as her mother loved her, she was nevertheless Sally's greatest critic. Look at her opinion of Sally's job, for example. Before Sally had been moved to the salvage depot, she had been based in the Town Hall, working in the Food Office, handing out advice about rationing and making sure that shopkeepers stuck to the rules. Mum had loved that – her Sally, an *office* girl! But she had regarded her working at the depot as a big step down, even though Sally was now the manager. As far as Mum was concerned, being manager meant Sally should wear a smart jacket and skirt and sit behind a desk, filling in forms and signing letters and telling Betty and Lorna what to do. The fact that Sally wore dungarees and mucked in with whatever tasks needed doing seemed downright wrong to Mum. She'd never actually said the word 'demeaning', but Sally knew that was what she thought.

As for the way in which she had responded to Sally's heartfelt question about life without Andrew – well, it had been dismissive, to say the least, but Sally hadn't fought back. There would have been no point. Mum would simply have said, 'But it's true, Sally. Andrew's your husband and you love him, but that doesn't alter the fact that you didn't know he existed this time last year,' and that might have made her previous words sound less dismissive, perhaps even more reasonable.

Sally wriggled slightly, moulding herself even closer to Andrew. He murmured in his sleep, but didn't waken. She let Mum's words sink in – well, not so much the words as the knowledge of how everything had changed in these past months. She and Andrew had met right at the beginning of August last year, which meant they were still three and a half months short of their first anniversary of his swiftly catching her when she had stumbled on the stairs in the Town Hall. She had been near the foot of the stairs and in the moment of falling had expected to land flat on her face on the foyer's tiled floor, but a strong pair of hands had caught hold of her and steadied her. How clearly she remembered looking up into a pair of warm, intelligent brown eyes; how clearly she remembered the tingles that had shivered across her skin. Her body had known even before her heart did that this was the one and only man for her, now and for always.

As for how she was going to manage without him – well, she just would, that's all. The same as every other wife of a serviceman. There was no choice involved.

You just had to get on with it.

Sally and Andrew were both on duty that night. Andrew was a member of a light rescue squad – as distinct from heavy rescue, which involved the use of machinery – and the squads had the job of digging people out when homes and other buildings were damaged during air raids. It took a lot of training to undertake what they did because they needed to understand both the nature of the building's construction and the way the high explosive could have affected it. As well as the relief and satisfaction of bringing the living to safety, the men also had to face the grim reality of digging out the dead, and also – the mere thought of which left Sally feeling squeamish – collecting body parts.

Sally's own war work was as a fire-watcher, as was Betty's. The two of them shared the same shifts, stationed on the salvage depot's flat roof, binoculars at the ready. When bombs fell and fires started, they had to deal with any small fires in their immediate vicinity, and also report larger fires to the ARP. As well as being responsible for the safety of the depot and its yard, they also kept an eye on a section of Beech Road.

Until tonight, Sally and Betty had always walked from Star House to the depot together, but now, for the first time, Sally made the short journey on her own. It added to her uneasy sensation that a great change that was about to occur in her life.

The sound of the siren lifted into the air, jerking Sally out of her introspection and sending her pelting along Beech Road. She dug in her pocket for her keyring and unlocked the wooden door in the depot's front fence. As she went in, picking up her feet to clear the plank across the bottom, the sound of hurrying footsteps told of Betty's arrival.

Together, they unlocked and unbolted the two big gates and pulled them wide open. Then they rushed across the yard to unlock the door and hurried up to the attics, where a ladder provided access to the roof via a skylight.

Betty climbed up while Sally waited at the bottom, nerves twitching. Tempting as it was to step onto the first rung the moment Betty's feet were out of her way, Sally knew better. One of the first lessons she had learned as a fire-watcher was that two people hurrying up the ladder made it bounce and jolt.

Soon they were both on the roof. Normally they had time to

bring folding chairs, blankets and hot drinks with them, but not tonight. Powerful beams from the searchlights raked the skies.

Turning in a slow circle on the spot, with her binoculars glued to her eyes, Sally said, 'There – over there – oh, Betty.'

A sharp intake of breath beside her told Sally that Betty knew exactly what she was looking at. The scene of tonight's attack was over Salford way. Betty had grown up in Salford and it was where she had lived first with her parents and then with her father and stepmother, until Grace, her father's devious second wife, had sneakily arranged for her to move all the way to Chorlton in the south of Manchester to take on a new job at the salvage depot.

'Do you know if your dad's out on duty tonight?' Sally asked.

'No,' said Betty. 'I lost track of his shifts in the build-up to the wedding.'

'That's only natural,' said Sally, not wanting her friend to feel bad about it.

A distant *whump* reached their ears as a bomb landed on Salford. Betty stifled an exclamation.

'So much for our wonderful honeymoon,' she said, lowering her binoculars to look at Sally. 'There's nothing like coming back to reality, is there?'

Sally also removed her binoculars. 'That doesn't stop your honeymoon being wonderful.'

'I know,' said Betty. 'I'm just upset at seeing what's happening tonight. Are your parents on duty?'

Sally's parents, who were the right sort of age to be the grandparents of the girls she had grown up with, lived in Withington. Mum was a proud member of the Women's Voluntary Service and her darling dad was an ARP warden.

'Yes, they are,' said Sally.

'Samuel is out on duty an' all,' said Betty. He too was in the ARP. 'I'm surprised at you and Andrew being on duty tonight.

Couldn't you have got out of it? Everyone would have understood.'

Sally put on a bright voice. 'I'm sure they would, but Andrew thought it was important to keep to our commitments.' She hesitated before adding, 'Between you and me, his decision for us to go on duty isn't the choice I would have made.' Her throat clogged with tears, making it impossible to continue speaking.

'Of course it isn't,' Betty said sympathetically. 'You want to spend every last moment you can with him.'

Sally nodded. The pain in her throat eased sufficiently for her to say, 'When we were engaged, and my mum said we could only get married if we moved to the countryside for safety, we agreed then that we wanted to stay put and see things through, come what may. It was all about duty and responsibility and doing what was right. Even though we were desperate to get married, we both knew that staying here was more important. Andrew says that being on duty tonight is part of that same commitment.'

'I was about to say, "Just like a man," but that sounds as if I think women are less patriotic or less involved in their war work,' said Betty. 'All the same, it would take a man to come up with a daft reason like that.'

Sally couldn't help smiling and a little of the weight eased from her burdened heart.

'Thanks for understanding,' she whispered, giving her dear friend a hug.

'That's what I'm here for,' said Betty.

CHAPTER THREE

Sally clutched Andrew's hand as they entered Victoria station. She had sworn to herself that she wouldn't cling and make this parting hard for him, but in fact she had to hold on tight simply to ensure they didn't get separated.

The long concourse was packed with passengers, many of them in uniform waiting to board a troop train of such length that it was going to be pulled by two engines. The sharp-sweet scent of steam and smoke wafted in the air and the sound of hundreds of voices lifted up towards the metal-edged glass canopy that covered the vast building, and thousands of echoes poured down again. An announcement was made through the tannoy but it was anybody's guess what was being said.

Andrew had been instructed where to report. As they pressed through the crowds, Sally walked more behind than beside him, taking quick, short steps so as to keep up without treading on the heels of his highly polished shoes.

Around her were the scents of tobacco and Evening in Paris perfume. Here and there, men stood alone reading newspapers, unable to hold the pages open as wide as normal. A young woman with a baby cradled in one arm and a toddler clinging to her other hand made her way through the crush, constantly glancing behind to ensure she was still followed by two older children, each of whom was weighed down with bags. An elderly couple stood together, peering short-sightedly at the timetable information on one of the boards in between the entrances to the platforms. A soldier suddenly turned round, blissfully unaware that the kitbag slung over his shoulder missed Sally by a whisker.

These weren't the final moments Sally had envisaged. She'd known the station would be busy, of course, but she had never pictured it as bad as this. It must be because of the troop train. She and Andrew made their way past the long line of ticket-office windows set in a graceful curve of wood. After that she glimpsed over people's heads the pale-yellow tiles on the exteriors of the station's buffet, restaurant and bookstall.

They had already decided to have a final cup of tea together in the buffet. Now they stopped and looked at each other.

'I hope we can get a table,' said Andrew. He led the way once more. 'Excuse us... Excuse me... Sorry, would you mind...? Thank you.'

They arrived at the buffet door just as it opened and a line of children in uniform streamed out, with a pleasant-faced nun at the front and another bringing up the rear. Andrew held the door for them, then ushered Sally inside. Behind a curved counter with a wood-panelled front, shelves of crockery lined the wall, and a glass display case of scones sat on the counter. Over on the far side of the room, there was a fireplace with a clock above it.

Thanks to the departure of the children, there were several free tables. A girl in an apron, armed with a tray, was already clearing away beakers and tea-plates.

'Go and nab a table,' Andrew said to Sally, 'and I'll fetch the tea.'

Sally chose a small table for two by the wall, wanting to feel as private as possible, though the privacy wouldn't last, not with the other tables filling so quickly. Chair legs scraped on the floor and luggage was stowed supposedly out of the way beside tables.

Andrew returned, carefully carrying two cups and saucers. There wasn't a sugar bowl on the table.

'I've put sugar in.' He set down the drinks and pulled out his chair. 'There's a bowl on the counter under the eagle eye of the lady doing the pouring, and a single teaspoon tied to a block of wood the size of a brick so no one can waltz off with it.'

Sally wasn't surprised. Shortages were biting hard and, like everyone else, the staff here had to hang on to everything they possessed.

'Well,' said Andrew with a sigh.

Sally gazed at him, anxious to savour every last moment, every last look. His brown eyes, always warm when he looked at her, were filled with tenderness. His build was slim but muscular – athletic. Oh, how she yearned for him not to be cannon fodder. He was such a good man, caring and hard-working, a loving son and the best possible husband. He deserved to *live*. Sally's heart was swollen with all the things she wanted to say but couldn't for fear of weeping, which was the last thing she wanted. Nothing must spoil these final moments and Andrew's last memory of her. The tears could flow later, when she was alone.

Reaching across the table, Andrew took her hand. 'I'm sorry about last night,' he said, 'about us going out on duty, I mean. I know it wasn't easy for you.'

'No, it wasn't,' Sally admitted.

'But it helped me to cope,' he told her. 'Being busy, having my duty to focus on, got me through.'

Sally nodded. It made sense, but, as she had told Betty, it wasn't a choice she would have made. Choosing to be apart from Andrew – *never!*

'If it helped you—' She had to stop to clear her throat. 'If it helped you, that's all I care about.'

His fingers gently squeezed hers. There was the slightest suggestion of roughness in his fingertips that came from working with wood. 'You're the best thing that ever happened to me, Sally Henshaw. You know that, don't you? You're beautiful and clever and you have the kindest heart. I admire your dedication to your job and I'm so proud of you. Being married to you has made me feel lucky every single day, and that feeling is never going to stop.'

'I'm going to miss you so much,' she whispered. Andrew's beloved features went out of focus as her eyes swam. She did some fierce blinking. She would *not* succumb to tears. She was determined to tell him how she felt, to send him on his way with her special words warming his heart. 'I shall hate it when you're gone. I'll miss you every single day and I'll never stop wanting you back. You're my whole world. I knew as soon as I met you that you were special, and nothing has ever made me question that. You're a remarkable man, Andrew Henshaw, and I'm proud to be your wife. And I've said this before, but it's important that I say it again, here, now, when you're on the verge of leaving: I understand why you felt impelled to join up. I respect your reasons, and I support the decision you made.'

'I'll never forget our wedding day.' Andrew's voice was throaty. 'When you arrived at the registry office looking so trim and lovely in your blue suit, I knew I was marrying the most beautiful girl in the world. My heart almost burst with pride. You've made me so very happy. When I arrived home every night – whether it was to my mum's house or to Star House – my heart always picked up speed because I knew you were going to be there.'

'Just come home safe to me at the end of the war,' Sally whispered. 'That's all I ask. Even though you're on the verge of leaving, I still can't imagine being parted from you. I can't picture my life without you – I can't picture my*self* without you.'

'It's the same for me.' Andrew's thumb rubbed gently over the palm of her hand. 'You're my world. You're the other half of myself. I'm a better person because of knowing you. I couldn't be happier having you as my wife.'

'And I couldn't be happier having you as my husband.'

Andrew's brown eyes were moist. 'I'm sorry I won't be here to help you celebrate your twenty-first birthday.'

She attempted to make light of it. 'Old Adolf isn't going to give everyone the day off for my benefit.'

'Just think. If your parents had stuck to their original decision not to let us marry while you were underage, we wouldn't have had these wonderful months as man and wife.'

A chill passed through Sally. Just imagine if Dad hadn't found out about Mum's attempt at emotional blackmail. After first refusing to give Sally and Andrew permission to get married, Mum had cleverly offered them the chance to marry if they would agree to move to the safety of the countryside, something they hadn't wanted to agree to because they wanted to stay in Manchester and do their duty. If Dad hadn't overheard that conversation, he would never have written the letter of parental consent for the registrar – and Sally and Andrew would still be unmarried. She shut her eyes briefly. That was all hypothetical. All that mattered was that Dad *had* overheard and he *had* written the letter.

Opening her eyes, Sally forced a smile. 'It didn't happen that way and we have had these wonderful months. It's been the best time of my life, even though we've had air raids and suffered the Christmas Blitz. I can honestly say that I've never been happier.'

'Nor have I,' said Andrew. 'I don't want to leave you. It means the world to me that you can see why I have to go.'

'I know.'

'It matters so much to me that you understand,' he said thickly.

'I do, I honestly do. I'd do anything to keep you at home in your reserved occupation, but it isn't what you want. I respect that. I respect *you*. I'll think of you every single day and I'll pray for your safety.'

'Write me lots of letters. I'll send you the address as soon as I can.'

'I will,' Sally promised. 'In fact…' She drew out an envelope from her handbag. 'Here's the first one. Put it somewhere safe and keep it for later.' With an attempt at light-heartedness, she added, 'Make sure you write back. I'll tell on you to your mother if you don't.'

'You'll go to see her often at Auntie Vera's, won't you? She's taken it hard that you want to stay on at Star House.'

'I know, and I'm sorry about that.'

'It's all right,' said Andrew. Gripping her hand tighter, he spoke with an intensity that startled her. 'I'm on your side – always. You and I will always be on the same side. Never forget that.'

Before she could answer, Andrew glanced across the busy room to the clock above the fireplace.

'I should go,' he said.

A wave of something akin to panic swept through Sally. She made a grab for her handbag and gas-mask box, but Andrew placed a firm hand on top of hers.

'No, you stay here.' His voice was low. 'It's bedlam out there. I don't want our last moment to be in the middle of that crush. This…' He wrenched his gaze from her to look around the buffet before returning his eyes to her. 'This is what I want to remember. A few civilised minutes in a station buffet. The two of us sitting together, talking, remembering.'

Sally could barely believe what she was hearing. She'd expected a few more minutes, and so what if the world outside the buffet would have squeezed and squashed them? She didn't care one jot about a bit of discomfort.

Andrew stood up and she shot to her feet, practically hurling herself into his arms, not caring that they were in a crowded room.

One last kiss – and one more last kiss – then Andrew picked up his things. He gave her a nod, anguish darting across his expression.

Then he headed for the door – and was gone.

Feeling cocooned inside a bubble of shock and distress, Sally joined the queue at the bus stop.

She didn't meet anyone's eyes. If she appeared upset, she didn't want a kindly stranger asking her if she was all right, or she might lose control and give way to a burst of weeping. The bus for Chorlton arrived and, after some passengers had alighted and walked off, the people who were waiting for a different bus stood aside as the Chorlton people edged forward to climb aboard. Sally stepped up onto the platform at the rear of the vehicle, grasping the long pole to steady herself. She made her way along the aisle and slid into a vacant seat, swaying slightly as the bus pulled away.

All the way back to Chorlton, she felt drained. She automatically alighted at the terminus and walked down Beech Road. It was a bright, cool day. In front gardens, newly thinned-out seedlings grew in neat rows. Many gardens also had a corner for a few favourite flowers. Normally, a glimpse of the rich, egg-yolk yellow of alyssum or a waft of hyacinth fragrance would have filled her with delight, but not today.

Mrs Beaumont and Mrs Henshaw had both suggested she call in at Star House upon her return, but she hadn't made any promises, which was now something of a relief. She headed past the end of Wilton Road, a short way down which lay Star House, and made her way to the depot.

As she walked through the open gates into the yard, Lorna and Betty looked round from where they were weighing sacks of metal in the far corner. Both of them wore dungarees, with their hair kept clean and tidy inside headscarves. They immediately stopped what they were doing and came hurrying towards her, concern written all over their faces.

'Come indoors.' Betty's blue eyes were troubled and sympathetic. 'I'll pop the kettle on. You look like you could do with a pick-me-up.'

It was on the tip of Sally's tongue to say she would rather get changed and crack on with her work, but she relented. After the emotional farewell, she was exhausted and her eyes felt gritty, as if she hadn't slept in ages.

While Betty saw to the tea, Sally and Lorna went upstairs to the staffroom. Through the colder months, they had taken their breaks in Sally's office, where a small fire had removed the chill from the air; but now that the temperature was kinder they had moved into this room, which was plain with bare floorboards, housing a table and chairs and a cupboard.

Except the room wasn't quite so bare today.

Sally turned to Lorna in surprise.

'I know it won't make you feel better,' said Lorna, 'but we thought today of all days it would be nice to cheer things up a bit.'

'It's lovely,' said Sally. 'Thank you. Where did you get the tablecloth?'

A twinkle appeared in Lorna's green eyes. 'Star House. Mrs Beaumont said we could borrow it, as long as we give it back after the war.'

That brought a chuckle to Sally's lips in spite of everything.

'Look,' Lorna added. 'An ashtray instead of a saucer.'

'We've gone up in the world,' said Betty as she walked in with the tray.

Lorna and Betty had already moved the table close to the window so that they would be able to see if anyone entered the yard below. The girls sat down.

'How are you feeling?' Betty asked. 'Or is that a stupid question?'

Sally pondered. 'I'm too stunned to feel anything – but that's a good thing, really, because I don't want to feel unhappy.'

'You've had this hanging over you for weeks,' said Lorna. 'Now that it's actually happened, it must be overwhelming.'

Sally made a decision. She sat up straight. 'Now that it's happened, I need to show some backbone. The country would be in a pretty poor way if all the wives whose husbands had gone off to fight collapsed in a heap, feeling sorry for themselves.'

'Don't be so hard on yourself.' Betty paused in the act of lighting a cigarette. 'You'd never do that.'

'I intend to keep busy by working hard,' said Sally.

'Hard*er*, you mean,' said Lorna. 'No one could ever call you a slacker.'

'Mrs Lockwood wouldn't agree with you if she could see us having an impromptu tea break,' Sally said wryly.

Mrs Lockwood, an upright, buxom woman with a parade-ground voice, was a stalwart of the local WVS. A bossy, not to say domineering woman, she had driven the local branch organiser, Mrs Callaghan, downright mad with her attempts to assume as much authority as she could. Mrs Callaghan had then had the clever idea of making her the branch's salvage officer, thus foisting her onto the depot.

She and Sally had had various tussles over who was in charge. Finally, Sally had won the day – or so she and her chums devoutly hoped – when the Lord Mayor himself had written Sally a letter of congratulation in acknowledgement of her contribution to the war effort. This had been after she had helped to unmask a thief in a factory in Seymour Grove. Really and truly, it had been Betty who had done it, but she had insisted upon letting Sally take the credit to pay Sally back for the time when she had done the same sort of thing for her. The Lord Mayor had also been made aware that Sally had in some way assisted in an Air Ministry operation, though he hadn't been furnished with any details, as the matter was extremely hush-hush.

'Let's talk about something happy.' Sally smiled at Betty. 'How's married life, Mrs Atkinson?'

A pretty flush entered Betty's peaches-and-cream complexion. 'Couldn't be better.' She laughed. 'Like all housewives, I'm learning the art of queuing.'

Lorna exhaled a stream of tobacco smoke. 'How do married women manage when they've got full-time war jobs? When do you find the time to queue up for ages outside the grocer's?'

'It's a juggling act,' said Betty. 'The butcher and the grocer both open early, so I can dash there very first thing, then come home and make breakfast. After I leave to come here, Samuel takes Mr and Mrs Kendall whatever meat I've bought for them.'

The Kendalls were an elderly couple whom Samuel, with typical generosity, had taken under his wing. Now they would have Betty looking after their interests, too.

'You'll soon get used to it,' Lorna told Betty reassuringly.

'When I worked on the production at Harris's factory,' said Betty, 'the married women were allowed to do split shifts so that they could have time off during the day to get their shopping done.'

'I suppose if you wanted to do that here...' Sally hadn't given it a thought until now. She had no notion if such a thing would be permitted.

'No, thanks,' Betty said cheerfully. 'I'd have to make up the time by staying later and I don't want to do that.'

'She wants to hurry home to Samuel,' Lorna said with a twinkle in her green eyes.

'Quite right too,' said Sally.

'Seriously, Betty,' said Lorna, 'we miss you at Star House. When is Mrs Henshaw moving out, Sally?'

'The beginning of next week,' said Sally, 'after my birthday. She wanted to stay for that.'

'It's going to be all change at Star House,' said Lorna. 'Two empty bedrooms. I wonder who we'll get instead?'

CHAPTER FOUR

Perching on the pale-blue candlewick bedspread that covered her bed, Deborah carefully wrapped Sally's birthday present in a creased sheet of Christmas paper. It was impossible to buy wrapping paper these days and this piece of paper was from the Christmas before last. Mum had let her have it for Sally because this was her twenty-first.

Twenty-one! And they'd been friends from the cradle. That was what they said when folk asked. They used to say, 'And never a cross word, either,' but they couldn't say that any longer. Last summer there had been a nasty falling-out after Sally, who'd been Deborah's brother Rod's girlfriend since the start of the war, had turned down his proposal. He'd been so sure of her response that he had proposed in public, at his birthday party in the spacious hut that belonged to the bowls club. Sally's refusal had come as a colossal shock to him – and not just him. Everybody had been stunned – both sets of parents, all the neighbours, *everybody*. They had all been so certain that Sally White and Rod Grant were meant for one another.

What had made it even worse was that it had happened at the same time as Sally had met Andrew Henshaw, the true love of her life. Sally had sworn that meeting Andrew and dumping Rod were two entirely separate things, and that she would have finished things with Rod even if Andrew hadn't come along, but nobody had believed her at first, including Deborah. Since then, she had winced many times at the memory of what she had said to her best friend.

But then Rod had shown his true colours, revealing the bully beneath the easy charm. Not only that, but he'd done it in front of the whole street. Deborah and her parents had been horrified. She and Mum had shed enough tears to float a battleship, certain they would never live it down. But presently local gossip had moved on to the next thing, thanks in no small part to the friendship and support Sally had shown Deborah in public. She'd got her mother to resume her friendship with Deborah's mum as well, and the fact that Rod now lived and worked up in Barrow-in-Furness helped, too.

Things were back to normal between Deborah and Sally these days... more or less. Deborah missed having her friend up the road. Sally now lived in Chorlton, while Deborah still lived with her mum and dad in Withington. They didn't work together either, which was sad because, until the falling-out, they'd worked side by side ever since leaving school, first in a shop, then in the Town Hall's typing pool, then lastly in the Food Office, giving out information about rationing and ensuring that all the rules and regulations were followed.

Now, Deborah finished wrapping Sally's present, a white clutch purse with a blue stripe across the width. She hoped Sally would love it. She'd always liked blue, and had even got married in a blue skirt and jacket.

Mum's voice called crisply from the foot of the stairs.

'Deborah! Are you coming to help me with this food or what?'

'What!' Deborah called back, the standard Grant family response.

She ran downstairs and joined her mother. She had the same heart-shaped face and friendly smile as her mum, but Mum's eyes were different. Both her mother and father had brown eyes, though they'd produced two blue-eyed children.

Deborah and Mum were going to make sardine rolls and fish-paste sandwiches to help with the catering for Sally's birthday tea. Mrs White, Sally's mother, was keen for everything to be perfect. She was making meat-paste sandwiches, nut tartlets and leek-and-potato balls. Sally's landlady was going to bring a lemon tart with home-made lemon curd. Mrs White had agonised over the possibility of a fancy birthday cake, but Deborah's mum had persuaded her that it might seem a bit too festive, what with Andrew having gone away just a few days ago, so Mrs White had asked Mrs Beaumont to bake the lemon tart instead.

Deborah made the sandwiches while Mum saw to the sardine rolls, which were the wartime equivalent of sausage rolls and could be eaten hot or cold. They were enjoyable enough, but nowhere near as tasty as real sausage rolls, in Deborah's opinion.

'Lay a damp tea-towel over the plate to stop the bread drying out,' Mum said when Deborah finished the sarnies. She opened the oven door and slid the tray of sardine rolls inside. 'They'll be ready in twenty minutes, but remind me to check them after fifteen. You know how fierce this oven can be.'

'It's going to be a delicious tea.' Deborah licked her fingertip, dabbed it on a tiny flake of sardine still in the can and popped it into her mouth.

'I hope Sally has a good time,' said Mum. 'It's not five minutes since Andrew left. She'll miss him even more, today of all days.'

Deborah felt sorry for the anguish her friend must be going through. 'We'll all make sure she has a lovely time.'

'She'll love the bag you got her,' said Mum. 'It's very stylish.

I hope she likes the taffeta rosettes from Dad and me. I wanted to get something special, but it's not easy finding gifts in the shops now.'

'They'll look lovely attached to a hat,' Deborah assured her. 'I'm glad you got her something.'

'Of course I did, you daft ha'porth,' said Mum. 'She's been like a second daughter to me, in and out of this house like she lived here.' She smiled reminiscently. 'Until marriage took her over to Chorlton.'

'You make it sound like she's gone to Timbuktu,' Deborah said with a grin. 'She's only gone a couple of miles or so up the road.'

'I miss the way things *used* to be.' Mum released a little sigh. 'Sally's gone. Rod's gone and we've never even met his wife.' Then she laughed at herself, cheering up. 'But I've still got *you* here, and that's perfect.'

She gave Deborah a hug and Deborah hugged her back, but at the same time her heart went plummeting into her shoes. The very last thing she wanted to do was hurt her mum, but the truth was that she'd got itchy feet. Now that Sally's chum Betty had got married and moved out of Star House, Deborah was longing to move there and have Betty's old room. Living here at home was all well and good, but this was wartime and, all around her, she could see girls acting with independence they would never have enjoyed before the war.

Now, that was what she wanted, too.

A little while later, Deborah and her parents walked the short way along the road to the Whites' house. It was a bright, sunny afternoon, and quite warm, although those cloudless skies promised a cool evening.

Deborah and her mother each carried a plate of party food. Deborah wore a coral-pink rayon-crape dress, its V-neck, cuffs and slender belt all in cream. She had slept in her rollers last night and her dark-brown hair was now attractively waved. She hoped it would hold its shape; it didn't always, because it was fine. Last year, she'd had a go at curling the ends of her hair at the back round a sanitary pad, something she'd heard of as a good way to create a plump and lasting roll of hair; but Mum had been outraged, and that had been the end of that.

Dad rang the bell and Mr White answered the door. The sweet scent of pipe tobacco clung to him and his kindly blue eyes crinkled at the edges as he welcomed them. He had bushy eyebrows, which Rod had privately joked to Deborah were to make up for the lack of hair on the top of his head. Mr White was heaps older than Deborah's father, who, though of no more than medium height, carried himself well and had a full head of light-brown hair.

As the Grants entered the narrow hallway, Mrs White appeared in the kitchen doorway at the end. She had the same hazel eyes as Sally. Her hair was, as always, neatly styled. It had been salt-and-pepper while Deborah and Sally were growing up, but there was no disguising how grey it was these days.

'We're a bit early,' Mum said cheerfully, 'but I wanted to bring our contribution along before Sally gets here.'

'Bring it through,' said Mrs White, standing aside to let Deborah and her mother into the kitchen. She moved one or two plates on the table to make space. 'Thanks for doing this.'

'It was our pleasure,' said Mum.

'There's more food coming,' said Mrs White, 'including the lemon tart.' She pressed her lips together, looking uncertain.

'You're not still worrying about whether you should have had a cake instead, are you?' Mum asked. 'We talked that over. More than once,' she added with a smile.

That made Sally's mum smile too. 'You're right. I'm being daft. I just want everything to be perfect. It's not every day your daughter turns twenty-one.'

'Sally will love the tart,' said Deborah. 'She'll appreciate the whole spread.'

Mrs White took off her apron and patted her hair. 'How do I look?'

'Very nice,' said Mum. 'I like that bit of lace trim you've sewn to your collar.'

Deborah didn't. She thought it made Mrs White look even older. She had often thought that, out of herself and Sally, she was the lucky one to have a mother who was of an appropriate age. Mrs White was old enough to be Mum's mother. As a youngster, Deborah had always loved it when Mum had said that Sally was a second daughter to her; but, when Mrs White had said the same thing of Deborah, it had been nice, of course, but also a bit strange because, really and truly, Mrs White was old enough to be her grandmother. Deborah had always secretly hoped that other people would never mistake her for the Whites' daughter. She knew that was horrid and ungrateful of her, but she couldn't help it.

'Where should I put Sally's presents?' she asked.

'In the parlour, please,' said Mrs White.

Deborah left the two mothers and went into the parlour, which smelled of pipe tobacco and lavender furniture polish. Although this house had the same layout as her parents' house, it felt different because Mrs White had her parlour at the back, unlike Mum and practically everyone else in the street, who had theirs in the front. According to Sally, her mother liked her privacy and wouldn't have liked having passers-by glancing in through the front windows and seeing the family, but Deborah thought that not overlooking the road outside gave the Whites' parlour a feeling of isolation – not that she would ever say so.

Soon more neighbours arrived, bringing food and extra chairs. Mrs Evans from across the road brought two bottles of her home-made elderflower cordial. Deborah helped to carry plates of cucumber sandwiches, fish croquettes, ginger fingers and savoury potato biscuits through to the kitchen.

'We're ready for the birthday girl,' said Mrs O'Keefe from next door.

'When are the Chorlton lot due?' Dad asked.

The 'Chorlton lot' arrived a few minutes later. When Sally appeared, everyone wanted to be the first to greet her. She was a good-looking girl with tawny-hazel eyes and neat features in a heart-shaped face. Her hair was fair but not in a light, creamy-coloured way. Deborah had heard Mrs White say more than once, 'Our Sally is a dirty blonde,' but after Sally had met Betty she'd told Deborah that Betty had said she was a *dark*-blonde, which sounded much more flattering. Deborah wished she'd dreamed it up herself.

Sally was followed into the room by her mother-in-law. Then came Betty. Deborah had felt interested in her ever since she had acted as Sally's other bridesmaid last year, even though she had been a new friend. She was a pretty girl with a curvy figure, her golden hair falling in an enviable tumble of curls. She was wearing a rather gorgeous royal-blue dress that made her eyes appear even bluer. With her was her new husband, Samuel Atkinson, a good-looking, bespectacled, hazel-eyed chap with an air of gentleness and modesty about him.

After the Atkinsons, Lorna entered the room. She was a real stunner, with her gleaming dark-brown hair and green eyes. Deborah had read about the occasional green-eyed girl in a romantic novel, usually the heroine, but it wasn't until she had first seen Lorna that she'd come across green eyes in real life.

With Lorna was Mrs Beaumont, the landlady of Star House. Deborah's pulse sped up a bit. She wanted to get Mrs Beaumont on her own so she could ask about Betty's old bedroom.

There was also a middle-aged couple who must be Andrew's auntie and uncle, the ones Mrs Henshaw was going to move in with. Mrs Henshaw and her sister couldn't have looked more different. Mrs Henshaw was tall and thin and exuded an air of competence. Her features were rather stern, though they relaxed when she smiled. Her sister, on the other hand, was shorter and rounder, with apples in her cheeks and a warm smile.

Sally was smiling too. If she had shed any tears earlier for Andrew on this special day, it didn't show. She looked trim and pretty in the forget-me-not blue suit she had worn at her wedding.

'These will be my best clothes for years to come,' she said, 'so I'll be wearing them every chance I get.'

'Which is more than can be said for me and my wedding dress,' Betty chimed in. 'I got married in traditional white,' she added for those who didn't know.

'Complete with full-length veil,' said Lorna. 'She looked beautiful.'

'The photographs will be ready next week.' Betty's blue eyes glowed. 'My dad is having them put in an album.'

'Oh, you've only just got wed, then?' Mrs Evans asked with great interest.

'On Saturday last week,' said Sally. 'Lorna and I were bridesmaids.'

'How lovely,' said old Mrs Uttley.

'Now then,' said Mrs White. There was laughter in her voice, but her eyes were definitely not laughing. 'Don't let's forget what today's special occasion is.'

Betty caught her breath in dismay. 'I never meant—'

'Of c-course you didn't.' Her husband slipped a protective arm round her.

'Let's give Sally her presents,' said Mr White, 'and get this party started properly.'

Everyone watched as Sally, a little embarrassed by all the attention but happy as well, opened her gifts. A pretty necklace from her parents, a powder compact from her mother-in-law. A handbag mirror from Lorna, a manicure-set in a little wallet from Betty and Samuel, a propelling pencil from Mrs Beaumont. There were small gifts from the neighbours – a hanky with an 'S' embroidered on one corner, some chocolate, a headscarf.

Sally was thrilled with the rosettes from Mum and Dad.

'They're for you to attach to a hat,' Mum explained.

'You'll look a right bobby dazzler,' said Mrs Evans with a smile.

With a glance at Deborah, Sally started to unwrap the Christmas paper. She exclaimed in delight when the clutch-bag was revealed.

'Thank you.' She gave Deborah a hug. 'I love it.' She looked around the room, her eyes shining. 'Thank you, all of you.'

'You haven't finished yet,' said Mr White, producing a small flat parcel wrapped in newspaper. 'This is from Andrew. He gave it to me to give you today.'

Sally looked startled and flustered.

'You don't have to open it now if you don't want to,' said Mrs White.

'Yes, she does,' said Mrs O'Keefe. 'We all want to see what it is. Don't pretend you don't,' she added when everyone looked at her.

After an emotional moment, Sally opened the present and revealed a book.

'Oh,' she breathed. 'Poetry.'

'Love poems,' said Betty.

Sally looked at Samuel. 'From your shop?'

Samuel nodded. 'Yes, but he ch-chose it himself. I d-didn't help him.'

Sally's hazel eyes brimmed with tears as she slipped the book inside her new clutch-bag. 'I'll put it in here for safekeeping and look at it properly later.'

She dabbed her eyes, and everybody murmured words of sympathy and affection, then a couple of conversations started up.

'Last week I had the pleasure of attending Betty's wedding,' said Mrs Beaumont, 'and today I'm honoured to be included in Sally's coming-of-age celebration.'

'It must be one of the joys of having girls billeted on you,' said Mrs White, 'getting to share all their special moments.'

'You must have an empty room now that Betty's got married,' said Mum.

'And next week it'll be two,' said Mrs Beaumont, 'because Mrs Henshaw will be leaving to live with her sister.'

'Two empty bedrooms,' said Mr White, removing his pipe from his pocket. 'That's the answer to the billeting officer's dream, that is.'

'I'm hoping not to involve him,' said Mrs Beaumont quickly. 'I'd much prefer to choose my own lodgers.'

Good. That was exactly what Deborah wanted to hear. But after the way Mrs White had been vexed when Betty had mentioned her wedding, Deborah couldn't possibly say anything this afternoon – could she? No, she couldn't. She'd imagined this would be a good opportunity to nab Mrs Beaumont, but now it was obvious she'd been mistaken. There were too many people. What if she ended up being overheard and stealing Sally's thunder?

Deborah knew her dream would have to wait a little longer, though that wouldn't be easy when she was so clear in her mind about what she wanted. She had grown up taking for granted, as all girls had, that she would live at home with her parents until she got married, but now she longed for something else in between.

Independence. Freedom. A wartime billet.

A room in Star House.

CHAPTER FIVE

The day after Sally's party, Lorna set off from the depot at a brisk pace, her hands protected by thick gloves as she pushed the sack-trolley along the path that cut diagonally across the middle of the recreation ground from the front gate on Beech Road over to the other one in the far corner, on Cross Road, opposite the entrance to Wilton Close.

As she passed between the allotments, she breathed in the pungent aroma of freshly turned earth and noticed with pleasure the young leaves on the trees around the edges of the rec. The sunshine brightened everything it touched and the feel of it on her skin was a pleasing sensation.

She made her way to the main road and headed for Samuel's bookshop, not far from the library, where she was going to collect some boxes of old books for salvage. Samuel's shop was a receiving point for masses of second-hand books, which he and Betty carefully sorted through and boxed up to be sent off to bombed-out libraries around the country as well as to the troops overseas. The tattiest volumes went for salvage, and it was the latest consignment of these that Lorna had come here to collect.

Standing in front of the shop door, she pressed down the thumb-plate that lifted the latch. As she pushed the door open, the little brass bell jingled cheerfully above her head. She turned her back to the doorway, pulled the sack-trolley up the step and walked backwards into the shop, taking care because there were more bookcases in here than there used to be, now that Samuel had turned the back room from a storeroom-cum-office into a proper parlour for him and Betty to live in.

'Only me!' Lorna sang out.

Samuel appeared and Lorna smiled to herself. With his tweed jacket with elbow-patches, his specs and his serious but sensitive face, he couldn't look more bookish if he tried.

'Good morning,' he greeted her. 'You're here for the s-salvage. I'll get the boxes.'

'D'you mind if I follow you?' Lorna asked, leaving the sack-trolley where it was. 'I've been hearing how smart the parlour looks now, and I'd love to see it.'

Samuel stood aside, waving her ahead of him, and Lorna entered the Atkinsons' parlour.

'Oh my,' she said. 'This is different to how it used to be.'

Bookcases had previously eaten up the floorspace, but now those that remained were out of the way against the wall. Over by the fireplace stood a pair of armchairs with a low table between them. On the other side of the room was a sideboard and a gateleg table with a pair of dining chairs. Other pieces – a standard lamp, a green-baize-covered card table – added to the cosiness, as did a selection of ornaments and a vase of pink tulips.

'I can see why Betty is so thrilled with it,' Lorna said admiringly.

'I w-wanted to please her,' Samuel said simply.

What a good man he was. So loving. Betty was a lucky girl – but undoubtedly Samuel would say he was the lucky one. Lorna smiled to herself. She knew all about being lucky. Just imagine how empty her life would feel now if she and George hadn't got back together. It didn't bear thinking about. Her life simply hadn't felt right without him. Now that they were reunited, she could admit that to herself.

Three boxes of books for salvage were stacked in the corner.

'C-can you manage them all at once?' Samuel asked.

'If I'm careful,' said Lorna. 'I'll need to avoid any bumps as I go. I'll pop the trolley outside and we can load it on the pavement.'

When she'd eased the sack-trolley down the step onto the pavement, Samuel was already behind her with the first box. He placed it on the metal shelf at the foot of the trolley.

Lorna would have followed him indoors but he said, 'No, I'll f-fetch them,' so she let him do the gentlemanly thing, contenting herself with stacking the boxes in the steadiest way. She smiled to herself. Samuel was such a decent, good-hearted chap. It was impossible not to like him. Lorna's heart gave a little bump. Samuel and Betty's obvious happiness and the way they each put the other one first made her want to picture her own future. She and George had agreed to take things steadily and not rush into anything, which was important after the way things had gone disastrously wrong for them first time round.

But even so, the temptation to imagine her future couldn't be denied...

On her way back to the depot, Lorna got caught in a light shower, but an ironmonger let her shelter on his premises among the fenders and fire-irons, copper goods and coal-boxes, birdcages and boot-scrapers. As she looked around, she saw that the quantity of goods was obviously depleted. Would he be able to get more? Lorna didn't like to ask, but she rather suspected not.

As soon as she saw a rainbow arching overhead she set off

once again, and was soon back at the depot. Indoors, Sally and Betty were sorting fabrics into piles.

'Good, you're back,' said Sally.

'I've been admiring your new parlour,' Lorna told Betty, who beamed, which made her dimple pop into view.

'I *love* it,' she said happily and her blue eyes shone. 'Samuel has done everything he can to make it comfortable.'

'So I saw,' Lorna agreed.

'I appreciate having it downstairs an' all,' said Betty. 'If Samuel had wanted to keep the room as a storeroom, we'd have had to use one of the upstairs rooms as our parlour and that wouldn't have been half so convenient for the kitchen.'

'Having the parlour on the ground floor must feel more natural,' said Sally.

'What are you two up to?' Lorna cast her glance over the various piles of fabric in front of her but couldn't make head or tail of them.

'Linen and calico for Admiralty charts,' said Sally, pointing. 'White shirt-collars for five-pound notes. Good-quality rags for army uniforms, poor-quality rags for mattress stuffing.'

Lorna grinned. 'It's a real education working for you.' She looked at her wristwatch. It was coming up for dinnertime. 'How about us all having our midday meals together this week? You've had a big change in your life, Sally, and a good natter with your chums will help see you through.'

Sally smiled at her, her tawny-hazel eyes softening. 'Thanks, that's a champion idea. I could do with a good chinwag.'

Soon the three of them were upstairs, seated at the table in the staffroom, a cup of tea beside each plate and the ashtray in the middle. Lorna and Sally peeled back greaseproof paper. Mrs Beaumont had made sardine sandwiches for Lorna and vegetable rolls for Sally. She always packed different meals for them to give them the option of sharing.

Betty had brought an oven-bottom muffin with cheese and tomato.

'More tomato than cheese,' she said ruefully, 'but you're both welcome to some if you want to do swapsies.' She picked up the knife and cut the muffin into three.

'How are you feeling, Sally?' Lorna asked when the food had been shared out and they settled down to eat. 'Don't think you have to be brave about it. Tell us the truth.'

'Well, things are feeling pretty grim for me just now with Andrew away until goodness knows when,' said Sally, 'but the last thing I want to do is take the gloss off your happiness, Betty. This is a wonderful time for you, being newly married. After being able to spend the early months of my marriage with my husband at home, I know how lucky you must feel.'

Betty paused in the act of raising her cup to her lips. 'It must be so hard for all the wives who are on their own,' she said quietly.

'And the girlfriends,' Sally said, looking at Lorna.

'My situation is a bit different,' said Lorna. 'George isn't away overseas. He's in London at the War Office, so we'll be able to see one another from time to time, even have the odd telephone call.'

'You must get something organised soon,' said Sally.

'Actually, I want my first visit to be to Lancaster,' Lorna said, and the others nodded understandingly. 'I know my father is making a good recovery because Mummy says so in her letters, but I still need to see him. It's as if I need to make sure.'

'That's understandable,' said Betty. 'I'd be the same if it was my dad.'

Lorna's family had undergone the most appalling shock some weeks earlier when her father, the stiff-necked, domineering Hector West-Sadler, had become paralysed after drinking a glass – a *single* glass! – of tainted alcohol made on the sly by criminals taking advantage of the wartime shortage of the real thing. When the paralysis had first happened, the doctors had been unable to say whether it was temporary or permanent. It really had been a case of wait and see. Fortunately, it had turned out to be temporary.

'I know how lucky he is to have recovered,' Lorna told her friends. 'You can be killed by drinking hooch, or you might lose your sight or become brain damaged.' She shuddered. 'The men who make the stuff are *evil*. It's the only word for them. Sorry,' she added wryly. 'This isn't exactly the cheery conversation I imagined when I suggested eating together.'

'The main thing is your father is doing well,' said Betty.

'Very true,' Lorna agreed as she opened the next greaseproof packet to find three fruit turnovers. Dear Mrs Beaumont had, of course, sent one for Betty, too. She offered them to her chums.

'Thanks,' said Sally, taking one. 'Do your parents know yet that you're back together with George?'

'Not yet.'

'You can tell them when you see them,' said Betty. 'It might be better to do it in person.'

Lorna smiled, her pulse quickening. 'As a matter of fact, I'm hoping George can come with me to Lancaster, War Office permitting, so it might be wise to share the news with my parents in a letter first. Then Daddy can get his explosions over and done with before we arrive.'

'Do you think he'll be angry?' Sally asked, her eyes clouding in concern.

'It's normal for Daddy to blow his top,' Lorna said airily. She respected her father as much as ever, but her wartime experiences meant she wasn't as in awe of him as she used to be. 'Explode first, think afterwards: that's my father for you. But that's enough about me.'

'We don't have to stop talking about the George situation,' said Betty. 'We understand how much it matters to you.'

'Believe me, you'll find yourselves fully immersed in it after the visit to Lancaster. I'll have the pair of you reliving every single moment and examining in microscopic detail every word that was spoken. There'll come a time when you're *begging* to talk about something else – anything else.'

Betty laughed, which made her dimple appear. 'Then let's talk about Sally's birthday party. That was such a lovely occasion. You seemed to enjoy it, Sally, though you must have been feeling sad underneath.'

'That pretty well sums it up,' Sally admitted. 'I was very touched by all the trouble everyone went to.'

'I'll tell you something that struck me about it,' said Lorna. 'I thought how lucky you were to spend your twenty-first surrounded by people you've known all your life. There must be heaps of girls nowadays celebrating all their special events with people who are new to them, whom they've met because of the war and the way so many people have been shunted around all over the place to do their war work.'

'Like us,' said Betty.

'I don't think you can include me in that,' said Sally. 'I was only shunted here from just up the road in Withington.'

'Actually,' Lorna answered, 'I think it applies to all three of us. We're all here at the salvage depot because of the war.'

'That's true,' said Sally. 'But for the war, you'd still be up in Lancaster.'

'Living in Lancaster under my father's thumb,' said Lorna. 'My move hasn't just been geographical. It's also been very much to do with growing up. I've moved on in an entirely personal sense from the girl I was brought up to be. And without the war, Betty would still be in Salford.'

Betty nodded. 'I'd still be working behind the counter at Tucker's. I would never have lost my job if it hadn't been for the war because there wouldn't have been any rationing. I'd still be living with Dad and Grace, knowing that Grace really hoped to get me out of the house for keeps.' She looked at Sally. 'But even without the war, you'd still have moved over here to Chorlton, wouldn't you? You'd still have met Andrew.' She grinned and her dimple popped. 'You'd still have fallen down those stairs straight into his loving arms.'

'Yes,' Sally agreed, 'because Deborah and I were already working at the Town Hall before the war.' Then she frowned a little and shook her head. 'Actually, no. I mean, yes, I'd have been in the typing pool at the Town Hall, but Andrew wouldn't have been there that day. He came to the Town Hall because of a wartime youth club he used to run.'

'So you'd have taken a tumble down those steps,' said Lorna with a grin, 'and ended up with a lump the size of an egg on your bonce.'

'Instead of a husband,' Betty added, chuckling.

'Give me the husband any day,' said Sally, smiling. 'And the mother-in-law,' she added.

'Even though things have been on the cool side since you had to tell her you didn't want to move with her?' Betty asked and Sally nodded.

'Even though,' Sally agreed softly.

'I hope Mrs Henshaw's move has gone smoothly today,' said Lorna.

'I'm sure it will have,' said Sally. 'It's not as though there's all that much to pack when you've been bombed out and lost almost everything.'

'I hope she'll be happy in her new billet,' said Betty.

'Bound to be,' Sally answered. 'She and Auntie Vera are going to divvy up the housework and the cooking.'

'The one thing Mrs Beaumont would never agree to – understandably,' said Lorna. 'Will it feel strange to you, Sally, not having Mrs Henshaw there? You've lived with her since you got married, haven't you?'

'Before that,' said Sally. 'I used to be the lodger. And yes, I will miss her, but...' Her voice tailed off and she looked at them earnestly, her hazel eyes serious.

'You know it won't go any further,' Betty assured her.

Sally nodded. 'Her leaving is a bit of a relief, to be honest. She was so upset when I said I'd be staying at Star House. She saw it as my family duty to go with her – the two Mrs Henshaws staying together no matter what.'

Betty placed her hand over Sally's for a moment. 'I, for one, am glad you stuck to your guns.'

'And Andrew is happy for you to keep on living at Star House,' Lorna added. 'Your happiness is what matters to him.'

'That's right,' Betty agreed. 'He adores you. Just look at how he got you that book of love poems.' She sighed. 'That was so romantic.' With a breathy little laugh, she added, 'I don't know how I kept it secret from you.'

'I'm glad you did,' Sally said warmly. 'It was the perfect surprise.' Tears sprang into her eyes. 'The party was wonderful. Everybody was so kind. I wasn't exactly in the mood to celebrate, but I ended up having a lovely time.'

'Something good to look back on,' said Betty.

'And I loved my presents,' Sally said with a smile.

'Especially the book of love poems?' Lorna prompted.

'Andrew wrote a special message inside it.' Sally's cheeks went pink. 'In the spirit of wartime rationing, I'm going to read one poem a day. When I reach the end, I'll turn back to the beginning and start again. I'll do that every day until Andrew comes home.'

None of them voiced it, but the question hung in the air between them. Lorna and Betty exchanged a look that was filled with the fondness and sympathy they both felt for their friend.

How many times would Sally read her precious book of love poetry before the war finally came to an end?

CHAPTER SIX

Anxiety made Deborah feel restless. Should she ask her parents for permission first? But what if they said no? They expected her to stay at home. Actually, they'd probably never given it a thought. They just took it for granted that she would – but things were different now. All over the country, plenty of girls had left home because of wartime jobs, and Deborah longed for her own slice of independence. She had started to think about it last year when Sally had left home.

Now, as she sat on the crowded bus on her way to work on Tuesday, Deborah frowned over the problem as she gazed unseeingly out of the window. She knew her parents weren't going to like it, but she badly wanted this to happen; she had started wanting it several months ago. Would Mum and Dad stand in her way? It felt almost inevitable that they would, but that didn't stop her yearning for independence. She hated the thought of missing out when other girls were benefiting from this new way of life.

She got off the bus and made her way to the Town Hall. It always gave her a boost to see the old building still in one piece, with its Gothic architecture and handsome clock tower. Plenty of other well-known landmarks had been severely damaged or destroyed outright in the Christmas Blitz. The Free Trade Hall was no more. Cross Street Chapel and Victoria Buildings were gone. Chetham's Hospital had sustained much damage. Many of the warehouses along Piccadilly had burned to the ground. Blast those Jerries.

It was important to remember the buildings that had survived. You could drive yourself mad if all you did was concentrate on the worst of what had happened. The Midland Hotel, which was a famous landmark, had survived untouched – mind you, there had been a rumour at the time that this was because Herr Hitler fancied it as his headquarters in Manchester, though there was no way of knowing if this was true.

Other buildings that had survived included Central Library, the railway stations and theatres and other hotels, including those on Lily Street. Deborah thought of the Lily Street hotels in particular because, when she and Sally were youngsters, their parents had taken them to Dunbar's Hotel each December for afternoon tea as a special treat before they went to the pantomime at the Palace. Looking back, those outings had been a funny sort of mixture. The afternoon tea of dainty sandwiches and tiny cakes had made the two girls feel very grown-up – and then they had attended the pantomime and joined in with every piece of audience participation and all the singing along, as happy and enthralled as all the other children in the auditorium.

She entered the Town Hall and crossed the lofty foyer's chessboard-tiled floor, heading for the staircase on which Sally had stumbled into Andrew's arms. Deborah thought of that sometimes. It had changed the course of Sally's whole life. Deborah, right beside her when it happened, hadn't had the first idea.

She made her way upstairs to the office where she had once

worked with Sally and now worked with Miss Rushton. That said it all, really. Although she and Sally had called one another Miss Grant and Miss White in front of other people, they always used first names when it was just the two of them, as befitted their status as lifelong chums. There was no such informality with Miss Rushton. She was pleasant enough and easy to work with, but they had never got on to Deborah and Rosalind terms.

Miss Rushton was already at her desk when Deborah walked in, and she looked up with a smile. She was a pretty, fair-skinned redhead with a smattering of freckles across her nose. She had a delicate, porcelain beauty that gave her the appearance of fragility.

'Morning,' she greeted Deborah. 'I'm off out soon. I've got some tests to do in Stockport, but I'll be back in ample time for you to go and do your advice desk.'

'Fine,' Deborah said, hanging up her jacket and gas-mask box. She put her handbag in her desk drawer and her hat on the shelf.

The two of them took turns to administer the tests, which involved visiting various grocers and butchers and spinning a sob story to try to get the shopkeeper to break the rationing rules. If he did, he'd find himself up before the magistrate. Sally had always disliked that aspect of the work, but Deborah took it in her stride and so did Miss Rushton. It was important to make sure that shopkeepers followed the rules.

Deborah spent part of the morning typing up reports for her boss, Mr Morland. She wasn't his secretary, but she and Sally had done a typing course at night-school back when they were still shopgirls. That had been Sally's idea. She'd had ambition even then, and their typing skills had enabled them to find jobs in the Town Hall's typing pool. They had been moved to the new Food Office at the start of the war. Sally had always displayed initiative when it came to work. As a Food Office clerk, she had collected recipes and shared them with the women she met during her advice sessions, even though that wasn't part of her job. No wonder she had ended up as the manager of the salvage depot in Chorlton. Deborah was proud of her.

After finishing her typing, Deborah read it through, checking for errors. When she had finished, she carried on bending her head over the sheets of paper, pretending to be reading when, really, she was thinking about the dazzling possibility of moving into Star House. If only she could get round her parents…

Then, dragging her mind back to where it ought to be, she put together a selection of leaflets to take with her that afternoon. Sometimes she or Miss Rushton visited a citizens' advice place to hand out rationing information; there was also a weekly session held here in a room on the ground floor. Helping housewives keep up to date was important. Everyone was still getting used to the meat ration having been reduced to the value of just one shilling a week.

Deborah liked her job, and she enjoyed the company of the other office girls in the canteen. Sometimes some of them went out dancing together. Today, as she sat with Miss Hill and Miss Brelland from Transport, chatting about films and fashion, she couldn't help imagining having conversations like this on a daily basis at home – and by 'home' she meant in a billet.

She found herself telling her colleagues of her hopes. The words spilled out, making her ambition feel more real.

'I've been wondering about leaving home and moving into a billet for single girls,' she said.

'Some hope!' Miss Hill responded at once. 'Decent billets are kept for war workers living miles away from home.'

'The place I'm thinking of is Star House – you know, where the landlady took in Sally Henshaw and her family after they were bombed out,' said Deborah, and her listeners nodded.

'One of the other girls has left because she's got married, and Sally Henshaw's mother-in-law moved out yesterday to live with her sister in Seymour Grove, so there are two rooms going begging.'

'Not for long if the billeting officer has anything to do with it,' said Miss Brelland, a lovely-looking girl with red-gold hair.

'Mrs Beaumont wants to fill the rooms herself,' said Deborah quickly. 'The thing is, I would kick myself afterwards if I didn't take a crack at this opportunity.'

'You'd better get your skates on, then,' Miss Hill advised. 'Didn't you once say that Mrs Henshaw is a stalwart of the Chorlton WVS? The WVS and the billeting officers are hand in glove. If Mrs Henshaw has changed her address, you can bet the billeting officer knows all about it.'

Deborah's heart was beating hard as warmth rushed into her cheeks. It was time to stop thinking about it and actually *do* something. But what if she was too late? She couldn't bear the idea of the billeting officer stepping in. She wouldn't have a hope.

If she was going to have a chance of making this happen, she had to act right away.

Deborah spent the afternoon in a state of mild panic. Every time she pictured missing the chance to move into Star House, her insides quivered. She knew full well that this was her one and only opportunity to leave home. Her parents would never let her move in with strangers.

The advice session that afternoon was to be held in a church hall near the big crossroads in Fallowfield. Before the war it would have been used for committee meetings, parish business and so forth. Now, it was full every day and every evening with all kinds of war business. As usual when Deborah came here, the Citizens Advice Bureau had a trestle-table at one end of the room and people with problems and enquiries awaited their turn, sitting on a line of wooden chairs along the wall.

Heels tapping on the bare floorboards, Deborah walked the length of the hall to where her own table was waiting for her. She arranged the pamphlets she had brought with her, then smiled at the first woman in her own queue to show she was ready.

The woman came forward and sat down.

'I'm Miss Grant from the Food Office,' said Deborah. 'How can I help you?'

'It's this business about golden syrup being on the ration, miss. How are you meant to get your eight ounces a month when you live on your own?'

Deborah gave a slight nod. This was an easy one. 'There's a pound in a jar, so you're allowed to buy two months' worth at a time. Your grocer really ought to have explained this to you. The same goes for jam and treacle.'

Deborah worked her way steadily through her queries, giving the people she helped her best attention. Even so, she couldn't stop herself compulsively glancing at her wristwatch in between enquiries. She wanted to do her job properly, but she also needed to get to Star House and speak to Mrs Beaumont. When there was no one left to assist, she started to pack away her remaining leaflets.

'Are you finishing early, Miss Grant?' Mrs Jasper came towards Deborah, dressed in the dark-green uniform of the WVS. Mrs Jasper was nicely spoken with a calm manner, but there was a note of disapproval in her tone just now.

'There's nobody else waiting,' said Deborah, 'and I have another appointment to get to.'

'Then let's hope no one else arrives in need of your help,' Mrs Jasper replied crisply and left her to it.

Deborah hoped so too. She didn't want to be reported, but

she couldn't afford to hang about. She caught the bus to Chorlton and walked to Star House. Her heart thumped as she opened the garden gate and she had to blow out a breath to steady herself as she stood on the step to ring the bell.

Mrs Beaumont answered the door. Her blue eyes looked even bluer, and her fair skin even fairer, thanks to her black hair. She wore a crimson blouse and a navy skirt. Well, if you were going to dye your hair jet-black, you might as well go the whole hog and wear vibrant colours too, Deborah reckoned. It was probably something to do with being theatrical.

'Hello, Mrs Beaumont. I'm Deborah Grant – Sally's friend. Do you remember me?'

'Of course I do. Sally isn't here. She's still at work.'

'I know,' Deborah said quickly. 'I'm not here to see her. I've come to see *you*.'

'Have you indeed? You'd best come in, then.'

Mrs Beaumont took Deborah into the parlour, where Deborah noted the presence of an old-fashioned gramophone with a huge horn on the side as well as an upright piano against the far wall. She remembered Sally's tale of the party Mrs Beaumont had thrown when her munitions girls were due to leave for pastures new, and how the furniture had ended up being pushed out of the way so everyone could dance their socks off while the landlady belted out tunes.

'Have a seat,' Mrs Beaumont offered.

Deborah waited for her hostess to sit before she followed suit. Mrs Beaumont leaned towards the table, where a cigarette, stuck in the end of a long cigarette-holder, was balanced over the rim of an ashtray. Mrs Beaumont picked up the holder and placed her elbow on the arm of her chair, creating an elegant pose.

'I take it you're here about a room?'

'How did you know?' Deborah asked, feeling a tingle of surprise.

'I'm a landlady. What else would bring you here but my empty rooms?'

'I'd love to live here,' Deborah gushed. 'I've only ever heard good things about Star House from Sally.'

'That's nice to know.'

'I've known her all my life. We used to work together until she went to the salvage depot. If you need references, I can get them from my boss at the Food Office and from the wartime mortuary in Withington.'

'The mortuary? That's the first time I've ever been offered a reference from one of those.'

'It's my voluntary war work,' Deborah explained. 'I'm not in the mortuary itself. When war broke out, Sally and I trained to decontaminate gas-attack victims, only there have never been any – so that's another thing I want to do: apply for different voluntary work.'

Mrs Beaumont treated her to an assessing look. 'It'll be all change for you, won't it? New billet, new war work.'

'I'll still be at the Food Office. I'm not a fly-by-night.'

Mrs Beaumont took a long drag on her cigarette-holder and tilted up her chin as she blew out a stream of smoke. She removed the cigarette from the fancy holder and stubbed it out gently so it could be lit again later.

Her heart beating quickly with nerves, Deborah clutched the handles of her handbag. What would Mrs Beaumont decide?

Coming to her feet, the landlady said, 'I'll show you Betty's old room, Marie Lloyd, and you can tell me what you think.'

Deborah had to stifle a broad grin as she followed the landlady. The wall alongside the staircase was decorated with signed photographs of the greats of the music hall. Marie Lloyd was at the front of the house. It was a pretty room, overlooking the former recreation ground on the other side of the road, and Deborah looked around appreciatively.

'Do you like it?' asked Mrs Beaumont.

'It's perfect,' said Deborah. 'Please may I have it?'

'I haven't told you the house rules yet.'

'I can promise you here and now that I agree to them.' Eagerness expanded inside Deborah's chest. 'I'd *love* to live in Star House, Mrs Beaumont, and I'd love to have this room. Please say I can.'

Deborah's mum was very upset. So was Dad, though he showed it by being annoyed. His brown eyes were grave and there was a tightness about his mouth beneath his moustache.

'I can't believe she'd do something like this behind our backs,' said Mum, her mouth twisting in distress.

'Well, she has, and it's come out of the blue,' said Dad.

Deborah pressed her lips together. They were talking about her as if she wasn't in the same room.

'I'm sorry about the way it's happened,' she began, and then stopped. She'd been about to say, 'It's come out of the blue for me as well,' as if the idea had struck her like a lightning-bolt that very afternoon. That had been how she had intended to explain it if she'd been able to have a private word with Mrs Beaumont on Sunday. But now she baulked at telling fibs. 'I really am sorry, but I've been thinking about it for a while.'

'And it never occurred to you to say anything to us?' Dad demanded, frowning darkly. It wasn't like him to be sharp with her – but then, it wasn't like her to be anything other than a dutiful daughter.

'I was only thinking about it. There's no harm in thinking.'

'It seems to me you've done a lot more than just think,' Dad retorted.

'I knew I should ask you first,' Deborah acknowledged, 'but today someone at work said—'

'Someone at work!' Mum exclaimed. 'Did you hear that?' she asked Dad. 'It seems we're the last to know.'

'It's just the way it happened,' Deborah said desperately. 'I had to get to Star House before the billeting officer did. I'm sorry for not asking you first. Won't you at least consider it? It's not as though I'd be moving in with strangers. I'd be with Sally, and she needs all the support she can get at the moment. And you've met Mrs Beaumont and Lorna.' She held her breath as her gaze flicked from one parent to the other.

Dad looked at Mum. 'She does have a point, Edith.'

'But her place is here with *us*,' Mum almost wailed. Slashes of colour appeared on her cheekbones.

'That's all there is to it, then.' Dad spoke in a tone of finality. 'I might have been prepared to stretch a point, but not if it means going against Mum's wishes.'

Deborah bit down on a sharp feeling of disappointment. She wanted to argue but that would only serve to make things worse. She thought of the lovely Marie Lloyd room and had to smother a sigh. Mrs Beaumont had said she could move in at the weekend.

Must she now creep back to Star House and undo the arrangements she had agreed to with such pleasure earlier on? No, she couldn't bear to. She would just have to hope against hope that she could talk Mum round. What were the chances?

If nothing else, her bitter disappointment gave Deborah something to say when she next wrote to Dulcie. It was strange having a sister-in-law she'd never met, but, through writing letters, they were gradually getting to know one another, though only in what felt like a superficial way. Deborah never felt she could write anything about Rod because on the occasions when she'd tried her mind had filled with the loutish way he had behaved during his showdown with Sally.

Now, however, the words flew onto the page as Deborah confided her woes. Only after the letter had been posted did she wonder whether Dulcie would share it with Rod. Whose side would he take?

The week went by slowly. Deborah's cosy bedroom, which she'd always loved, now merely seemed full of things she wasn't allowed to pack. How long could she decently leave it before she had to come clean to Mrs Beaumont? She couldn't bear the thought of having to say she didn't want Marie Lloyd after all. That would spell the end of her dream…

There didn't seem to be any hope of talking Mum round, not least because she refused to discuss the matter.

'There's nothing to say,' Mum insisted, her lips settling into a narrow line.

Deborah arrived home from work on Thursday to find Mrs White and Mum in the parlour, having a cup of tea and a cigarette together. The way the pair of them looked up when she walked in made it obvious what they'd been talking about. After saying hello, Deborah withdrew, then stood outside the room with her ear close to the door. Eavesdropping was wrong, but she simply had to know.

'Believe me, I have nothing but sympathy,' said Mrs White. 'I remember what it was like for me when Sally flew the nest. I was very hurt, but—'

Deborah's breath caught. But it was for the best? But Sally's happiness was all that mattered?

'—your husband has said it's up to you. That's more than Sally's father did.'

Deborah slumped and almost banged against the door. She crept away, her heart heavy. Mrs White had just knocked the last nail in the coffin.

. . .

Deborah came home from the Town Hall on Friday feeling very down in the mouth, but she'd already decided she had to put on a brave face. If she took this setback on the chin, it would make her look grown-up. She needed Dad and Mum to think well of her in case another opportunity arose in the future for her to move to Star House – assuming Mrs Beaumont would give her a second chance. She had to go over to Chorlton this evening and break the news.

The herby smell of oatmeal sausages greeted her as she entered the house. Mum came out of the kitchen, wiping her hands on her apron.

Before Deborah could show how cheerful and mature she was, Mum said, 'Come and sit down. No, not in the kitchen. In the parlour. I've turned the heat down on the sausages.'

Deborah followed her mother and they both sat down. Mum took a letter from her apron pocket.

'What is it?' Deborah immediately feared someone must have died.

'It's from Dulcie. I wrote to her about you announcing you wanted to move out.'

'Oh.' It had never occurred to Deborah that Mum would have done the same thing as she had.

'She's written back to say she thinks I should let you.'

Deborah didn't know what to say – didn't know what to feel. She didn't dare feel pleased yet, let alone excited.

'Here, read it for yourself,' said Mum but then hung on to the letter and read from it. '*I know it's the done thing for girls to stay at home until they get married, but times have changed and I can understand Deborah's wish to move in with her friends. It would be a shame for her to miss out. After all, she won't be far away, and you know the people. Just imagine if she'd wanted to join the Wrens!* That's what Dulcie says.' She sighed.

Deborah kept quiet, sensing Mum was on the brink.

'I thought she'd agree with me,' said Mum. 'Everyone else

has, but then I've only asked women with daughters the same age as you. Dulcie has made me see things differently. So – I suppose you can go to Star House.'

'Oh, Mum,' breathed Deborah.

She gave her mother a big hug, but really it was Dulcie she was hugging. The best sister-in-law in the world.

Excitement poured through Deborah. Against all the odds, she'd got what she wanted.

Freedom!

CHAPTER SEVEN

Lorna spent Saturday on duty with the WVS, doing a long stint at the British Restaurant in town. She was proud to be a member of the Women's Voluntary Service, which undertook all kinds of work to support the civilian population, from shopping for the housebound to training women to drive, from making billeting arrangements for air-raid victims to organising clothing exchanges, from helping the nit-nurse to running mobile laundries in areas where the water had been cut off by enemy bombing.

She spent much of the morning peeling her way through a mountain of potatoes until her hands ached; peeling and chopping carrots; and removing the stones from the prunes that had soaked overnight, ready to be made into prune pudding today. Later, she was on washing- and drying-up duty, after which it was time to help prepare the meals that would be available at teatime. The restaurant was busy all day, with members of the public coming in for a two-course meal and a hot drink, all for under a shilling.

When she arrived home shortly before teatime, there was an air of excitement in the house – what, again? They already knew that Sally's chum Deborah was moving in. Something else must have happened today.

'Lorna!' Sally greeted her, appearing in the sitting room doorway as Lorna hung up her things. 'Come and hear the news.'

'What's happened?' Lorna asked, following her into the room.

Sally looked at Mrs Beaumont, who said, 'The munitions girls came round this afternoon.'

'Oh, and I missed them,' said Lorna. 'What a shame. How are they? I haven't seen them since that awful night in town.'

She shut her eyes for a second, remembering the explosion, those poor people being flung up into the air... and the corpses that had landed. She had been to the flicks earlier that night with Stella, Mary and Lottie, the munitions girls. They'd gone their separate ways afterwards, which meant that Lorna had ended up experiencing the air raid alongside Virginia Lawrence, whom she knew through George. The three munitions girls hadn't been hurt in the raid and nor had Lorna, but poor Virginia had suffered concussion and a broken arm.

'They're fine,' said Mrs Beaumont. 'They send their best.'

'They brought another munitions girl with them,' said Sally, clearly unable to hold her tongue any longer. 'A Miss Dayton – Louise.'

'They want her to move in here with us,' said Mrs Beaumont.

Lorna's interest quickened. 'What did you tell her?'

Sally laughed. 'She said, "The rest of you can go out for a walk while Miss Dayton and I have a chat," so we all had to clear out.'

Mrs Beaumont smiled. 'But you came back to good news. She will be moving in next weekend.'

'What's she like?' Lorna asked at once. 'Is she nice?'

'I'd say so,' Sally answered. 'She seemed friendly and pleasant. Good-looking, too. Lovely hair: light brown and fluffed up in lots of waves. She said she likes to wear it that way when she's not at work.'

Lorna nodded. 'If she's in the munitions, she'll have her hair scraped back at work, with not so much as a curl on show.'

'So we'll have a full house again,' Sally said, pleased.

'I think she'll fit in,' said Mrs Beaumont. 'She's a little bit older than you two. Twenty-five? Twenty-six?'

'If Stella and the others like her, she must be a good egg,' said Lorna.

'Something I've learned about running a wartime billet,' said Mrs Beaumont, 'is the importance of everyone getting along with one another. It didn't matter so much if a few sparks flew when I took in theatricals. They stayed a week and then moved on to their next booking, although some stayed longer. But in wartime, we all need to pull together.' She looked at the girls. 'Why don't you two nip along to the depot and tell Betty the news before she closes up? I'm sure she'd like to know.'

A few minutes later, Lorna and Sally set off.

'It's going to be like London Road station at Star House next Saturday, with two new girls moving in,' Lorna remarked.

'It's my Saturday for the depot,' said Sally, 'so I shan't be around to lend a hand.'

'I can't wait to meet this Miss Dayton,' said Lorna. 'I hope she'll let us call her Louise.'

'Bound to,' said Sally. 'It's one of Mrs Beaumont's rules. When Betty moved in and it was just her and the munitions girls, who were already great pals, Mrs Beaumont insisted on first names so Betty wouldn't feel left out.'

They walked into the yard, to find that Betty had changed out of her dungarees back into her own clothes and was about to close up.

'Good job I didn't shut up shop early and sneak off,' she joked when she saw them.

Lorna and Sally told her the news.

'That's good to hear,' said Betty. 'I'm pleased.'

'It's jolly good luck, if you ask me,' said Lorna. 'Getting Sally's friend, and now a pal of the munitions girls, is much better than having somebody foisted on us by the billeting officer.'

Betty laughed. 'Steady on. I was foisted onto Mrs Beaumont by the billeting officer, I'll have you know.'

'We'll help you lock up,' said Sally. 'Then you can get home to Samuel.'

'Actually, I'm coming round to Star House,' said Betty. 'Come indoors a minute.'

Inside, she produced a cloth shopping bag, from which she withdrew a flat package wrapped in brown paper.

'I can't open it to show you,' she said, 'but it's the photograph of the three of us with Mrs Beaumont on my wedding day. Samuel had it framed.'

'You shouldn't have said,' Lorna protested. 'Now all I want to do is rip the paper off and look at it.'

Sally laughed. 'Then we'd better get it home quickly.'

They locked up and returned to Star House, where the aroma of herbs greeted them. Mrs Beaumont appeared from the kitchen, wearing her wraparound apron with its exotic pattern of peonies, roses and huge daisies against a background of foliage in apple green and forest green.

'Betty,' she said, pleased, 'it's nice to see you.'

The girls took her into the sitting room and sat her down.

'We've got something for you,' said Sally.

Betty handed over the parcel. 'We hope you like it.'

Mrs Beaumont opened it and gave an exclamation of delight.

'Is this for me? When the photographer wanted us to pose, I never thought...'

'It's from the three of us,' Betty told her. 'We wanted you to have something to remember us by.'

'As if I'd ever forget my salvage girls,' said Mrs Beaumont as she wiped away a tear. 'It's lovely – and all the lovelier for being unexpected. Oh, you are such dear girls. I think of you as *my* girls, you know. I think of the munitions girls in the same way, even though they don't live here any more. It was a real blow for me at the beginning of the war when the government ordered all the cinemas, theatres and concert halls to close for the duration. Of course, with no theatrical people in need of digs, I had to start taking in war girls. Then the government relented, and places of entertainment opened up again. I was so fed up with being stuck with war girls. But now... well, it's been a new experience for me to look after the same guests for months on end. You've all grown on me. Having you here is like living with family.'

'Oh, Mrs B,' said Lorna. 'You're a second mum to us.'

Mrs Beaumont sniffed daintily and dabbed at her nose with a lace-edged hanky. 'And now you've given me this beautiful photograph. Thank you. Thank you all so much.' She stood up. 'Now come here and let me give you all a kiss.'

On Monday Lorna received a letter from George confirming that he would be able to get up to Lancaster the coming weekend. She was thrilled. During her morning tea break at the depot, she dashed off two letters, one to George, the other to her mother, then went over the road to the post office to send them on their way.

The three girls talked about it while they flattened empty cardboard cartons. Lorna knew that five medium-sized cartons could be made into one shell fuse, and twenty breakfast cereal boxes could end up as the case for a three-pound shell: you couldn't work alongside Sally Henshaw for long without knowing these things.

'So you've just written to tell your mother to expect you and George this weekend?' asked Betty.

'Tell me to mind my own business,' said Sally, 'but I hope this isn't the first she's hearing of you and George being back together.'

'No, it isn't,' Lorna confirmed. 'I wrote last week after the three of us talked it over. Her reply was waiting when I got home on Saturday. I didn't say anything because everyone was so happy about the new girls and the photograph.'

Betty looked at her. 'Does that mean your mother isn't pleased about George?'

'Not necessarily. She's just concerned. Her letter was full of words like "jilted" and "breach of promise". You get the idea.'

Last year Lorna's parents had taken her down to London, hoping she would find a husband – which she had, very quickly. George Broughton was handsome, charming and clever and Lorna had thought herself the luckiest girl in the world. She'd been aware, of course, that her father was chuffed to bits because George was the heir to a title – but nothing had prepared her for the gossip that had sprung up, saying that the West-Sadlers had come to town specifically to bag a title for their daughter. Everything had got out of hand, and George had ended up breaking off the engagement. Like the gentleman he was, he had offered to spread the word that Lorna was the one who had made the decision, thus enabling her to save face.

But Lorna's father had then insisted upon opening a breach-of-promise case against George and the matter had gone to court. To Lorna's horror, the judge had castigated her for daring to bring such a frivolous matter to court during a time of national emergency. The newspapers had enjoyed the proverbial field day at her expense. That was how she had ended up here in Manchester at the salvage depot – it had been Daddy's way of hiding her from any more publicity.

'I can understand your mother feeling concerned,' Betty said gently.

'It's only natural,' Sally added.

'I know,' said Lorna. 'She wrote, *Daddy and I want to know that you're sure – and that George is sure.* Well, this weekend they'll see for themselves, won't they?' She didn't miss the glance that the other two exchanged. 'I hope you aren't about to pour cold water on things.'

'Of course we aren't,' Betty assured her at once. 'We want everything to go as well as possible for you. You know that.'

'Our only concern,' Sally went on, 'is that it might not happen as easily as you make it sound. I could be wrong – I hope I am. I just want – *we* just want you to be prepared for whatever comes.'

Lorna sighed. 'I know. You're quite right. I might sound all bright and breezy about it, but I'm well aware it might not be that simple. Everything was downright *awful* last year and it's a big thing to ask my parents to put it behind them. I'm sure no parents would find it easy to forgive the man who broke off his engagement to their only daughter.'

'When they see how dearly you and George care for one another,' said Betty, 'surely they'll come round.'

'We'll keep our fingers crossed for you all weekend,' Sally added.

'Fingers, arms, legs and eyes, if you can manage it,' Lorna said with a smile.

Lorna took Friday off to travel home to Lancaster on the train. The journey dragged on for double the time it would have taken in peacetime, which was the way of things these days, with goods trains and troop trains taking priority over passenger trains. Her mother had said she was going to be on WVS duty all day so wouldn't be free to meet her at the station, which was something of a relief. It meant she would get the third degree from both parents together instead of having to go through it twice.

In the event, because of the train being so late, Lorna reached home just a few minutes in advance of her mother. Her heart turned over when she saw her father. His muscular frame was less beefy and his wide shoulders, instead of being squarely thrust back, were curved slightly forward. A walking-stick was propped beside his armchair. Daddy – needing support! It made sense, of course, after the way the hooch had temporarily paralysed him from head to toe, but it was still a shock, and it gave her an unpleasant fluttery feeling in her stomach.

Her father pushed his hands down hard on the arms of the chair and shoved himself to his feet. Lorna pretended not to notice the effort, but evidently she wasn't entirely successful.

'There's no need to look at me like that,' Daddy said sharply. His voice lacked its usual boom but there was no denying the vexation in his eyes. 'I hope you don't imagine you've come here to play Florence Nightingale.'

Lorna remembered what her mother had said when Daddy was in hospital and they had sat by his bedside, waiting for him to wake up.

'You mustn't be sorry for him. He'd hate that. You and I shall have to be tough and ruthless. He says that if you feel sorry for someone, it's because they're weak – so we mustn't be sorry for him. We have to be strong and determined and matter-of-fact. Then he'll know we still respect him.'

It had been true then and it remained true now.

Lorna lifted her chin and gave her father a straight look. 'It's good to see you on your feet, Daddy. A big improvement on the last time I saw you. How long before you're completely recovered?'

He made a harrumphing sound. 'It's driving me mad, this getting better lark. They've given me exercises to do and I do *double* the number I'm supposed to, but I'm still not back to normal.'

Lorna wanted nothing more than to hold him in her arms and offer reassurance and understanding. She tried not to look sympathetic.

'Have the doctors said you'll get back to how you were?' she asked crisply.

'No reason why I shouldn't,' he replied, though whether this was his own assessment, or that of the doctors, wasn't clear.

Sensing that at this point he wasn't prepared to lean on his walking-stick in front of her, Lorna sat down. Daddy did the same, descending onto his seat with a sort of controlled thud. His body might not be back to normal yet, but his temper was. Mind you, that had never gone away.

Mummy walked in, pulling off her gloves. Lorna had inherited her mother's height and slenderness, which she always joked was a big improvement on Daddy's beefy build. While Lorna was lucky enough to have eyes of pure green, her mother's were greeny-hazel.

'Oh, good. You're here, darling,' said Mummy with a smile. 'Was the journey frightful?' She leaned down, presenting her cheek for Lorna to kiss. 'It's so good to have you home – and what's this about George?'

'Yes!' barked Daddy, the old power suddenly returning to his voice. '*George!* After what he did—'

'As I explained in my letter,' Lorna put in, 'we met up again during the Christmas Blitz and we've been seeing one another since then.'

'And he's come to his senses and realised what a mistake he made by jilting you,' Daddy said forcefully.

'Please don't say that in front of George,' Lorna begged.

'Lorna's right,' said her mother. 'We mustn't frighten him off.'

'No, indeed,' Daddy agreed. 'Does this mean the engagement's on again?'

'No, it doesn't.' Lorna employed her firmest voice. 'We're taking our time – unlike last year, when we couldn't get engaged fast enough.'

'I hope you know what you're doing,' Mummy cautioned her.

'What's that supposed to mean?' Lorna asked, stung.

'It means that you should examine your feelings carefully. Don't reunite with George just to show the world that you can.'

'I wouldn't dream of it!' Lorna cried.

'It would be understandable after what the press put you through,' said Mummy.

'Don't remind me.' For a moment the unpleasant memories assaulted her. 'I've invited George here because we're both serious about rebuilding our relationship.' She looked from one parent to the other. 'I hope you'll both want to support us in that.'

Please, please, she thought.

'We only want what's best for you,' her mother replied, her eyes serious. 'Isn't that so?' she asked, looking at Daddy.

'Well, of course,' was his gruff response, as if this ought to have been obvious. 'The question is, is George right for *you*?'

'Yes,' Lorna declared in her firmest tone. 'He always was, but events got in the way.'

Her father snorted. 'It's no use blaming it on "events". That's taking the easy way out. The fact is that George let you down in the worst possible way, and that was *not* the act of a gentleman.'

It was high time for Lorna to stand her ground. 'It's not as though you cared about George one way or the other, not in a personal sense. What mattered to you was that he will one day inherit a title and the family estate. That was what you cared about – and that wasn't the act of a gentleman, either, Daddy.'

'She's got you there, Hector,' Mummy said wryly before Daddy could start blustering.

Lorna glanced at her mother, feeling impressed. Not so long ago, she wouldn't have dreamed of speaking so frankly to Daddy. Engaging in war work had been good for her.

'The thing is this, Daddy,' Lorna said quickly. 'I love George, and he loves me. We're absolutely certain of one another – and we want you and Mummy to feel certain too. That's the reason I asked him to come here this weekend. The good opinion of you and Mummy means the world to both of us. We hope that, by the end of this visit, we'll have earned it.'

The next day Lorna was overjoyed to be with George once more. The way his grey-blue eyes deepened in intensity when he looked at her made her heart do funny things.

Her happiness seemed to rub off on Mummy. Lorna had worried that she might be frosty, but she had evidently taken Lorna's words to heart and decided to give George a chance. Her eyes, though watchful, were kind. Frankly, she was probably on the lookout for anything Daddy might say or do, as much as George was.

Lorna, too, was concerned about Daddy and George being together again. Their last meeting had been on the day of the breach-of-promise court case. Lorna still wanted to curl up with shame when she thought of Daddy demanding that she be permitted to keep the engagement ring and then, when it was made clear to him that she couldn't because it was a Broughton family heirloom, demanding that she ought to receive financial compensation instead.

Daddy and George couldn't be more different. Daddy was heavy-jawed and thick-set with an overbearing personality, while George was tall and lean-faced with an air of quiet authority. He had a keen intelligence, while Daddy was shrewd and manipulative.

The first meeting between George and her parents had gone better than Lorna could have hoped. He had presented Mummy with a colourful bouquet that must have cost a pretty penny.

'How beautiful, George. Thank you,' said Mummy.

'My pleasure, Mrs West-Sadler. A small token of my gratitude to you for welcoming me into your home after I was foolish enough to break off my engagement to Lorna last year. I hope you're prepared to give me another chance.'

'Yes, well – this is what Lorna wants,' said Mummy. The words sounded stilted, but Lorna could see that Mummy was both charmed and impressed by the gentlemanly way in which George had assumed the blame for what had gone wrong.

His first meeting with Daddy – which Lorna had fretted over for long hours the previous night – went surprisingly well, too.

Daddy was already on his feet, standing up straight, when George entered the well-appointed sitting room.

George spoke immediately. 'Mr West-Sadler, I was' – and Lorna's heart thumped: Daddy would be furious if George said *sorry* – 'very angry when Lorna told me what had happened to you. Dashed bad luck on your part to be handed tainted alcohol.'

'Dashed bad crime on the villains' part,' Daddy replied gruffly.

'I'm pleased to see you're recovering, sir. That takes strength of will as well as of body.'

'Flattery won't wash with me,' Daddy retorted.

George wasn't discomforted. 'No flattery intended, just the plain truth. I have reason to know of the devastating effects hooch can have on the body and the mind. One day I might be able to go into detail about it – and about what a gem of a girl Lorna is.'

The shrewd look in Daddy's dark eyes showed that he was intrigued. Lorna felt grateful. It seemed George had struck just the right note.

The war provided the two men with plenty of safe conversational ground.

'Lancaster City Council has sent a deputation to Merseyside to see how the bombings have affected the place,' Daddy said later over pea-and-mint soup followed by rabbit pie, 'and to see the work done by the volunteers.'

'The war effort relies on everybody mucking in together,' said George. To Mummy he added, 'You must see that all the time in your work with the WVS.'

'There's so much to be done,' said Mummy, 'and our responsibilities are expanding all the time. We have a lot of evacuated children in the countryside round here and we have launched a new scheme for the care and welfare of those who are due to leave school this summer. In the wartime world, it'll be easy enough to find jobs for them. We're compiling a card index of information supplied by teachers and foster-parents.'

'Don't their parents want them to go home again?' Lorna asked.

'Some do, some don't,' said Mummy. 'They're unquestionably safer here and many of them are billeted with younger brothers and sisters. We want to make it possible for them to stay, if that's the best thing.'

'I'd no idea the WVS found itself *in loco parentis*,' George remarked.

Mummy sighed, but it was a crisp sound, not a sorrowful one. 'We simply respond to circumstances.'

Afterwards, George and Lorna sat outside together on a bench facing what had once been Mummy's prized flowerbeds and was now a vegetable garden. The air was cool, and the scent of their tobacco mingled with the green tang of spring.

'Today went well, don't you think?' said George.

'I'm exhausted,' Lorna replied. 'I was so worried that they wouldn't make you welcome or that Daddy would blow up about what happened last year, but in the event it turned out all right.'

'More than all right. This has been a strain on all of us, but especially on you, my love. I want you to know how deeply I appreciate this chance to build bridges with your parents. They must have been beside themselves with fury at me for ending our engagement and hurting you so badly, but they have been nothing but gracious and civil to me today. It must have cost them something to do that, especially—I was going to say, "especially your father", but that wouldn't be fair. It must have been just as hard for your mother. It must have broken her heart to see you so unhappy last year.'

'It must have done,' said Lorna, thinking about it, 'but she didn't really let it show. She was still very much under Daddy's thumb in those days, and she took her lead from him in all matters, the same way I was brought up to do. If Mummy was hurt on my behalf, and I'm sure she was, she simply hid it. She didn't even comfort me on the sly, as it were. She didn't so much as slip into my room, sit on my bed and open her heart – you know, woman to woman.'

'I'd like to think, for both your sakes,' said George, 'that those days are behind you now.'

'I hope so too,' Lorna murmured.

George slid his arm round her shoulders and drew her closer. 'It's so good to be with you again. Everything falls into its rightful place when we're together. I'd have put up with any number of explosions from your father just to be in your company for these two days. I hate having to be apart.'

'War work,' said Lorna. She angled her face to look up at

him. 'Do you think it's good for us to have time without one another?' she asked curiously.

'As part of taking things slowly second time round?'

'Yes.'

'Frankly, no,' said George. 'I'd much prefer to take things slowly with you close by than with me in London and you in Manchester. I'm finding it rather hellish, truth be told.'

Lorna felt a ripple of surprise. 'I thought you were going to say that being separated was good for us, that it was giving us time to be sure of our feelings.'

'I'm already perfectly sure of my feelings, thanks very much,' said George.

Lorna snuggled closer, happiness radiating throughout her body. She felt confident of their relationship now, in a way she hadn't last year.

'One thing I'm completely sure of,' she said, 'is that things are much better second time round.'

'That's an interesting theory,' said George. 'I think we should test it.' His lips brushed over hers. 'Is this better second time round?'

He covered her mouth with his, softly at first, then deeply. Lorna's senses sang with pleasure and desire. Oh, this was so much better than first time round.

CHAPTER EIGHT

At six o'clock on Sunday morning, Sally and Betty climbed down from the depot roof and locked the big front gates before setting off for home. It had been a busy night. The siren had gone off shortly after half past ten and the all-clear hadn't sounded until a quarter to five. The raid had felt as if it was going to go on for ever.

It had been the third night in a row for air raids. On the first night, Chorlton-cum-Hardy had been hit and people had died on the corner of Chatsworth Road and Cavendish Road, not a stone's throw from where the temporary wartime mortuary was situated. Seven had been killed in all. It had made Sally go hot and cold all over to picture how near Cavendish Road was to MacFadyen's, the building used by the local WVS. A photograph had appeared in the *Manchester Evening News* of a Mr and Mrs Mooney looking commendably calm outside the wreckage of their house on Egerton Road South. They had been in their indoor shelter, presumably a Morrison shelter, when their house had been hit, and had escaped injury.

On the second night, there had been further casualties and fatalities in Stretford. And then last night – Saturday night into the early hours of Sunday morning – the raid had lasted more than six hours. The bombs that fell had been further away this time, but Sally knew from her own experience what it would have been like for the people in the affected areas – that all-too-familiar sound as the bomb hurtled to the ground, the fear that it might have your name on it, followed by the terrific explosion that jolted buildings from their foundations, clogging the air with dust and the smell of burning.

Now that it was all over, Sally and Betty walked together along Beech Road towards Wilton Road. There were various routes Betty could take to go home to the bookshop, but she liked the one that took her past Star House. They said a quick goodbye at the gate before Sally went indoors.

Would the other girls think her unsociable if she had a bit of a lie-in before church? No, of course they wouldn't. Staying up all night was always tiring, of course, but Sally felt more tired than usual.

She smiled to herself as she peeled off her clothes and pulled on her nightie. It was nice to think of the house filling up again. Yesterday, with Lorna away in Lancaster, Sally had woken up as Mrs Beaumont's sole lodger. After spending the day at the depot, she'd arrived home to be one of three, Deborah and Louise having taken up residence during the day.

She hoped Louise Dayton hadn't felt left out when she and Deborah had greeted one another with hugs and squeals, but Louise had seemed to take it in her stride, giving no sign of feeling left out. As she had shaken hands with the new girl and welcomed her to Star House, Sally had taken a moment to admire her looks. Her rather square face had a delicate jawline, and her brown eyes were clear and intelligent. She'd given Sally a friendly smile.

'Welcome to Star House,' Sally had said warmly. 'Sally Henshaw. Pleased to meet you.'

'Louise Dayton. Likewise.'

'I assume you've been told the rule about first names, so it's Sally.'

'And Louise.'

They'd exchanged smiles and Sally had immediately liked the new girl.

Now, she snuggled beneath the sheets, her body dog-tired but her brain still buzzing, sure that she wouldn't manage more than a light doze... and the next thing she knew, Mrs Beaumont was beside her bed with breakfast on a tray.

'Golly.' Sally sat up. 'I don't remember the last time I had breakfast in bed.'

'I thought you could do with a bit of spoiling,' said Mrs Beaumont, laying the tray across her lap.

Sally couldn't imagine her landlady wanting to fuss over anybody who wasn't top of the bill at the music hall, but she wasn't about to argue. This was a great treat, and she was all appreciation.

After breakfast she got dressed in a plain blouse and skirt suitable for church, adding her linen jacket and felt hat. Then she set off with the others. Just before they entered the porch of St Clement's, a voice called to them.

'Mrs Beaumont! Sally!'

It was Betty. She and Samuel were at the bottom of the path, hurrying to catch up with them.

Mrs Beaumont introduced Louise to the Atkinsons and Betty wished her well in her new home.

'The best billet in Chorlton,' Betty said. To the group in general she added, 'Samuel heard something exciting about last night's raid.'

'A Junkers 88 w-was brought down near Northwich,' Samuel told them.

'What a thrill for the ack-ack gunners,' said Sally.

'What happened to the crew?' Louise asked.

'They bailed out but they w-were all c-captured.'

This gave everyone a boost, but the mood sobered in church when prayers were said for the souls of those who had been killed in Chorlton a couple of nights previously: Charles and Ida Casper of 1 Chatsworth Road, and four women next door at number 3; and David Herbert of 19 Cavendish Road.

Afterwards, the Star House residents said goodbye to the Atkinsons and returned to Star House. Louise read the newspaper while Mrs Beaumont put the dinner on.

'Come and see my bedroom,' Deborah invited Sally.

'Because, of course, I've never been in Marie Lloyd before,' Sally teased, following her up the stairs.

They sat on the bed in Marie Lloyd.

'I love it,' Deborah said enthusiastically. 'I'm so excited to be here.'

'Was your mum upset?' Sally asked.

'Yes, but she knows it's the right thing for me. Three cheers for Dulcie. It was her letter that swung it.'

'Well, I'm glad it did,' said Sally. Happiness radiated through her. She was going to love having her friend here at Star House. 'Are you going to transfer to the Cavendish Road mortuary?'

Deborah pressed her lips together for a moment in an expression Sally recognised of old. It meant Deborah had made up her mind about something.

'I'm going to see if I can join the WVS instead.'

'Why?'

'Oh, you know what it's like at the mortuary. You have to change into the decontamination suits and prepare yourself mentally for the possibility of dealing with the bodies of people who have died in a gas attack... and then none arrive. We've been having raids for the best part of a year now and we've yet to suffer one. Thank heaven,' Deborah added quickly. 'The last thing I want is for there to be any gas attacks. I want to do something different, something that involves keeping busy all the time.'

'I understand,' said Sally. 'It'll be a bit of a shock for your parents, you instigating another big change in your life.'

'They never wanted me to do gas-attack work in the first place,' said Deborah, 'any more than yours did. Mum's part of the WVS, so I hope she'll be glad for me to join, too.'

'When you tell her, make sure the first thing you say is that you'll be joining the Chorlton branch, not Withington,' Sally advised. 'Otherwise, she might end up being disappointed, and you don't want that.'

'No, I don't,' Deborah agreed. 'She really didn't want me to leave home, and I've spent all week feeling guilty.'

'Believe me, I understand,' said Sally. 'Feeling guilty is horrid, but you have to stand firm.'

'Are you talking about me or yourself?' Deborah asked.

'Both,' Sally admitted, smiling. 'I'm going to visit Andrew's mother at Auntie Vera's this afternoon. Wish me luck.'

Sally felt a twist of anxiety in her tummy. Things had once been so warm and relaxed between her and her mother-in-law. The very first time they'd met, Mrs Henshaw had welcomed Sally into her home and done everything she could to make her feel comfortable. Sally had been both thrilled and deeply touched – all the more so because her own mum hadn't given Andrew the same sort of welcome, since she was still miffed over Sally ditching Rod Grant. But, however spiky things had been at first between Andrew and Sally's parents, the relationship between Sally and Andrew's mother had been nothing but cordial and affectionate.

Sally missed that and would dearly love to get it back. But was that possible?

. . .

Auntie Vera lived in a neat house in Seymour Grove. The front room was furnished with heavy-looking pieces that Andrew had told Sally Uncle Mick had inherited from his parents, and which Auntie Vera had painted white, wanting them to look modern. Sally privately considered that she'd have done better to leave them be.

She experienced a surge of affection at the sight of her mother-in-law and the way her austere face softened when she smiled. Sally gave her an extra hug.

'That's one thing I do miss now Andrew's gone,' said Mrs Henshaw. 'The hugs. He's a great one for hugging, is Andrew.'

'That's true,' said Sally.

Andrew hadn't hugged them one at a time. If they were both there, he drew the pair of them to him and all three would hug one another. The sweetness of the memory was piercing as well as precious, and Sally felt close to her mother-in-law.

'How have you settled in?' she asked.

'Fine, thank you,' said Mrs Henshaw. 'We had it all worked out before I came – didn't we, Vee? We're sharing all the household jobs.'

'How is everything at Star House?' asked Auntie Vera.

'Deborah has moved in – you remember her from my party, don't you, Auntie Vera? And there's a new girl called Louise Dayton. She works in the munitions at Trafford Park.'

'Your friend Deborah,' said Mrs Henshaw with a look at her sister. 'That gives you another reason to stay put there, I suppose.'

'It'll be lovely for us to live together,' Sally said, keeping her voice neutral, though her heart gave a thump of expectation at what was coming next.

'I just want to make it clear,' Auntie Vera said in her warmest voice, 'that you can still move in here any time you like. You'll always be welcome, Sally dear.' She looked at her husband. 'Won't she, Mick?'

'She will indeed,' he confirmed.

'Thanks,' said Sally. 'You're so kind.'

Auntie Vera meant well, she knew, but all at once she felt put upon. Only this morning, she'd advised Deborah not to feel guilty, but it was easier said than done, a lot easier.

Still, she reflected on the way home, the visit had been a good one. Yes, Mrs Henshaw had shown her disappointment about Sally's living arrangements, but she hadn't laid it on with a trowel; and Sally had shown she intended to stay where she was, so maybe they would accept it now and let the matter drop. Even if they didn't, future visits would be easier, she was sure, and that was something to be thankful for.

She alighted from the bus at the terminus and walked along Beech Road, feeling optimistic. Living under different roofs had marked a significant change in the relationship between her and Mrs Henshaw, but she had high hopes that they would feel their way back to their old closeness and would look forward to living together again when the war was over. It couldn't come soon enough for Sally.

She turned the corner into Wilton Road and walked to Star House. As she opened the garden gate, she caught a movement in the sitting room window and glimpsed Mrs Beaumont moving away. The landlady met her at the front door when she walked inside.

'Might I have a word, Sally?'

'Is something wrong?'

'Not at all. In fact, quite the opposite – assuming I'm right.'

'About what?'

'Come in the sitting room, where we can be private.' Mrs Beaumont shut the door behind them and huffed out a little breath. 'There's no delicate way of saying this, but, being responsible for the laundry, I'm aware of when you girls have your monthly visitor.'

Heat poured into Sally's cheeks and her shoulders curled

over in embarrassment. Her own mother had never said anything so blunt to her, and now here was her landlady talking boldly about – about something that nobody ever referred to.

'And you haven't had yours, dear,' said Mrs Beaumont gently.

Astonished to find herself in the middle of such an intensely personal conversation with her landlady, Sally said, 'It's the worry of the last few weeks, with Andrew going away. It's no wonder I'm late.'

'That would be understandable but... If you'd missed just the once, we wouldn't be having this little talk, but you've missed twice now, Sally, so don't you think you ought to find out for certain why?'

'Why...' Sally's mouth dropped open as understanding dawned.

'Haven't you had any other indications?' Mrs Beaumont asked her. 'Has your bosom felt tender? Or have you been tired?'

'Everyone's tired,' Sally said automatically. Then it hit her. 'Oh, but I have been feeling more tired than normal...'

'For some girls, that's one of the signs.'

'D'you think I...?' The question faded away. For a moment, Sally closed her eyes in wonderment. *Could this really be happening?* 'I never imagined...'

'Well, I don't see why not,' Mrs Beaumont replied, sounding both sensible and amused. 'You are a married woman, after all. I think you need to make an appointment with the doctor.'

Tears rose in Sally's eyes. Might she really be having a baby? She'd heard – everybody had – of wives who had deliberately got themselves pregnant when they knew their husbands were going away. Sally hadn't set out to do that, but might it have happened on its own?

She clasped her hands beneath her chin as hope bubbled up

inside her. She clamped down hard on it. She couldn't afford to hope, just in case she was wrong.

Too late. The hope was already there.

Sally touched the green ration book with reverent fingers. It was true. It was *real*. She was going to have a baby and the green ration book proved it.

Her heartbeat raced in sheer elation that was quickly followed by profound sorrow. More than anything in the world, she wanted Andrew here. That was out of the question, of course, and it was no use being silly about it.

She wanted him to be the first to know. That was the right and proper way to do it. It was natural to tell your husband first.

Except in wartime.

There was a joke doing the rounds that when a girl was in the family way, the first person to know was the milkman. This was because of the extra milk available to mothers-to-be at a reduced price. After reading the government leaflet provided by the doctor, Sally found she was also entitled to vitamin tablets and extra meat as well as an additional egg per allocation. She could also get concentrated orange juice from the welfare clinic.

There was absolutely no possibility of keeping this quiet at Star House. Mrs Beaumont was already in the know and was just awaiting confirmation; and, as soon as the extra milk appeared on the doorstep, the other girls would start to put two and two together. That meant Sally would have to inform her parents and Andrew's mother pretty sharpish, because they would be understandably hurt if they thought the Star House residents had known before they did.

So much for Andrew being the first to know, and the two of them hugging their precious knowledge close for a while before sharing it with the world.

That evening, Sally wrote a long, loving letter to Andrew

and dropped a kiss on it before she posted it. Then she caught the bus to Withington to see her parents, her mind boggling all the way there at this profound change in her life.

As she walked down the road to Mum and Dad's, Mrs Grant popped out of her front door.

'On your own, Sally? Deborah not with you?'

'Just me,' said Sally, feeling obscurely guilty.

Mrs Grant nodded. 'Just asking.' Her tone sounded casual but the way she bit her lip was a dead giveaway of how much she was missing her daughter.

Mrs Grant went back inside and Sally carried on past the next few doors to her mum and dad's house.

Dad let her in. 'This is a nice surprise.' His kindly features softened with love as he gave her a hug. Knowing she was going to be a parent herself gave Sally an insight into the depth of his feeling for her. 'Come in and sit down. Your mum's not here at the moment.'

That upset her plan. Should she tell Dad and leave him to tell Mum? Would Mum be miffed to hear the news second-hand? Sally knew her mother well enough to know she would be. Then again, why shouldn't Dad be the first to hear the wonderful news?

All these thoughts passed rapidly through her mind before she took a seat in the parlour.

Dad sat in his armchair. 'Mum won't be long. She's only gone next door.'

'How are you?' Sally asked.

'Not so bad. These early-morning raids, short as they are, are keeping us all on our toes.'

'Jerry has been dropping flares all over the place, looking for targets – the docks, the factories.'

'And the railway lines,' Dad added. 'Bridges make a good target for them. And how are you, Sally? You're looking well, I must say.'

Sally was saved from replying when they heard the back door open.

Dad called, 'Come and see who's here.'

Mum walked in, unfastening the buttons on her sage-green crocheted cardigan. Sally knew that she would have fastened the cardy before she went out. It was essential to her to be as neat as possible when she left the house, even if she was just nipping next door.

'Sally!' she said, pleased. 'We weren't expecting you.'

Sally stood up and kissed her.

'Did you come with Deborah? Is she at her mum's?'

Crikey. Clearly she'd have to tell Deborah to go home for a visit in the very near future.

'Just me,' she said, for the second time that evening.

'I'll put the kettle on.' Mum started to turn away.

'Before you do that,' said Sally, catching her mum's hand and gently pulling her back, 'I've got something to tell you.' Excitement trembled inside her as she looked at her parents. 'I'm having a baby. You're going to be grandparents.'

It took a moment to sink in, then Mum uttered a delighted cry and threw her arms round Sally. A moment after that she was in Dad's arms.

'This is marvellous news,' he declared, 'the very best.'

'It makes up for Andrew going away,' said Mum. 'I bet he wouldn't have gone if he'd known.'

Sally hadn't expected that, but she quickly rallied, her loyalty to her husband surging to the fore. 'Or he'd have been even more determined because of having a child to fight for.'

'This calls for a sherry,' said Dad.

'Tea first,' said Mum.

She practically dragged Sally into the kitchen.

'We can talk properly now,' she said. 'Women's talk. How far gone are you?'

'Just past two months.'

'It's a bit early to be telling people,' said Mum, never slow to criticise; but then she puffed out her bosom. 'But you wanted us to know.'

'Yes,' said Sally.

'Have you told Andrew's mother?'

'Not yet. I'm going round there tomorrow.'

Mum nodded, obviously pleased to have taken precedence over Mrs Henshaw. 'And what does Andrew think?'

Sally's heart dipped. 'He doesn't know yet. I've only just posted the letter to tell him.'

'Then we really are the first to know,' Mum said proudly. 'That's grand, Sally. Thank you.' She jutted out her chin, looking more than a little pleased with herself. 'It shows how right I was at Christmas to give you that christening robe.'

That made Sally laugh. 'Well, yes, I suppose it does.'

She was thrilled to have told her parents. It was also a big relief. It had been important to tell them first, as Mum's reaction had shown. Her parents' delight meant the world to Sally. It couldn't make up for not being able to tell Andrew to his face – nothing could come close to doing that – but witnessing Mum and Dad's joy had filled her with emotion and excitement and a sense of how the family was going to grow, thanks to her baby.

Her baby. Hers and Andrew's baby.

When Sally got home from Withington, she found Lorna had arrived back from Lancaster, the glow in her creamy, smooth skin showing how happy she was. Sally settled down in the sitting room with the others, tingling with the awareness of her pregnancy and the thought that here in Star House it was still her secret. Although she longed to tell her chums, that would have to wait until after she'd shared her news with Andrew's mother. After Sally's parents, she was entitled to be told next.

'How is your father coming along?' Mrs Beaumont asked Lorna.

'He's doing very well, thank you,' she answered. 'He isn't as fit and strong as he used to be, but he'll get there in the end, I'm sure. He definitely will if sheer willpower has anything to do with it.'

'Has he been ill?' Louise asked. 'I'm sorry to hear that.'

Lorna hesitated before saying, 'If you're going to live here, you might as well know.'

'I don't mean to pry,' Louise put in at once.

'It's easier if you know – you and Deborah,' said Lorna. 'With alcohol being in short supply, there are rogues out there who make their own, and it's dangerous stuff, I can tell you. My father and a couple of colleagues unknowingly drank some illegal alcohol, and it made them very ill.'

'I had no idea.' Deborah shot Sally a *Why didn't you tell me?* look.

'As a matter of fact, they were paralysed,' said Lorna.

'How awful – how frightening,' said Louise. 'That's the first I've ever heard of such a thing. What your family must have gone through…'

'It has been pretty grim at times,' Lorna admitted. 'Not knowing if the paralysis was going to be permanent was hard to live with. But Daddy and the others are well and truly on the mend now, and that's what matters. Anyway, if you'll all excuse me, I must get changed. I'm on WVS duty tonight.'

Sally followed her upstairs and into Vesta Victoria. There were two rooms called Vesta. Sally and Andrew had been given the other one, Vesta Tilley, because that one was a double.

'You look happy,' said Sally, 'and I don't just mean about your father.'

'You could say that.' Lorna's green eyes sparkled.

'I'm glad for you,' said Sally. 'There's no time to talk about it now, but I hope you're going to spill the beans tomorrow.'

'All over the place, I promise. I can't wait to tell you and Betty everything.'

Sally left her to get ready to go on duty. It might seem selfish but, if Lorna had lots of details to share involving George, that would make it easier for her to keep the lid on her own news for the time being. But she was, of course, genuinely keen to hear all about Lorna's visit, and she knew Betty would be too.

'Especially the George bits,' Betty said the next morning as the three of them started on the daily salvage sacks. There were more than usual and sorting through the contents was going to take some time.

'How did he get along with your parents?' Sally asked. 'Was it awkward?'

'At bit, at first,' said Lorna, 'but he acted with charm and straightforwardness, which seemed to do the trick.'

'Have your parents forgiven him?' Betty asked.

Lorna stopped with a saucepan in her hand. She thought for a moment before placing it in the correct pile.

'The honest answer is I don't know – and I don't *want* to know. When George dumped me, all sorts of things had gone wrong. There was all that gossip, especially about my parents wanting me to marry into a titled family. You can imagine what George's people felt about that, and you can imagine what they said to George.'

'It sounds horrid,' said Betty.

For an instant, Lorna's lovely green eyes clouded over. 'Everyone played their part in what happened – including George and me. I'm not suggesting we're blameless. But that was then and I don't want to keep harping on it. What matters is now: George's and my second chance.'

'Well said,' Sally applauded.

Lorna delved into her sack again. 'All I can say is that, in spite of all my fears, of which I had a great many, the visit went well. My parents started off civil and ended up warm. Now it's up to George and me to prove to them that we belong together.'

'That should be easy,' said Betty, 'because anyone can see that you do.'

Lorna smiled wryly. 'We thought that the first time round and it didn't work out too well. But it's different now – especially for me. I've been through a lot since last year. I've become independent.' After a moment she added, 'I hope that will stand me in good stead when we go to visit George's parents.'

Sally gave that some thought during the day. She too had grown in independence. They all had. It was because of the war. Far more was being asked of young women now and the result was that they had spread their wings, often in obvious ways, such as by joining the services or the land army, but also in smaller ways – such as when she had opted to stay at Star House instead of dutifully tagging along with Mrs Henshaw when she decamped to Auntie Vera's.

Her independence was now a large part of who she was. It was something that Andrew respected in her. And now she had her unborn child to look after, it was going to be even more important, especially with Andrew away for heaven knew how long.

Mrs Henshaw surprised Sally by weeping when she heard about the baby. It was the last thing Sally had expected from her sensible, capable mother-in-law, and she found it deeply touching.

'Don't mind me.' Mrs Henshaw blotted her tears with her hanky. 'I'm sorry, but after all the worry and upset of Andrew joining up, and you choosing not to come here with me, this feels overwhelming.' She gave Sally a watery smile. 'Wonderful but overwhelming. I'll write to Andrew at once.'

'Would you mind waiting a few days?' Sally asked. 'I haven't heard back from him myself yet.'

'Then shouldn't you have waited before you started telling people?' Mrs Henshaw asked, surprised.

Sally explained about the additional rations she was entitled to. 'It's going to be obvious at Star House very soon, so I wanted to tell you and my parents before that.'

'Oh, well, that's understandable,' said Mrs Henshaw. 'Of course, you wouldn't have been under that kind of pressure if you'd moved here with me. I'm sorry. I know I shouldn't keep harping on about that. I don't want it to come between us – especially now.'

Sally's heart swelled. 'We've always got along so well. I want that to continue.'

'I miss living with you,' said Mrs Henshaw. 'I care about you, Sally, and not just because you're married to my son. I care about you for yourself. And so I'm going to ask you again, because you're carrying Andrew's child: please will you reconsider and come to live here?'

Sally held in a sigh. 'I care about you too. I couldn't have asked for a better mother-in-law.'

'But you don't want to live under the same roof as me,' Mrs Henshaw stated flatly.

'I do,' Sally answered without hesitation. 'After the war, I want us to live together just like we used to, the three of us – except that by then it'll be the four of us.'

'Four of us,' Mrs Henshaw whispered wonderingly.

'What could be better?' Sally asked.

The next day, Sally received a letter from Andrew, who was both astonished and thrilled. After what Mum had said, Sally had been unable to prevent herself from wondering if he might express a wish that he hadn't joined up after all, but he didn't.

This is just wonderful. I'm more happy and proud than I can say. You must take great care of yourself and our baby. This time last year, you and I hadn't even met and now I'm going to be a father!

Sally felt better after that. Now it felt all right for the others to know. She decided to tell them all together – including Louise. It wouldn't be fair to leave her out and Sally wanted her to feel she was part of the Star House community.

First of all, she went into the kitchen while Mrs Beaumont was busy at the stove. She slid an arm round the landlady's waist and kissed her cheek.

'Guess what?'

Mrs Beaumont gave a little gasp and turned her face to Sally's, her blue eyes widening. 'Is it definite?'

A huge smile spread across Sally's face as she nodded.

'To be honest,' Mrs Beaumont said quietly, 'I thought you must have had good news because you didn't say a word to me. If it had been a false alarm, you'd have told me, but instead you went dashing off to Withington and then to Seymour Grove.'

'And now I've come dashing into your kitchen to tell *you*,' Sally finished. 'Will it be all right for me to stay living here in Star House? You shan't mind having a baby here?'

'Mind?' Mrs Beaumont exclaimed. 'Of course I shan't mind. When are you going to tell the other girls?'

'This evening,' said Sally. 'I've invited Betty round. We aren't on fire-watching duty tonight; and Lorna, Deborah and Louise are all at home, so it's the perfect time.'

'Fancy everyone being in all at once,' said Mrs Beaumont. 'That doesn't happen often.'

'I've told the others that it's so we can get to know Louise,' said Sally, 'so don't let on you know different.'

Sally could hardly wait for Betty to arrive. The others were in the sitting room when the doorbell rang. Sally went to answer it. She drew her friend inside and helped her off with her jacket.

As the two of them entered the sitting room, Lorna said, 'This is a good idea of yours, Sally, getting us all together so we can become better acquainted with Louise.'

Sally sat on the arm of a chair and looked around her at her pals. Soft-hearted Betty, golden-haired, with that lovely dimple when she smiled. Dark-haired Deborah with those bright-blue eyes, who'd been her friend all her life. Clever, generous Lorna whose eyes were that wonderful green. And Louise, brown-eyed and good-natured, who showed every sign of fitting in well.

Emotion thickened in Sally's throat. These were the girls who would be beside her through her pregnancy. She couldn't ask for a better bunch.

'Actually,' she said in answer to Lorna's remark, 'that was a fib. I just wanted to get you all together without saying why.'

They all looked at her.

'Has something happened?' Betty asked.

Sally couldn't keep a straight face any longer. Her smile broke free and she half-laughed.

'You could say that,' she answered. 'I'm happy, oh, so very happy, to tell you that – I'm going to have a baby.'

There was half a moment of silence. Then the others jumped up, all exclaiming at once. Sally found herself surrounded. They all wanted to touch her, to hold her. She came to her feet and let herself be hugged.

'This is so exciting!' cried Betty. 'Congratulations!'

'I'm going to be an auntie!' said Deborah.

'We're *all* going to be aunties,' said Lorna.

'Yes, you are,' Sally said at once. 'That means you as well, Louise. You're a Star House resident, so you're one of us now.'

'Thanks,' said Louise. 'Being included in this special moment means a lot.'

'We'll all help to look after you,' said Deborah.

'Lorna and I will do all the heavy work at the depot,' Betty offered.

Sally laughed. 'I'm not poorly. I can carry on doing what I've always done.'

'Until you grow too huge,' Lorna teased.

'This is such wonderful news,' said Betty. 'I couldn't be happier for you.'

'I don't want it shouted from the rooftops,' said Sally. 'Before the war, nobody talked about their happy events until they were at least three months along, and I'm not that far yet.'

Unfortunately, she hadn't thought to give the same caution to her mother. The next evening Deborah went over to Withington and, when she came back to Star House, she sought Sally out.

'My mum knows about the baby,' she said. 'I swear I never breathed a word. She said your mother told her.'

'Oh well,' said Sally. 'No harm done.'

'You don't mind?'

'It's a bit late for that.'

'It's because your mother is so happy,' said Deborah.

'I know.' Sally smiled. 'I'm happy too.'

'So am I,' said Deborah, her smile spreading all over her face. 'I'm going to love being an auntie.'

'Auntie Deborah,' said Sally and they hugged one another.

It was marvellous that everybody was so pleased for her. When Mum turned up at Star House the following evening she was greeted with congratulations, which made her hazel eyes dance, a show of happiness Sally had never witnessed before.

'Sally will have the best possible care,' said Mrs Beaumont. 'You need have no fears on that score.'

'You're right,' said Mum. 'I won't – because she'll be moving back to Withington to be with her dad and me.' She looked straight at Sally. 'Won't you, dear? Now that Andrew's gone, and with you needing special looking after because you're a mother-to-be, where else would you want to be other than at home?'

A strong feeling of déjà vu swept over Sally. This was just like when she'd had to tell Mrs Henshaw she wasn't going to Auntie Vera's with her, except that this was harder because it was her own mum.

'I'm staying here,' Sally said gently. 'I've still got my job, don't forget.'

'This war!' Mum exclaimed. 'It's turned everything upside down.'

The next thing Sally knew, both mothers wanted to know what was going to happen after the baby came along. Unless she chose to be evacuated, the war effort would require her to keep on working one way or another, either by – what was that new word that people were using? – childminding, so that another mother could work, or by carrying on working herself. And if she stayed on at the depot, then she would herself need someone to care for her baby, and who better than a grandmother?

'So, it makes perfect sense for you to live with Dad and me,' said Mum, and Sally felt obliged to promise that she would think about it, because it was the only way to close the subject for the time being, not to mention the fact that an immediate refusal would have been deeply hurtful.

'I know you've made it clear that you want to stay on at Star House, but I wouldn't feel right if I didn't remind you that there's plenty of room for you and the baby at Vera's, and she and Mick would be only too happy,' Mrs Henshaw assured Sally the following day, and Sally promised to think about that too.

Then a letter from Andrew had her dissolving into tears at the breakfast table. The others clustered around her in concern.

'It's all right,' she managed to assure them. 'They're good tears.'

'That's a relief,' said Lorna. 'Are we allowed to ask why?'

'It's this letter from Andrew.' Sally waved the sheet of paper in the air. 'He says... He says that because he's a skilled carpenter and joiner, they're going to keep him here in England for the foreseeable future.'

'Oh, that's marvellous,' breathed Deborah.

'He's going to be stationed somewhere on the south coast,' said Sally. 'I can't tell you how relieved I am.'

'That's perfect,' said Louise, 'especially with a baby on the way. I know it's not the same as having him here, but it's a jolly good second-best.'

Yes. Yes, it was. Sally floated through the day on a cloud of happiness and gratitude. That night, she lay in bed, counting her blessings.

She laid a hand on her tummy.

'Your daddy is going to be a lot closer to home and a lot safer than he might have been. He's still going to be away for heaven knows how long, little one, but you'll have other relatives who love you to pieces. You'll have your grandparents, three of them. They can't wait for you to get here.' She chuckled, feeling warm inside. 'Not to mention a host of ready-made aunties. You already have so many people who are going to love you – and your daddy is staying in England – and I'm the luckiest girl in the whole world.'

CHAPTER NINE

Ever since the letter to Mum from Dulcie supporting her wish to be allowed to move to Star House, Deborah had felt closer to her sister-in-law. She was certain that, when they finally met, they would instantly bond. She had sent Dulcie a long, cheerful letter about being given permission to leave the mortuary and join the WVS, and looked forward to receiving her sister-in-law's approval and encouragement in reply.

To her chagrin, Dulcie's reply contained the words, *Rod wants me to say...* Did he, indeed? Then he should jolly well put pen to paper himself! Deborah used to think the world of her big brother, but not any more, not since he'd behaved like a loutish bully and shown up her family in front of the whole street. His conduct that day had shocked her and their parents deeply. They simply hadn't known he'd had it in him. She felt a pang of sympathy for Sally, who had not only been on the receiving end of Rod's callous and vengeful behaviour that day, but who had also silently put up with all the times he had treated her in a supposedly loving, but actually domineering, way.

And now he wanted to stick in his two penn'orth about her

change of wartime voluntary work. It would serve him right if she didn't bother reading that part of Dulcie's letter and just skipped over it, but of course she did read it.

Rod wanted to remind her of the nasty insinuations that were made against girls in various areas of war work. The land army slogan 'Back to the Land' had been changed by some coarse men into '*Backs* to the Land', a slur on the morals of these hard-working women and girls. Even those who had joined up weren't immune to it. 'Up with the lark and to bed with a Wren' was another aspersion; and as for the nasty thing that was said about the girls attached to the Air Force – well, the less said about that the better.

Members of the WVS, on the other hand, were known to all as 'the ladies in green' or 'the voluntary ladies', which was respectful, so Rod approved of his little sister joining the WVS ranks.

Deborah wasn't sure how to feel about that. It was as if Rod had given his permission, which was obscurely unsettling. Even before he'd let his family down so badly, she wouldn't have felt any need to have his consent.

But she wasn't going to let that spoil her new venture for her. Even though Mum hadn't wanted her to leave home, she and Dad had helped Deborah pay for her WVS togs, and she had all but burst with pride the first time she had put on the distinctive green uniform. As well as being smart, it had evidently been designed with practicality in mind. The pleat-free skirt stayed smooth without ironing and when Mrs Callaghan, who ran the Chorlton branch, said, 'Roll up your sleeves, ladies,' she meant it figuratively, not literally, because the blouses were short-sleeved.

Mrs Callaghan was a tall woman with dark eyes in a pale, strong-featured face. She had interviewed Deborah in her office inside MacFadyen's, the building the WVS had taken over for the duration. The office was tiny and crowded, but spotless and in good order.

'It didn't look like this last year,' said Mrs Callaghan. 'I always meant to tidy it up and give it a good spring-clean but never had the time. Then an elderly woman, seventy-something, came to see me, wanting to do her bit. It turned out she'd been a charwoman all her life. She took one look at my office and took it on as her war work.'

Deborah couldn't wait to get started on her own war work, though she was taken aback when her first job was nit-spotting at the infant welfare clinic. That gave everyone a good laugh at Star House, which made her feel better.

Deborah was paired up with Lorna a few times while she learned the ropes. Mrs Henshaw had previously been a member of the Chorlton WVS, but had transferred to Seymour Grove when she moved in with her sister.

'I overheard Mrs Callaghan say Mrs Henshaw has asked if she can transfer back,' Lorna told Sally. 'Apparently she feels she'll get more opportunities to see you if she does.'

'And I expect she explained why as well.' Sally groaned humorously. 'So now both the Chorlton and Seymour Grove branches know about the baby.'

'You might as well take out a full-page advertisement in the *Manchester Evening News*,' said Deborah, 'just in case there's anyone left who doesn't know yet.'

But Mrs Henshaw didn't appear at MacFadyen's, so presumably she either didn't receive permission to transfer or else she'd been asked to wait for the time being.

'It makes sense,' Lorna said to Deborah. 'You join the branch closest to where you live. If they let Mrs Henshaw pick and choose, others might want to as well. There's too much work to be done to have time for that sort of faffing about.'

There were indeed many jobs to be tackled. After months spent constantly building herself up to face the arrival of the gas-dead at the mortuary, Deborah had believed herself to be tough, but her first night on rest-centre duty left her emotionally drained. There was a ceaseless stream of folk in need. Some had been bombed out and were glassy-eyed with shock. Others, more than a hundred of them, had been evacuated thanks to an unexploded bomb. Then another hundred arrived because of a ruptured gas main.

Lists of names and addresses. Tea, sandwiches, cigarettes. Wafer-thin mattresses and blankets for the exhausted. Cutting up newspaper in squares for lavatory paper. Telling people over and over again, who were too shocked to take it in the first or second time or the third time, what the procedure was when you lost your home. More tea and sandwiches for delivery to the public shelters. Tea urns being sent out in wheelbarrows or prams. Hot water for people whose skin was encased in a thick layer of dust. Children curling up close to their mothers. The smell of disinfectant. And someone playing the piano quietly in the background, a small piece of comfort and normality in a topsy-turvy world.

At the end of the shift Lorna said to Deborah, 'You look as dazed as if you'd been bombed out yourself.'

'I feel as if I've gone twice through the mangle,' Deborah replied bluntly, quoting an expression her nan used to use. 'I'd no idea it would be like this.'

'You'll get used to it,' Lorna said matter-of-factly.

'Yes,' Deborah answered with quiet determination. 'I will.'

CHAPTER TEN

'Let me push that for you,' said Lorna, trying to take the handles of the sack-trolley from Sally.

But Sally held on. 'There's no need. I'm not an invalid. I'm having a baby. As a matter of fact, I've never felt healthier in my life.'

'That's good to hear, but you still need to be careful. It's like Betty said when you told us you're expecting. Some of the work we do here at the depot is heavy. There's no other word for it. No one wants you to overdo it.'

Sally laughed. 'You sound like my mum – and my mother-in-law,' she added.

Betty joined in. 'You've got a lot of mums at the moment. We all want to take care of you.'

'Make the most of it,' Lorna teased. 'The moment the baby is born, all the attention will be transferred to him or her. You won't get a look-in.'

Later, while Sally was on the telephone in the office, Betty asked Lorna, 'You aren't really worried about her, are you?'

Lorna considered. 'Not worried, no. It's just that nobody wants to see someone in her condition doing heavy lifting.'

'She certainly looks healthy,' said Betty. 'Her skin is glowing.'

Lorna gave her a nudge. 'You'd better watch out or she'll knock you off your perch as the Radiance girl.'

Betty laughed. A few weeks earlier, she had been chosen by Radiance, the face cream people, to appear in an advertisement. They had become interested in her thanks to a photograph that had appeared in the *Manchester Evening News*, showing her sitting, laughing, on top of a pile of salvaged tyres in the depot yard. The Radiance advertisement had appeared shortly before Betty and Samuel's wedding and Lorna was proud of her friend. If the advertisement was a success, there was the possibility of another one later in the year. That would be champion.

'Sally is sensible,' said Betty. 'She would never do anything she thought she shouldn't.'

'True,' Lorna agreed. 'We must just keep our eyes peeled so we can step in and do the heavy jobs before she gets a chance.'

Betty's dimple appeared when she chuckled. 'Oh aye, I can imagine that. While we're shoving one another out of the way to get there first, Sally will be ahead of us.'

Lorna laughed as well. 'Probably. She's nothing if not dedicated to her work.' She decided to confide. 'Her having this baby makes me wonder what lies ahead for George and me.'

Betty looked at her. 'Well, you're back together, so...'

'Oh, I know,' said Lorna. 'I'm as sure as I can be without a ring on my finger that we're going to get married. Mind you, I had a ring on my finger once before and look how that turned out.'

'Things are different now,' Betty said staunchly.

'Yes, they are. I just hope others see it that way. I'm sure there will be those who'll be watching and waiting for everything to go wrong again.'

'More fool them,' said Betty. 'It just shows they don't know you.'

'Thanks,' said Lorna. 'You're a pal. I just wish I could shake off the feeling that George and I have something to prove.'

'Only to your families,' Betty replied, 'and you've already won over your parents, haven't you?'

'True,' Lorna agreed.

Not wanting to sound downbeat or whiney, she didn't add that her parents had been relatively easy to win over. It wouldn't be so easy with George's parents. It was the prospect of having to face Sir Jolyon, and especially Lady Broughton, that she was worried about.

It was almost the end of May and there had been no let-up in the air raids. Incidents in Moss Side and Withington accounted for most of the casualties. The injured were taken to Withington Hospital or Manchester Royal Infirmary and most of the dead to the mortuary in Cavendish Road. Incendiaries and high explosives fell in both Salford and Stretford; and Eccles had a bad night, with many houses suffering damage and a petrol station being set ablaze when it took a direct hit.

As part of her WVS work, Lorna sometimes worked on the ambulance-cars. These were ordinary motorcars that were used to ferry minor injuries to hospital, thus freeing up the real ambulances for the seriously injured. Each ambulance-car was manned by two WVS women, the driver and a helper.

'All this time, I've been the helper,' Lorna told Louise, 'but I'm having driving lessons now. It's a good skill to have. It'll make me more useful.'

Louise nodded. 'Learning to drive is on my list of things to do.'

'There can't be much time for you to take on a lot,' said Lorna. 'You work such long shifts at Trafford Park, and you have to travel to and fro on top.'

'At the moment I'm putting in a few hours a week repairing

hoses for the fire service,' Louise told her. 'When a raid is on, miles of hoses have to be led from rivers and canals, and a lot of big buildings have giant water-tanks in the cellars for the firemen to use. Hoses end up snaking all over the show. Inevitably, some get burned through by flying embers, so lots of teams are needed to do repairs on a regular basis.'

'Important work,' Lorna commented.

'But with compulsory overtime making the munitions shifts longer, it isn't always easy to fit it in.'

'I know that when Stella and the others left Star House, it wasn't because they didn't want to live here any longer. It was in order to move closer to Trafford Park and save themselves the travelling time. I hope you don't end up feeling you have to do that.'

'Thanks,' said Louise. 'That's kind of you to say.'

'I want you to feel welcome here,' said Lorna. 'We all do. Sally and I know one another well; and she and Deborah have been chums all their lives. Nobody wants you to feel excluded.'

Louise nodded. 'I appreciate it.'

Lorna felt drawn to Louise. It had been a lucky day for Star House when Stella, Mary and Lottie had recommended her to Mrs Beaumont. Lorna was rather intrigued by Louise's looks. With brown eyes, you might have expected her to have hair of a darker brown than she did; or, looking at it the other way, with that light-brown hair, you might have expected hazel eyes.

'Do you feel you've settled in?' Lorna asked.

'Yes, thanks. Stella and co told me it's a top-notch billet and they're right. I couldn't be more comfortable.'

'Or better fed,' Lorna added, smiling.

'True. I'm going to ask Mrs Beaumont if she'll kindly write down some of her recipes for me to give to my mother next time I go home.'

'Your mother must miss you.'

'So does my father. They were dead against me leaving home, and they hate it that I work in munitions.'

'It's dangerous work,' said Lorna.

Louise smiled. 'If they'd had their way, they'd have made working in a dress shop a reserved occupation.'

'Is that what you used to do?'

'Since the day after I left school,' said Louise. 'What did you do?'

'Rich father. Life of leisure,' Lorna said lightly.

'Plenty would give their eye-teeth for that.'

'I know. It sounds ideal, doesn't it?' said Lorna. 'It's only now, with my wartime experience, that I look back and realise how restricted it was. But I do know,' she added quickly, 'how fortunate I was, how privileged.'

Louise's mouth formed a thoughtful line. 'That's interesting. Your privilege came from before the war, whereas I see my privilege being in the here and now.'

'How d'you mean?' Lorna asked, intrigued.

'Living away from home. Working in the munitions. I'm not going to stay there indefinitely. I intend to find a skilled profession that I can train for in wartime and, with luck and a prevailing wind, stay in afterwards in peacetime. I want to do something interesting and worthwhile with my life – not go back to working in a dress shop.'

'Don't you want to get married?' Lorna asked.

'I'm not taking it for granted.'

'Oh, but you aren't as old as all that,' Lorna exclaimed, wanting to offer encouragement. 'You're not on the shelf yet.'

'I like working,' Louise replied. 'Being on the production line in the munitions is repetitive and exhausting, but it gives me such a sense of purpose, and I want to keep that after the war. As for getting married – let's just say I'm not banking on it.'

'You will if you ever meet the right person,' said Lorna with a smile.

'Are you talking about me – or about yourself and your chap?' Louise asked perceptively.

'Both, I suppose,' Lorna admitted. 'I'm happy with George and that makes me want my friends to have their own happy-ever-after as well. George and I haven't had it easy. We were engaged last year, but then it all fell apart, and we separated. Now we're together again, thanks to the Christmas Blitz of all things, and being together feels wonderful and precious.'

'And better than first time round?' Louise suggested.

'That too,' Lorna agreed.

'Does that mean you've found your happy-ever-after?' Louise asked her.

'I hope so,' said Lorna. 'With all my heart, I hope so.'

The last day of May fell on a Saturday, and it was Lorna's turn to open the depot. The day couldn't pass quickly enough for her because Sally had given permission for George to place a telephone call to the depot just after it closed.

Lorna's heart pounded as she sat behind Sally's desk, awaiting the call. When the instrument rang, she answered it with a professional-sounding, 'Chorlton-cum-Hardy Salvage Depot,' and spoke to the operator to accept the call. The next moment, she was talking to George.

'It's wonderful to hear your voice,' he said.

'And yours,' she replied. 'I miss you.'

'Same here.'

'I'd love to arrange to come down to London to see you.'

'Best not to, just for the present,' said George.

That meant one of two things – or possibly both. It could mean that George was tied up with War Office commitments or it might be a reference to their shared past. It was early days for them to be seen together in London. Neither of them wanted to resurrect old pressures. In any case, it would be wrong to do so before they had received George's parents' blessing.

Something so important and deeply personal wasn't really a subject for the telephone, just in case the operator was earwigging. They weren't supposed to, but you never could tell.

'I know,' said Lorna. 'I'd love us to be together again, that's all.'

'I'll sort out some possible dates for a visit to my family,' said George. 'That's the next thing we need to do.'

Lorna felt a quiver of pleasure, not unmixed with alarm at the prospect of being in Lady Broughton's company.

As she walked home a short while later, she pushed her ladyship from her mind and concentrated on herself and George. How lucky they were to have this second chance. It was sobering to remember that they owed it to the Christmas Blitz, which had caused so much damage and so many fatalities and injuries.

When she got home, she popped her head round the sitting room door. Mrs Beaumont was knitting, with the wireless playing orchestral music.

'Hello, dear. I'll finish this row and then do your tea. It's just you today.'

'Did Sally and Deborah have theirs earlier?' Lorna asked. The two friends had planned to see their mothers for the evening; and Louise was at work and wouldn't be back until later.

'Deborah did,' said Mrs Beaumont. 'She's gone off to Withington. Sally's having a lie-down. I'll take her up a tray when I do your meal. She might fancy a bit of soup.'

'Is she all right?' Lorna asked.

'She told Deborah she's got a bad head.'

Lorna picked up on her landlady's choice of words. 'She *told* Deborah? D'you mean it isn't true?'

'She just needs a rest, that's all. She didn't want her mother racing round here.'

'Is there a reason why she would?'

Mrs Beaumont finished her row and pushed her knitting along towards the bottom of the needle. She stood up.

'She's had a bit of spotting.'

'What does that mean?' Lorna asked.

'I shouldn't have said anything. Single girls aren't meant to know about these things.'

'You've said it now,' Lorna answered, 'so you have to tell me.'

'It means there's been a bit of blood, like when you have your monthly visitor,' said Mrs Beaumont carefully. 'After Deborah left, I had the doctor round—'

'The *doctor*!' Lorna exclaimed.

'—and he said Sally needs to stay in bed and not exert herself.'

'But she's all right?' Lorna pressed.

'It's something that happens to some girls in her condition,' said Mrs Beaumont.

Lorna felt reassured. 'Maybe this will persuade her to take things easier at the depot. You know what she's like: so hard-working.'

'You're on WVS duty tonight, aren't you?' Mrs Beaumont asked. 'I'm going out presently, but I'll be back before you go, and Louise will be home by then as well, so Sally won't be on her own. You'll see, she'll be right as rain tomorrow.'

While Lorna was eating her pilchard salad, Mrs Beaumont took a tray upstairs, and brought it back down again two minutes later.

'Sally says she isn't hungry. I told her she's eating for two, but she still didn't want anything.'

'I'll pop up and see her after I've had this,' said Lorna.

'I'd leave it for now,' said Mrs Beaumont. 'She said she's going to see if she can have a doze. Best thing for her.'

When Lorna had finished her fruit turnover, Mrs Beaumont washed up and soon afterwards left the house. At first Lorna felt she ought to creep about, but then told herself not to be silly. Sally's room, Vesta Tilley, was on the second floor, above Betty's old room, which now belonged to Deborah.

Around half past eight, Louise arrived home. Lorna sat her down and produced the meal Mrs Beaumont had left for her.

'You look tired,' said Lorna.

'I am,' Louise admitted. 'It's not just a physical thing. It's mentally taxing. All that concentration.'

'You can't afford to make even a tiny mistake,' said Lorna.

'I've seen girls with fingers missing, and with terrible facial scars; I've heard of women being blinded or killed. I don't want any of that to happen to me. The trouble is, you can be as careful as you like but if the next girl slips up… Sorry. Not the most cheerful subject. Where are the others? Oh, I remember. They've gone to Withington, haven't they?'

'Deborah has,' Lorna confirmed, 'but Sally's upstairs in bed.' In answer to Louise's enquiring expression, she said, 'The doctor said she needs a rest.'

'She's had the doctor?'

'Mrs Beaumont thought she looked a bit peaky.' That was easier than explaining about the spotting, which would be embarrassing to talk about.

'I'll make sure not to disturb her,' said Louise. Her room, Florrie Forde, of 'Down at the Old Bull and Bush' and 'Pack Up Your Troubles in Your Old Kit Bag' fame, was next to Sally's.

The two girls sat chatting for a while, comparing notes on films they'd seen recently. Then they listened to the news on the Home Service. After the shock and distress of the sinking of HMS *Hood* off the coast of Greenland recently, with the loss of all but three out of more than fourteen hundred lives, the sinking of the German battleship the Bismarck was still being discussed, as was the withdrawal of British forces from Crete. One piece of very welcome news was that the first shipment of food sent by the American people had been received.

'I hope that will make life a bit easier,' said Lorna.

'Fingers crossed.' Louise stood up. 'I'll go and have my bath now and pretend I'm up to my neck in rose-scented bubbles. Then I'll hit the sack. That long shift is catching up with me. I don't envy you going out on duty tonight.'

'Shall I bring you up some cocoa when I come up to get changed?' Lorna offered.

'That would be wizard. Thanks ever so.'

A while later Lorna went up to the second floor with Louise's hot drink. She knocked softly on the door and opened it. Louise was in bed with the light on. She placed her book on the bedside cupboard and raised herself on her elbows.

'This is awfully good of you,' she said.

'You're welcome.' Lorna moved *Murder in Mesopotamia* to put down the cocoa. 'I'll sneak a look in Sally's room and, if she's awake, I'll offer her one.' She glanced at the book. 'I love Agatha Christie. *Peril at End House* is my favourite—'

A sharp intake of breath from Louise cut her off.

'*Sally!*' Louise sat up, throwing aside her covers and sending her drink tumbling to the floor.

Lorna turned quickly. Sally was in the doorway, clinging to the doorframe, practically doubled over.

Lorna darted over to her. 'Sally! You're in pain.'

Louise joined them. 'Come and sit on my bed.'

She tried to put her arm round her, but Sally groaned and bent further forward, then reared up. Her eyes were huge, her face completely colourless.

'Oh my goodness, you're... *bleeding*,' said Louise.

'It... hurts,' Sally managed to say. 'It feels like my insides are tied in knots being pulled tighter and tighter. I didn't know anything could... hurt so much.'

She uttered a small cry and lurched forward. She would have slumped to her knees had the others not caught her and taken her weight. Lorna had never felt more useless in her life.

'Sally?'

Mrs Beaumont appeared at the head of the stairs and Lorna's knees almost buckled in relief. Sally gave a cry of pain.

'You poor child,' said Mrs Beaumont, her voice a mixture of sympathy and the matter-of-fact. 'I fear your baby is in danger. Now then—'

Her voice broke off, and Lorna and Louise stared at one another, as the air-raid siren began to wail.

After a stunned silence, Louise said, 'We have to evacuate the house.'

'How are we going to get Sally out?' Lorna asked, horrified at the way an already desperate situation had suddenly escalated.

Sally uttered a cry that she cut short by clamping her teeth. Her legs folded. Lorna and Louise, unable to hold her up, sank to the floor with her.

Mrs Beaumont slid past and knelt in front of Sally, gently grasping her chin to look into her eyes.

'Could you get down the stairs if we all helped you?'

Sally sucked in a breath and nodded, but then she again bent over with a strangled cry.

'That answers that question,' Louise said briskly. 'Right, here's what we'll do. Lorna, you and I will grab hold of each other's wrists and make a chair out of our arms. We'll have to carry Sally down like that as best we can. Did you hear that, Sally? It'll be bumpy but we'll manage.'

'Let's get you wrapped up in your dressing gown, Sally,' said Mrs Beaumont. 'You'll need yours as well, Louise.'

Gradually, Lorna and Louise carried Sally downstairs. Mrs

Beaumont went first, walking backwards, holding Sally's hand and talking to her, encouraging her, and looking daggers at Lorna and Louise each time they jolted her. The journey down the first staircase was hairy, but then they got into the swing of it and the descent to the ground floor went more smoothly, with Lorna and Louise sidestepping their way down in time with one another.

Mrs Beaumont ran to fetch a dining chair. The others eased Sally onto it. Stepping away, Lorna realised her forearms were covered in blood. She exchanged a silent, terrified glance with Louise.

'We need an ambulance,' said Louise. Behind Sally's back, she raised her bloodied hands to show Mrs Beaumont.

'The quickest thing would be to get an ambulance-car from MacFadyen's,' said Mrs Beaumont. She hurried to open the front door. 'Go on, Lorna!'

Lorna flew from the house on slippered feet. As she raced down Beech Road, she was dimly aware of the drone of engines overhead and the bursts of rapid fire from the ack-ack guns on the meadows at Turn Moss.

She was breathless, her chest burning, when she reached MacFadyen's and ran inside to ask for a motor.

'We have one available,' said Mrs Callaghan, 'but no driver – though that doesn't matter. You can drive, can't you?'

'*Me?*' Alarm streamed through Lorna. 'I've had lessons, but—'

'You've had lessons,' was the bracing reply. 'Now is the time to put them into practice. Come with me.'

Lorna gritted her teeth as she followed Mrs Callaghan outside to where a motor was parked. Feeling as if she was an observer watching herself, she inserted the rotor arm, which had to be removed every time the motor was left so as to prevent the enemy from using it. Then she got behind the wheel and set off, leaning forward, her shoulders rock hard with tension.

She jerked the motor to a halt outside Star House and stepped into the road, but she knew she mustn't leave the vehicle unattended even for a minute. She practically hopped from one foot to the other as Louise and Mrs Beaumont assisted a stumbling, hunched-over Sally, now wrapped in a blanket, down the path.

She helped them get Sally into the vehicle.

'I'll sit in the back with her,' said Louise. She'd had time to fling some clothes on.

'So will I,' said Mrs Beaumont.

'No,' said Louise. 'You have to stay here. If something happens to the house, you need to be here to tell the ARP there's nobody in need of rescue.'

She didn't need to add, 'And if the motor goes for a burton, you'll be able to tell our families what happened.'

Lorna and Louise got in and Mrs Beaumont called her good wishes to Sally before stepping away, one hand pressed to her throat.

Filled with resolve, Lorna set off once more, trying to change gears smoothly and praying that she wouldn't have to make any detours because of craters in the road. Enemy planes streamed overhead, pursued by searchlights, and the fire of the anti-aircraft guns shattered the night. Every time a bomb fell to earth, the motorcar trembled, but fortunately the road didn't pick itself up in a series of giant ripples, as Lorna had seen happen more than once.

When they finally reached Withington Hospital, Louise sprang out of the motor while Lorna shifted it out of the way so that an ambulance could get past. Louise returned with a nurse and a porter, one on each end of a hospital trolley. They helped Sally from the vehicle.

Meanwhile Lorna had thrown up the bonnet so she could remove the rotor arm, but Louise stopped her.

'You need to take the motor back. Someone else might need it.'

'But—'

'You're on duty tonight. I'll stay with Sally.'

'I don't want to leave her!' cried Lorna.

Louise grasped both her hands and held them tightly as she gazed into Lorna's face. 'You have to. You have a job to do. You've been a marvel, Lorna, driving like that through the bombing, and I know how much you care about Sally. But now you've got to get that motor back to the WVS and do whatever they need you to do for the rest of the night – and it's going to be a long one.'

It was a dreadful wrench, but Lorna was forced to agree. With a nod, Louise hurried away and vanished inside. Lorna stared after her and then, sniffing hard and pressing her lips together to fight back the tears, she climbed into the motor.

CHAPTER ELEVEN

The bell rang for evening visiting and the ward door opened. Sally turned her head on the pillow and saw her parents. Tears sprang into her eyes.

Losing her baby last night during that heavy air raid had felt like living through the end of the world. Now, she felt spent and she could hardly bear to think. She felt sore and bruised inside, but she didn't care about her own discomfort. Her baby was gone, ripped from her. The future had been ripped from her, too. Her life had been returned to how it had been before she knew she was expecting a baby – except that it hadn't really gone back to how it had been. It was different. *She* was different.

Mum pulled up the chair beside her bed and reached for her hand. Dad stood behind, the vertical lines between his bushy eyebrows deeper than normal, his cheeks more sunken, highlighting his cheekbones. He looked older; and so did Mum. Her face was drawn, her hazel eyes bleak.

She squeezed Sally's hand. 'Sally, how dreadful. What a shock. We're both so sorry – aren't we?' she asked over her shoulder.

'The main thing is that you're all right.' Dad's voice was thick with emotion.

'Mrs Beaumont and Lorna came round to tell us this morning,' Mum went on.

Staggering to Louise's room... being carried downstairs, the world swooping around her... Finding herself in the back of a motor... voices... the long-drawn-out whistle of incendiaries streaming to earth... The sounds of the raid and the agonising twists of pain in her belly somehow mixing and becoming one and the same...

'Mrs Beaumont says she is happy for you to recuperate at Star House,' said Mum, 'but she's not your mother. When you're discharged, you'll come home to Dad and me, and I'll look after you.'

'I'm not an invalid,' Sally whispered.

'*I'm not an invalid,*' she'd said to Lorna when Lorna wanted her to stop using the sack-trolley. '*I'm having a baby.*'

'Maybe not,' said Mum, 'but you need your rest.'

Sally pictured it, the fussing, the hushed voices. She'd already lost her future with her and Andrew's child. Now her mother wanted to restore her to the home of her girlhood. She loved her parents dearly, but returning home to them would feel bizarre.

Besides, she didn't deserve to be looked after. She hadn't looked after her baby, had she? She hadn't taken proper care of him or her. If she had... Oh, if she had...

The ward sister came to see Sally. 'You lost a lot of blood, so Doctor wants to keep you in tonight just in case. You're going to be moved to the maternity ward.'

Sally could barely breathe. Did this sister not know? 'But – I *lost* my baby...'

'I know it sounds harsh, but it makes sense. The hospital is full to bursting with air-raid casualties and this bed is needed. We can't put you in surgical because you haven't had an operation, and we can't put you in medical or burns. Anything to do with babies means maternity. Don't worry. They have a couple of small side-rooms at one end of the ward. You can have one of those.'

Don't *worry*?

'Hospital isn't really the place for miscarriages,' said the sister. Her voice was businesslike, but sympathetic too. 'Generally speaking, women have them at home.'

'Shouldn't I have come to hospital?' Sally asked in a small voice.

'Your friends did the right thing in bringing you, because of the blood loss. I meant more as a general rule. Miscarriages are more common than you think, I'm afraid.'

Sally immediately pictured herself for ever afterwards looking at strangers in the street and wondering, *Have you had one? What about you?* Then she thought of Mum. Deborah's mum had told her that Mum had lost several babies. It wasn't something Mum had ever talked about – but that was the whole point, wasn't it? No one discussed it.

Sally dreaded being taken to the maternity ward, but the small room she'd been allocated was immediately inside the doors, so at least she was spared having to pass between the lines of mothers and mothers-to-be. Belatedly it occurred to her that she was being tucked away not simply for her own sake but also for theirs, so that they didn't have to think about the possibility of their babies dying.

Sally could feel her strength returning. There was something wrong about recovering when her baby was dead and gone. She had insisted on being taken to Star House. She knew it would hurt her mother, and she was truly sorry for that, but she couldn't face being in her childhood home just now.

Mrs Beaumont soon had her on the sofa in the sitting room, legs stretched out, her upper half propped up by cushions and pillows, a small table beside her with a drink and even a little bell.

'You're to keep your feet up for the next few days,' she said, 'and you're not even to think about the salvage depot. Lorna and Betty can manage.'

'But it's my Saturday this week—' Sally began to protest.

'No, it isn't. The others are doing it for you. Lorna's doing the morning and Betty's doing the afternoon.'

'I'm sure there's no need,' Sally tried again.

'There's every need,' Mrs Beaumont replied in a voice that brooked no argument. 'They want to look after you and this is their way of doing it. Everyone wants to look after you.'

'It feels very public,' Sally whispered. She thought again of all the secret miscarriages that never got talked about. Was it a good or bad thing that her misfortune had occurred with such drama?

The doorbell rang.

'That will be Mrs Henshaw,' said Mrs Beaumont and went to let her in.

Andrew's mother immediately perched on the edge of the sofa and put her arms round Sally, who tried desperately to hold in her tears, but they leaked out anyway.

Mrs Henshaw rocked her. 'My dear Sally, I'm so very sorry. It's tragic, and even worse with Andrew not here. Mrs Beaumont came over to Seymour Grove to tell me what happened, so I'm well aware of what a bad time you had, you poor love. Here, take my hanky. It sounds as if Lorna and Louise were remarkable, getting you safely to hospital the way they did.'

'Yes, they were,' Sally said softly, 'though I don't really remember that part of it all that clearly.'

She might have talked through some of the bits she did remember, but Mrs Henshaw said, 'That's probably for the best,' and Sally felt she'd been silenced – or was she just being hyper-sensitive? Probably the latter...

After a moment Mrs Henshaw said, 'I want you to know that I've written to tell Andrew, so you don't have to concern yourself with that.'

Sally experienced a little ripple of shock. Surely she should have been the one to tell her husband, but, then again, how would she ever have found the words?

'Do you think he'll get leave?' she asked, hope daring to raise its face for a second.

'Not for one moment,' Mrs Henshaw answered. 'If you hadn't had such appalling blood loss, if you'd had your miscarriage privately at home like most women, afterwards those in the know would have patted you on the shoulder and that would have been the end of that. The sad fact is, Sally, that miscarriages don't count.'

Sally felt as though she'd had cold water dashed over her. 'It matters to *me*.'

'Of course it does,' Mrs Henshaw said soothingly, 'and it matters to everyone who cares about you. A lot of people have your welfare at heart, Sally. You have good friends. There are your parents. There's me. There's Auntie Vera and Uncle Mick. We're all deeply sorry for what you've been through.'

A thick wodge of guilt expanded in Sally's throat. There was so much heartache on her behalf, and she didn't deserve it. What would they all think if they knew the truth – that losing her much-wanted baby was all her fault?

'I feel as if I ought to apologise for all the trouble I've caused,' said Sally.

There were immediate objections not only from Lorna and

Louise, but also from Deborah and Betty, who were with them in the sitting room.

'We're just glad to see you in one piece,' said Lorna.

'And we're all terrifically sorry about the little one,' Betty added, her blue eyes swimming.

A fist squeezed Sally's heart. 'I need to think about something else. I might go mad if I go on and on thinking about... Anyway, please tell me what's been happening.'

The others looked at one another, then Lorna spoke up.

'That raid when we took you to hospital was the worst since the Christmas Blitz,' she said. 'There were a lot of deaths and injuries.'

'And a lot of buildings were damaged or destroyed or burned to a crisp,' said Deborah.

'Jerry homed in on us by five different routes, is what I heard,' said Louise.

'The Gaiety Theatre was damaged,' said Deborah. 'The Café Royal, the Theatre Royal, the YMCA.'

'The College of Technology and the police headquarters,' Louise added.

'There were major fires all over the place,' said Lorna, 'and lots of people have been left homeless.'

'It was bad in Salford an' all,' said Betty. 'Nurses were killed at Salford Royal Hospital, and one of the stations was damaged. Have you heard of Threlfall's Brewery? That was damaged too.'

'Stretford, Swinton, Eccles,' Louise added. 'They got hit too.'

'This sounds cheerful,' Mrs Beaumont said drily as she walked in.

The girls looked at one another and the mood lightened. Louise, who'd been in one of the armchairs, went to sit on the hearthrug so their landlady could sit down.

'The other news,' said Lorna, 'is that clothes rationing has started – and nobody knew in advance.'

'Clothes rationing?' Sally looked at Deborah. 'Did you know?'

'Just because I know about food rationing, you mean? Nobody knew except for the people who organised it.'

'Presumably so there wouldn't be a run on buying clothes before it started,' said Mrs Beaumont.

'How will it work?' Sally asked. She didn't care in the slightest, but she had to take her mind off her personal loss if she could.

'We'll all get sixty coupons,' said Louise, 'which have to last a year. Each item of clothing is worth a certain number – a blouse is worth five, a dress eleven – and you have to hand over the requisite number when you buy something.'

'The most bizarre thing,' said Lorna, 'is that this first year, a certain number of coupons are going to be unused margarine coupons. Imagine that!'

'It's all anyone can talk about at the Town Hall,' said Deborah. 'Clothes rationing, I mean, not margarine coupons.'

'Likewise at the depot,' Betty added. 'People have been popping in all the time, not to bring us salvage, but to have a chat about clothes rationing and how it's going to work.'

'It's the same when I'm queuing at the shops,' said Mrs Beaumont. 'It's caused far more of a stir than when Rudolf Hess parachuted into Scotland last month.'

A feeling of unreality crept up on Sally. How had Rudolf Hess got into the conversation? And why had she imagined that trying to dwell on something other than her baby was a good idea?

Something must have shown in her face, because Mrs Beaumont said, 'Sally?'

They all looked at her. She made a decision.

'I'm going to say it, because I'm sure you must all be thinking it. Everyone told me to leave off the heavy side of the depot work and I didn't.'

She heard a jumble of protests but didn't let them sway her.

'I didn't listen, and I should have. It's my fault I lost my baby. But I felt so *healthy*, you see. I thought I could carry on as normal, so that's what I did. You all told me to go easy on the heavy lifting, but I didn't listen. I thought you were all fussing and I loved you for caring, but I believed you were all wrong. I carried on doing whatever was required at the depot, and in the end... in the end... I don't know... my baby came loose. The effort of lifting – which didn't feel like any sort of effort at all – made my baby come loose.' Anguish burst out of her in a storm of tears. 'I'm so sorry I didn't listen to you... I'm so sorry...'

CHAPTER TWELVE

As midsummer approached, the sunrises brought a glimmer to the beads of dew, and the undersides of the clouds glowed as the shadows receded.

Deborah had seen many a sunrise since taking on voluntary war duty. As far as she was concerned, the best thing a new day could offer was for the crisp scent of night-time not to be tainted by the stench of smoke and cordite.

Her heart ached for her friend. She felt guilty for not having realised, when Sally had ducked out of the Withington visit by claiming to have a bad head, that there was more to it. She spent as much time as she could with Sally, anxious to give her support. She couldn't help but be aware of the stark contrast between Sally's grief and her own happiness. She loved living at Star House and she loved working for the WVS.

Sally, always a good friend no matter what, said, 'It's nice to see you in high spirits.'

Deborah immediately felt guilty again. 'It doesn't mean I'm not thinking of you.'

Sally took her hand. 'Just because I'm down in the dumps

doesn't mean I want to drag everyone else down with me. I'm glad things are going well for you.'

'I feel as if my life has opened up,' Deborah confided. 'I enjoy living in a billet and feeling independent.'

'The WVS has been good for you, too,' said Sally. 'I remember what a difference becoming a fire-watcher made to me. At the start of the war, I was so scared at the thought of gas attacks. My stomach turned over every time the siren sounded. But there were no gas attacks – and please God there never will be – but waiting for them became more and more of a strain. You went through that for several months longer than I did. Being a fire-watcher is a big responsibility and there are times when it's downright frightening, but from the outset I loved the feeling of being busy and useful.'

'Busy and useful,' Deborah repeated. 'That's how I feel with the WVS.'

Busy and useful: that summed it up for her. Being among the first to arrive at the scene of a collapsed building had its scary side, but it was also something to be proud of. She was impressed that Lorna had learned to drive and now that was her ambition too, though perhaps she ought to wait a bit before saying so. She didn't want to look like a copycat.

The last day of the month was due to be Sally's first day of working alone at the depot, which was the subject of several whispered conversations at Star House. Sally had made a good recovery, but the others still watched over her.

'It wouldn't do any harm to drop in at the depot,' said Lorna. 'Unfortunately, I can't because I'm on WVS duty all day, and Betty's already arranged to go over to Salford to see her folks. She offered to cancel it, but that would be the very last thing Sally would want.'

'I'd offer to ask for the guided tour,' said Louise, 'but I'm working that day.'

'I'll pop in during the morning,' said Mrs Beaumont, 'just to make sure she's all right.'

'I work until one on Saturdays,' said Deborah, 'so I can call in during the afternoon.'

'She won't like being checked up on,' said Lorna.

'She doesn't have to *like* it,' said Mrs Beaumont. 'I'll tell her that if she doesn't want her friends keeping an eye on her, I'll send her mother round to do it.'

When Deborah walked into the depot yard on Saturday afternoon, Sally waved from the window before coming outside.

'Don't tell me,' she said, raising her eyebrows. 'You just *happened* to be passing.'

Deborah wasn't going to let that put her off. She gave her friend a cheeky grin. 'Be grateful Lorna, Louise and Betty are all spoken for today, or they would have "just happened" to be passing as well.'

'I've already had Mrs Beaumont and Samuel.'

'Samuel?'

'He was under orders from Betty that when he shut the shop for dinner he had to leg it round here.'

'Well, I'm the last one,' said Deborah, 'so once I've gone, you can breathe freely. Are you annoyed with us?'

'No, I'm grateful.'

'Nothing can make up for what happened to you,' said Deborah, 'but you have friends who care about you.'

'I know,' said Sally.

'And I really *am* passing by,' Deborah added. 'I'm on my way to one of the roads off Chorlton Green to help do up some of the houses. Do you have a spare pair of dungarees I could borrow? If I'm going to be slapping paint around, I don't want to get it on my clothes.'

'We've got several pairs in the cupboard,' said Sally. 'I'll show you.'

Inside, they went upstairs, their footsteps loud on the bare floorboards. In the room where Sally's dress was hanging from the picture-rail, she opened a cupboard in which was a pile of pairs of folded dungarees.

'Those are the unused ones,' she said. 'But they're men's dungarees and they'd swamp you.'

Deborah looked at her. 'Yours fit pretty well.'

'Thanks to a considerable amount of altering. Instead of taking enormous dungarees, why not have an altered pair? You're not tall enough for Lorna's, but you could borrow Betty's. She won't mind.'

'You're a brick.'

'Feel free to get changed here,' said Sally. 'If you aren't back before I shut the depot, I'll take your things home with me.'

Downstairs, the telephone rang and Sally went to answer it, leaving Deborah to get changed. It felt odd to be in dungarees. She wished there was a proper mirror instead of the tiny one on the wall. Mum wouldn't be pleased to see her dressed like this. She was old-fashioned about girls wearing trousers, even though it was happening more and more now for practical reasons.

Wearing dungarees made Deborah feel modern and independent and rather proud as she headed for Chorlton Green, but she felt self-conscious too. It was a prickly mixture.

A group stood about outside a run of old terraced cottages that clearly dated from the last century. Even though she didn't want to be shallow, the first thing Deborah did was scan the group to see what the girls and women were wearing. Spotting a couple of girls in slacks made her feel better, not to mention grateful that she was wearing Betty's dungarees instead of looking ridiculous in a man-sized pair.

Mrs Callaghan, the leader of the WVS branch, called for everybody's attention.

'Good afternoon, ladies and gentlemen. Thank you all for turning out to help today. These four cottages in the middle all suffered bomb damage. They've been repaired and now our job is to make them habitable, and not merely habitable but as attractive as we can. The residents are currently all crammed in with friends and family and, as you can easily imagine, are looking forward to coming home. Let's make these cottages as good as we can for them.'

There was a lot to do. To start with, each cottage had to be thoroughly scrubbed from top to bottom. After that, 'wallpaper' was painted on, as were 'curtains' round the windows.

'It's a shame we can't provide the real thing,' one woman commented, 'but this will cheer up the room no end.'

Through the wall came the sound of hammering. Having finished her share of the painting in the first cottage, Deborah was sent next door, where she found a couple of young men putting together some blackout frames, which would fit into the windows so there was no need for blackout curtains.

One of the young men, a good-looking chap with slicked-back dark hair and dark eyes in a squarish face, called, 'Here, mate! Come and hold this steady for me, will you?' It was only when he added, 'Oh – sorry, I thought you were a man,' that Deborah realised she was the one being addressed.

The other young man burst out laughing. 'Mistaking a girl for a man isn't exactly a good start.'

'Sorry,' the first chap said again to Deborah. 'I glimpsed the dungarees and assumed... No offence.'

She managed to say, 'None taken,' and hoped her voice didn't sound too hollow.

She wished he hadn't explained. Now everyone had stopped what they were doing to take a good look at her, including a girl in slacks. All of a sudden, slacks seemed pretty and feminine, while dungarees were chunky and masculine. Deborah was mortified.

One of the middle-aged women said, 'Very workmanlike,' which made it worse, even though she'd meant it approvingly.

Deborah's face was aflame. She wished she could escape upstairs and get painting, but she felt obliged to give the assistance that had been asked for. Kneeling on the floor, she held the pieces of the frames as instructed so they could be fixed together. She kept her gaze glued to the frame on the floor and didn't look at the young man even once.

The moment the job was done, she fled up the stairs, her heart bumping with every step. She'd felt so modern and independent when she'd dressed in Betty's dungarees, but now she felt clumsy and gauche, not to mention a complete idiot. Everyone had looked at her and drawn their own conclusions. And as for those two young men, the one who had inadvertently insulted her and his friend who'd enjoyed a hearty laugh at her expense, she could have crowned the pair of them, especially the one who had started it by mistaking her for a man.

A *man*. She'd never been more embarrassed in her life.

CHAPTER THIRTEEN

Towards the end of June, German armed forces started to invade Russia. It was chilling to think that Hitler had so much power and military might that he could afford to open up the war on yet another front.

'Let's hope it means he'll pay less attention to us,' Sally's dad commented.

Sally hoped so too. Now that Andrew was in the army, she had even more reason to wish for the war to be over. She missed him every single day, but sometimes an extra wave of longing would pour over her and rip her breath away, leaving her wondering how she was to live her life without him by her side for goodness only knew how long.

The fine weather continued. When Sally went for walks on the meadows alongside the River Mersey, golden buttercups, thistly-looking knapweed and early harebells of softest blue caught her eyes; all plants she had imagined showing to her child and telling him or her their names.

From her bedroom window, she could see people hard at work on the allotments, thinning carrots, parsnips and lettuces, examining leaves for blackfly and working on the next sowing of salad crops so there was always salad for the table.

Life was going on all around her and, while Sally knew that this was a good thing, it also sometimes meant that a quiet despair crept into her heart. She thought of the long lists of casualties that had to be published after each and every air raid – lists of fatalities, too. All those names and addresses of people who had lost their lives.

Her baby had never appeared on a list. Her baby didn't have a name. She didn't even know if she'd been carrying a girl or a boy.

Mum came to see her at Star House one evening at the beginning of July.

'You're looking well, Sally.'

'I'm fine,' she replied.

It was true. Physically she was. It was shocking that her body could recover from something so momentous. That wasn't a thought she had shared with anyone, not even with Andrew in their letters. Quite the opposite, in fact. She had written of her deep sorrow and also of her concern for him, but at the same time she hadn't wanted him to worry about her, so she had emphasised her recovery. There was an unwritten rule that those left behind at home should send cheerful, encouraging letters to the troops, not letters full of gloom and anxiety.

Mum nodded. 'I'd like you to take a day off work, or half a day at least.'

'I don't need it,' said Sally.

'It's so you can come to see Dr Carney with me.'

Sally drew in a sharp breath that scorched her throat. 'Are you poorly? What's the matter?'

But Mum wouldn't be drawn. 'Just say you'll come with me.'

'Of course I will.'

What could be wrong with her? She was a good twenty

years older than the mothers of Sally's contemporaries, but she had always enjoyed good health.

A day or two later, they sat in Dr Carney's house, where the front parlour acted as his waiting room. When it was their turn, he popped his head round the door and called them through.

Sally's heart was beating quickly as she took a seat in his surgery. Mum still hadn't told her what this was about. If Mum hadn't been using both hands to grasp the handles of her handbag, Sally would have reached across in a gesture of loving support.

The doctor sat behind his desk. He was a short, tubby man whose hair was considerably thinner than it had been when Sally was a little girl.

'Thank you for seeing us,' said Mum. 'Please will you tell Sally what you told me?'

Now Sally's hand reached towards her mother of its own accord. She ran her tongue over her lower lip. Mum had clearly brought her here because of bad news.

'Well, young lady,' Dr Carney said as if Sally was six years old, 'your mother has brought you here because she's concerned about you.'

Sally's hand fell away as she glanced at Mum with a frown.

'I wanted you to hear it from the doctor,' said Mum. 'I knew you'd believe him when you might not believe me.'

Dr Carney stepped in. 'I understand that you've had a miscarriage. I also hear that you blame yourself because of the physical nature of your war work.'

Sally was silent. With warning, she might have had something to say, but caught unawares like this…

'The truth is that nobody ever knows for certain why a miscarriage happens,' the doctor continued, 'but given that you are strong and healthy, it seems unlikely that your work was the cause. It is far more likely that you have inherited some… defect from your mother.'

It took a moment for the words to sink in.

Sally's voice came back. 'A *defect?*'

Mum hung her head.

'Your mother had one successful pregnancy, of which you are the result, but there were other pregnancies that ended in spontaneous abortions.'

Abortions? Pictures of gin and knitting needles dropped unbidden into Sally's head.

'He means miscarriages,' Mum said quietly.

'Your mother was fortunate to have you,' said Dr Carney. 'There is no knowing why her other pregnancies ended in the way they did, but I'm afraid it is possible that you have inherited that defect.'

Later that afternoon, Sally and her mother sat in Mum's parlour with cups of tea beside them. They were both smoking. Sally had smoked for pleasure for years, but now she understood why some people smoked to settle their nerves.

'Was I right?' Mum asked in a brittle voice. 'Was it easier to believe Dr Carney than if I'd said it?'

Sally nodded. 'If you'd said it, I'd have thought you were just trying to make me feel better, but hearing it from him...' Something deep inside her quivered at the thought of the *defect.*

'I'm sorry,' said Mum.

'Whatever for? You've helped me.' Being told she had a defect didn't help, but it was something she would have to get used to. How did you adjust to something like that?

'I mean I'm sorry I've passed on whatever it is to you.'

'It's not your fault. You couldn't help it.'

'I never imagined... It never occurred to me you might have the same problem.'

'It's better to know the reason than not know,' said Sally.

Was it? Could it be called a good thing to know she might have some sort of defect?

'I was horrified when I heard what had happened to you. All those memories came flooding back. I don't mean I was horrified because of the memories. I was horrified because I knew what you'd gone through – the pain and the anguish. I never suffered anything like as badly as you did in physical terms, but it isn't the physical pain that's the worst part anyway. It's the feelings... the desolation.'

Sally dashed away a tear. 'Desolation. That's a good word for it.'

'When you were growing up, I used to look at you and think of the brothers and sisters you should have had.' Mum put her cigarette to her lips and inhaled deeply, then blew out a long stream of smoke. 'People would sometimes say to me, people who had no idea about the miscarriages, that I was lucky to have just the one child, because children are so tiring, and especially with me being an older mother.'

'Oh, Mum...'

'People are always quick to make their own judgements about the lives of others. They probably thought I was glad to have just one. They probably thought I was grateful not to have more.' She breathed in deeply and shook her head.

'I keep thinking about the future,' said Sally, 'the one I thought I was going to have with the baby. I'd imagined bringing up him or her to look forward to the day Daddy came home. And now that future is all... gone.'

Mum nodded. 'After a miscarriage, you're supposed to go back to normal and carry on as if nothing has happened; but it has happened, and it never quite goes away. And listen. Here's something important. I don't want you blaming yourself, d'you hear me? You *mustn't* blame yourself. You did nothing wrong. I know how much you longed for that baby, how much you were looking forward to being a mother, and you would *never* have done anything to place your child in jeopardy – any more than I would have done with mine.' After a moment she added, speaking rapidly as if to prevent herself from changing her mind, 'Shall I tell you what I envy about the way it happened to you?'

'*Envy?*' Sally couldn't believe her ears.

'I don't know if that's the right word but it's the closest I can get,' said Mum. 'In my day, folk didn't talk about pregnancy.'

Sally smiled. 'I remember you telling me Dr Carney brought me in his black bag.'

'It's different now because of green ration books and pregnant ladies being evacuated. But back then it was all very private, and the most secret thing of all was if you lost a baby. That was the hardest part, that I knew that this terrible thing had happened to me but almost no one else knew. I'm sorrier than I can say that you suffered as much as you did and that you lost all that blood, but at least it means your loss was seen and acknowledged. What I wouldn't have given for that when it happened to me. You didn't have to put on your best face and pretend nothing had happened, Sally.' Mum took another drag on her cigarette. 'I'm sorry I used the word envy. That was the wrong thing to say. I just mean that I'm so very grateful to think of you having the support I didn't have. It isn't appropriate that those girls you live with – single girls – should know what happened, but I can't be sorry about it. I'm glad you haven't had to go through all this on your own.'

'The way you did,' Sally said sombrely, having to speak past an ache in her throat.

'I wish you'd come here after you left hospital,' said Mum.

'I did what seemed right at the time,' Sally said softly. 'But if I had come here, we might have had this conversation sooner.'

'Or we might not have had it at all,' said Mum. 'If you'd come here and let me fuss over you, I wouldn't have fretted in the same way and I might have ended up keeping my secret.'

A wave of compassion swept over Sally. Mrs Grant knew about Mum's sorrows, so presumably other neighbours did too, but Mum wouldn't thank Sally for saying so. Even though Mum wished she'd had the support she had needed at the time, she would be horribly embarrassed if she thought her misfortunes were common knowledge.

All Sally could say was, 'I'm glad you told me.'

Such simple words, but they contained a wealth of love, understanding and gratitude.

CHAPTER FOURTEEN

'I'm glad you and George have finally managed to arrange a visit to his parents,' Betty told Lorna as they sorted the contents of the daily sacks one morning of hazy sunshine towards the end of July.

'I don't know whether to be excited or nervous,' Lorna confessed. 'A bit of both, I suppose. George swears I'll be made welcome by his parents, but I'll still wonder what they're thinking...'

'Won't it be like when George went to Lancaster?' Betty asked. 'Your parents were iffy to start with, but then they came round because they want what's best for you, and that means being with George. His parents must want what's best for him too. What was that for?' she added as Lorna gave her a quick hug.

'For being *you*, Betty Atkinson; for being a generous soul who looks for the best in other people.'

Betty swatted her away. 'You daft thing. For your information, I don't always see the best in others. Look at the way I've talked about Grace in the past.'

'That's different,' said Lorna. 'You knew she wanted to prise you out of your own home, and even after she'd achieved it she did her level best to stop you being alone with your dad. It would have been strange if you *had* found nice things to say about her after all that.' She looked into Betty's face. 'But things are better between the two of you now, aren't they?'

'They seem to be,' said Betty. 'Me being a married woman living miles away helps as far as she's concerned; and Dad knowing that she wasn't all sweetness and light to me behind his back helps as far as I'm concerned.' She smiled ruefully. 'That sounds very ungracious, doesn't it? The most important thing to me is that Grace and I are on reasonable terms now.'

'You're a better person than I am,' Lorna told her. 'I'm not sure I could have put all that behind me the way you have.'

Betty gave her a sweet smile. 'It's very simple, really. I don't want Dad to be miserable. How did we end up talking about Grace, anyway?' she asked with a laugh. 'We're meant to be discussing you and George. Anyroad, I meant what I said: George's parents must want what's best for him.'

'But who's to say what the best is?' Lorna put on a bright voice, but really she felt taut with worry. 'I'm not sure the Broughtons will see me as best.'

'Why not?' Betty challenged her. 'After all, your parents have accepted George back into the fold.'

'It was easier for my parents,' said Lorna. 'All they ever had against George was that he jilted me. I don't mean to make it sound as if that was a trifling thing. It was dreadful in all kinds of ways, not least because of the way the press dragged me through the mud.' She took a moment to focus her thoughts. 'What I mean is that George was a dream come true for my parents, especially my father, before the jilting; but the same can't said for how George's family viewed me, especially his mother.'

'How so?' Betty asked.

'George is out of the top drawer, which is exactly what

Daddy wanted. I expect he couldn't believe his luck when I fell in love with a man from a titled family,' Lorna explained. 'But I'm not out of the top drawer, so I'm not what his family was hoping for.'

'You're as good as anyone from the so-called top drawer!' Betty declared staunchly.

'Try telling Lady Broughton that,' Lorna answered with a laugh she was far from feeling. 'She wants a girl with a perfect pedigree, who had exactly the right sort of upbringing.'

'This reminds me of Grace,' said Betty. 'When I first took Samuel home to introduce him, she couldn't wait to tell me what a good catch he was. Then she said that he was too good for me and I'd better reel him in quickly before he could see sense.'

'How unkind,' said Lorna, shocked.

Betty shrugged it off. 'The point is that when two people are right for one another, they shouldn't let another person tell them what's what.' She laughed, which made her blue eyes twinkle. 'And you can tell Lady Broughton I said so!'

Lorna might be torn between anxiety and excitement at the thought of visiting the Broughtons, but there was no doubt as to her feelings at the prospect of being reunited with George.

How everything had changed. Just a matter of months ago, she would have sworn she had got over him and managed to move on from her heartbreak. She had truly believed that to be the case at the time, but now, as she looked back, it seemed as if she had been only half-alive back then. It had taken their meeting up again during the horrors of the Christmas Blitz to make her realise, to make them both realise, that they were meant to be together.

After all the emotional upheaval and uncertainty they had gone through, taking their relationship steadily was without doubt the right thing to do for the time being, but it was hard when all she wanted was for them to be together, enjoying one another's company and getting to know everything about one another in a way they hadn't done the first time round.

'If he had carried on living in the Claremont Hotel like he was doing before Easter,' she confided to Sally, 'then taking things slowly would be a doddle. It's being apart because he's back in London that makes it so difficult. Letters and the occasional telephone call can never make up for not seeing one another. – I'm sorry. I shouldn't say that to you when Andrew is away indefinitely. I know he's on home soil, but it's not as though you can see one another.'

'Don't ever feel you have to tiptoe around me because of Andrew being away,' said Sally. 'I want you to be happy and I'm glad George is in London and not abroad. I'm glad Betty has got Samuel at home too.'

Typical Sally. She was always sensible. She had made a good recovery from the ordeal of losing her baby – on the outside, at any rate. She kept her feelings on the subject to herself, though she had given the others a glimpse.

'You're all so kind to me and it really helps,' she had told them. 'I'm still getting used to what happened and I've got a lot to think about. It'll take time.'

She didn't ask them in so many words to leave her alone, but that seemed to be what she hoped for. Or maybe it wasn't a question of being left alone so much as one of being allowed time to reflect on everything without interruption.

'She knows we're here if she needs us,' Lorna said to Deborah. 'That's what counts.'

'I know you're concerned about her, but you mustn't let it overshadow your trip to Yorkshire,' said Deborah. 'That's the last thing she'd want. She has the rest of us to keep an eye on her, don't forget.'

That made Lorna feel better about preparing for her visit.

She had a week off. A whole week in George's company! Her heart lifted in anticipation. That was worth the price of a dozen Lady Broughtons. The arrangement was that George would arrive the day before Lorna.

'That way, no matter what the hold-ups are on our respective journeys,' he had told her over the telephone, 'I'll be there first, and I'll meet you off your train.'

George and his father, Sir Jolyon, who were both with the War Office, were to travel together from London on Friday, and Lorna would make her journey across the Pennines on Saturday. Sir Jolyon would have to return to London on Sunday, while George and Lorna were to remain until the following Saturday.

Lorna was aware that Sir Jolyon had offered Platt House for war service back in the spring of 1939.

'He didn't want to wait for the old place to be requisitioned,' George had explained to her.

These days the house was a hospital, but the picture that had instantly appeared in Lorna's mind of gallant troops bravely bearing their injuries had soon been tempered.

'Evidently, khaki dye brings on a severe reaction in some chaps,' George had told her. 'That might sound amusing, but it can be quite serious. They go to Mother's hospital to have their skin treated.'

'Mother's hospital?'

'Yes, she runs the show. Her official title is Commandant, which makes her sound very fearsome.'

And deservedly so, in Lorna's unspoken opinion. She was less worried about Sir Jolyon. His big beef had been with Daddy, not with her. But Lady Broughton, though civil, had always been cool. What were the chances of winning her over?

. . .

Like so many other passengers since the names of the stations had been painted over, Lorna was concerned about getting off at the right place, but luckily there were some locals on the train and they told her when her stop was coming up. As the train ran alongside the platform, there was a loud hissing noise, then the brakes shrieked and some of the carriage doors were thrown open, before a deep clunking sound signalled that the mighty engine had come to a halt. Holding on to the door, Lorna stepped down onto the platform.

George came striding towards her and she dropped her bag and ran into his arms, her heartbeat drumming excitedly inside her chest. They clung together for a few moments, then George released her, taking a long moment to gaze into her eyes.

He shook his head with a smile. 'It's good to see you.'

'You too,' she answered, brushing his cheek with her fingers and releasing a deep sigh. This was one of those special moments she wanted to remember for always.

'We'd better get going.' George moved round her to rescue her case from where she'd dumped it.

A gleaming Bentley stood outside the station. George opened the passenger door for her, then saw to her luggage. Before driving off, he sat with his hands on the steering wheel, smiling at her, his lean, serious features looking good-humoured and loving.

'Nervous?' he asked her.

'A little,' she admitted.

'Don't be. I've made it very clear to my parents that I have no doubts about our relationship.'

Although she was glad to hear it, Lorna's mouth went dry with anxiety. Would Lady Broughton be swayed by his confidence?

They drove through beautiful countryside and turned in through a pair of tall gateposts, each topped with a stone pineapple, onto a drive with substantial shrubberies on either side. Presently, the drive formed a graceful curve and headed for the house.

Beneath a roof dotted with ornate chimneystacks, tall windows on the ground and first floors suggested high ceilings, while the second floor had smaller square windows. In the middle of the ground floor, shallow steps led to a pair of double doors. All in all, Lorna thought it an orderly and handsome building and not overbearing.

In front was a spacious lawn on which a game of croquet was in progress, played by two nurses and two men in untucked shirts that were open at the neck. More patients and one or two nurses sat at circular tables or on benches that had arms and legs of ornamental ironwork. A couple of hammocks had been erected in the shade of some cedar trees. The lawn was surrounded by flowerbeds. Lorna formed a swift impression of fuchsias, hollyhocks and stately grasses that wafted gently in the breeze.

George drove past the front of the house and round the side, where he stopped the motor. Ahead, beyond the back of the building, Lorna glimpsed one end of a vegetable garden, so close to the house that it had to have been a real garden before the war.

George indicated a side door.

'This is where we go in and out. The entrance hall at the front is a socking great space and it would have been criminal for the hospital not to make use of it. In any case, the main parts of the house belong to the hospital now. The family has been shunted into the nether regions.'

'You make it sound as if you've been relegated to the coal-hole.'

George laughed. 'Perhaps not. There's a suite of rooms on the ground floor and the corresponding rooms above. Bradshaw will show you to your bedroom. She's one of the two remaining servants. She's been here all her life, and she tells off the land girls for talking about the vegetable garden, which she still insists on referring to as the rose garden. When you've had time to freshen up, come downstairs and see my parents.'

The elderly Bradshaw, kind-eyed and as sturdy as a pit pony, showed Lorna the way upstairs to a carpeted landing with closed doors along either side. Lorna's bedroom was old-fashioned but comfortable and spotless. It was easy to imagine Bradshaw taking no prisoners where the cleaning was concerned.

Soon she was ready to go down. She found George hovering near the foot of the staircase. Her heart gave a happy little bump. He hadn't wanted her to walk into the room on her own.

Sir Jolyon and Lady Broughton were waiting for them in a sitting room in which the prevailing colours were cream and light green. Lorna was too intent upon making a good impression to notice more than that.

Sir Jolyon came forward to greet her. He had the same lean features and grey-blue eyes as his son.

'Welcome to Platt House, my dear.'

'Thank you,' said Lorna.

Then it was time to be greeted by her ladyship. Her once-dark hair was now liberally threaded through with silver, and her eyes were deep blue. She had a patrician look – 'good bones,' Lorna's mother would have said.

'Yes, indeed,' said Lady Broughton. 'Welcome.'

'Thank you,' Lorna said again. 'It's a great pleasure to be here.'

The door opened and Bradshaw trundled a wooden tea-trolley into the room.

'I expect you're parched after your journey,' said Lady Broughton. 'Was the train crowded?'

Her civility was faultless. The little group made a few remarks about Lorna's journey while the tea was poured and passed round. It all felt very polite.

Lorna asked about the hospital. 'It must have been strange giving up most of your home to it.'

'It isn't the first time,' said Lady Broughton. 'Platt House was a hospital in the last war as well, though we had a general hospital for officers back then.'

'But, yes, it was strange to start with,' said Sir Jolyon. 'The blue drawing room is now the nurses' common room.'

'The red drawing room and the three largest bedrooms were packed full of paintings and the best furniture and then shut up for the duration,' said Lady Broughton. 'The dining room is now a recreation room for the patients.'

'The ballroom, God help us, is now the canteen,' Sir Jolyon added. 'Not that I begrudge it. We all have to do our bit.'

'We have possibly the most luxurious air-raid shelters you'll ever see,' George added. 'All the biggest sofas were hauled downstairs into the cellars.'

'I saw patients on the lawn when we drove up,' said Lorna.

'They have the freedom of the grounds,' said Sir Jolyon, 'except for the part the army uses for grenade-throwing practice. So don't be alarmed if you hear explosions.'

'You may also see children creeping about,' said Lady Broughton.

'They sneak in, you mean?' asked Lorna.

'On the contrary, I made it clear at the outbreak of war that they were welcome,' Lady Broughton replied. 'They love searching for German spies. And of course, with the children roaming around, it makes it harder for the patients and nurses to do any canoodling in the shrubbery.'

Lorna blushed, but George threw back his head and roared with laughter. '*Canoodling* in the shrubbery! Whatever next?'

'Laugh if you wish, George,' said his mother, 'but I haven't had to dismiss a single member of staff since before Dunkirk.'

Presently Sir Jolyon invited George to join him in the estate room to look over some plans for crops, which left Lorna with Lady Broughton.

'You're the last person I expected George to bring home,' said her ladyship.

Lorna braced herself. 'We've decided to put last year behind us.'

'I'm sure your parents must be delighted.'

'Yes, they are,' Lorna replied steadily. 'They think very highly of George.'

'I'm sure they do,' said Lady Broughton. 'He is an excellent man, intelligent, cultured, hard-working and patriotic. Any family would be fortunate to have him among their number.' Her face softened – or was that a ploy to make Lorna trust her? 'But I would think that, wouldn't I, the proud mother? Unfortunately, I don't believe the same can be said for you. I always had my doubts about you even before I discovered your father's plot to bag the heir to a title as his son-in-law. You haven't been born to it, you see. All this...' She made an elegant gesture that encompassed Platt House and all it stood for. 'With your background in trade and your social-climbing father, how can you possibly have what it takes?'

Lorna gave a small gasp that seemed to get lodged in the back of her throat. Having Lady Broughton throw Daddy's social ambitions in her face was especially hurtful. She was shocked too. She had known all along that George's mother wasn't keen on her, but never had anything been said openly.

Lorna now knew beyond doubt that she didn't stand a chance of winning her ladyship over.

Lorna didn't breathe a word to George of what his mother had said. It would have smacked of telling tales. Moreover, it would have created friction, which she didn't want. In a strange way, if she had told George it would have seemed like a victory for her ladyship. It would have made Lorna look as if she lacked backbone.

No, as hard as it was, the best thing to do was take it on the chin and conduct herself as if all was right with the world. The main thing was to concentrate on enjoying time with George in this special place where generations of his family had lived.

But on Sunday, Lorna's hopes were shattered. She and the Broughtons attended church together and Lorna pretended not to notice the glances that came her way. She was introduced to various people outside afterwards. No one was crass enough to refer to the engagement of the previous year, but the bright light of curiosity in several pairs of eyes made it clear that everybody knew precisely who she was.

When they returned to Platt House, there was a message for George to contact the War Office. He disappeared for a while and when he returned, his face was grim, his eyes positively stormcloud-grey.

'I've been called back,' he said, looking at Lorna, before turning to his father. 'You aren't the only one who'll be heading to London this afternoon, sir.'

Lorna bit back an exclamation of disappointment. George had to do his duty, and she wasn't going to make it difficult. In the lightest voice she could manage, she asked, 'How long will you be gone?'

'Not sure,' he replied. 'I'll return as soon as I possibly can. In the meantime, you and Mother can get to know one another.'

Crikey. The very last thing Lorna wanted was to be stranded at Platt House with Lady Broughton. She didn't imagine that her ladyship felt any different. But she was careful to keep these thoughts to herself when she and George were able to snatch a few minutes before he had to take his leave.

'I'm sorry about this, my love,' George said, the backs of his fingers brushing their way softly down the side of her face.

'It can't be helped,' she replied.

'No, it can't, but it's still dashed unfortunate timing,' said George. 'We've had barely any time together.'

'Let's hope that whatever it is can be dealt with promptly, so you can get back here toot sweet,' said Lorna. 'Then it'll be an even better visit because we'll appreciate it more.'

I know I will, she added silently as she pictured being here on her own with Lady Broughton.

After George and his father had departed, Lorna told her hostess that she would like to make herself useful.

'Is there anything I can do in the hospital?' she offered.

'Do you have any nursing experience?' Lady Broughton enquired. 'No, I thought not. The patients are always glad of company.'

'That wasn't quite what I was hoping for,' Lorna said. 'I had hoped for more of a job. As well as my salvage work, I'm in the WVS at home.'

'Then I'll ask the local WVS if they can use you,' said Lady Broughton.

Lorna thought that would suit both of them. It would get her out of Lady Broughton's hair while enabling her to fill her time doing something useful.

As a result, Lorna found herself as a volunteer on the pie scheme, which involved working as part of a busy team to prepare and bake scores of pies and pasties and then travelling around the countryside to deliver them to people scattered about, working on the various farms. A girl called Barbara, who had dark hair and a clear-skinned outdoorsy look, was put in charge of her. Together with another girl called Angela, they drove around in a battered old van, chatting as they went from farm to farm and village to village.

Barbara's husband was in the army. He had dashed home for a quick wedding and then gone back again more or less immediately.

'That sounds very romantic,' said Lorna.

Angela didn't have a boyfriend, but she wrote to a dozen servicemen.

'Just as a friend,' she told Lorna. 'Letters mean a lot to our boys overseas.'

When Lorna arrived on the second day, looking forward to more of the same, she found Barbara frowning as she shunted pieces of paper around on her desk.

She looked up and saw Lorna. 'I don't suppose you can drive, can you? There's a tummy bug doing the rounds and I'm two drivers down.'

'I had some lessons but—'

'But you don't feel confident about driving down country lanes in a strange place,' said Barbara. 'Fair enough.'

Lorna thought of the agricultural workers and land girls who relied on the pie scheme. She thought too of taking Sally to hospital.

'Look,' she said. 'If you send me out with someone who knows the route inside out, and who won't mind if I crunch the gears, I'll do it.'

'Good show,' said Barbara. 'It'll be good driving practice for you. I'll give you the shortest route.' She grinned. 'You'll be driving as smoothly as Sir Jolyon's chauffeur by the end of the day.'

Except for knowing how important this was, Lorna might have wished she hadn't offered. As it was, she was determined to do her best. By the end of the day, her confidence behind the wheel had increased no end.

It was disappointing, therefore, to be asked the next day to do something different.

'An infants' hospital is being moved out of London,' she was told by the WVS branch organiser, 'and a house here has been requisitioned. We have two days to make it ready – and when I say "we", I mean *you*, Miss West-Sadler.'

'Me?' Lorna's voice came out almost as a squeak.

'Yes. It's this wretched tummy bug. I have plenty of highly competent women, but a lot of them have been laid low. I heard about you taking that motor out on one of the pie routes even though you're an inexperienced driver. That's the sort of attitude that's needed for this project. I've got some volunteers for you. You'll be able to manage, won't you? Jolly good!' she finished briskly, giving Lorna no time to express any reservations.

Lorna was shocked when she saw the state of the requisitioned house. Talk about filthy! She had arrived half an hour before the volunteers so she could form a plan, but now the work that was needed seemed overwhelming. All she wanted to do was turn tail and run.

Instead, she walked purposefully to the nearest telephone box, put a call through to Platt House and asked to speak to Bradshaw.

'It's Miss West-Sadler,' she said when Bradshaw came on the line. 'I urgently need some advice.'

When the volunteers arrived, Lorna knew what was needed.

'The house needs scrubbing from top to bottom. We're collecting the furniture from storage tomorrow, but there are some wooden tables here that are badly stained. If we sprinkle lemon juice on the stains, they'll clean up nicely tomorrow. And the gratings over the outside drains are grimy, so we must make a fire outdoors, then pick up each grating using a poker and place them one by one in the flames. That will take off the grime.'

As her volunteers got to work, Lorna smiled to herself. Anyone would think she knew what she was talking about!

By the end of the next morning the house had been transformed, but her work wasn't over yet. She chanced to overhear a remark from one of the volunteers about 'the poor mothers left behind in London while their little ones are brought all the way up here,' and it set her thinking.

'We ought to help the mothers if we possibly can,' she said to the volunteers when they all stopped for a tea break. 'They really need to be able to visit their children while they're up here in hospital – and I'm sure the children will need to see their mothers, too. I wondered about the possibility of arranging accommodation for the mothers?'

'Assuming they could afford the train fare,' piped up one of the women, though not in a negative tone. On the contrary, she sounded the same as Lorna, as if she was thinking things through.

'The Public Assistance Board could help,' said another lady. 'The WVS works with them regularly.'

'And this is a worthy cause,' said Lorna. 'Do you think local people would open their homes to mothers whose infants are in hospital? It would be like taking an evacuee but just for a few nights.' She wanted to make it clear that she wasn't going to swan off into the sunset leaving everyone else, with their depleted numbers, to put her ideas into action. 'Help me make a list of what needs doing and you can advise me on who best to speak to. I'll devote the rest of the day to it and see what I can come up with.'

After a busy afternoon, things started to fall into place, not least because her volunteers had no intention of letting her organise this all on her own.

By the time she headed back to Platt House, she felt as if she was surrounded by a golden glow of sheer wonderment at what marvels the women of the WVS were. Something needed doing and so they organised it. Simple as that.

Now she had to prepare for a final evening in Lady Broughton's company. There had been guests each evening. Was that so that the two women wouldn't be alone together, or would these others have been invited anyway? Lorna didn't know.

All that mattered to her was that George was still in London – and she was returning to Manchester in the morning. So much for their longed-for holiday in each other's company.

CHAPTER FIFTEEN

'D'you mean to say you've been away for a whole *week* and George wasn't there?' Deborah could hardly believe her ears. Together with the other Star House girls and Betty, who had come round especially to hear all about Lorna's holiday, she was in the sitting room.

Lorna shrugged. 'Yep, 'fraid so.' Her voice was breezy, as if it didn't matter, but then she sighed and the sadness showed in her green eyes. 'It was rotten luck. I hoped he'd only be gone a day or two, but he didn't come back at all, though he telephoned me each evening.'

'It's hardly the same thing, though,' said Louise.

'What a shame,' said Betty.

'I wondered once or twice about cutting short my trip and coming home, so as to save some of my annual holiday,' said Lorna, 'but what if I'd done that and then George had been able to get away from London? Besides,' she added, 'I was busy helping the WVS and I couldn't let them down. There was illness in the ranks, so they needed every pair of hands they could get.'

'I'm sure they appreciated everything you did,' said Louise, her clear brown eyes showing she meant it. 'If nothing else, it kept you occupied.'

'Just not in the way I'd expected,' Lorna said ruefully.

'Poor you,' Sally said sympathetically.

'And poor George,' Betty added.

'I keep telling myself,' said Lorna, 'that what matters is that he's now been to my home, and I've been to his, so we've fulfilled that particular duty.'

Deborah sat forward. 'Yes – his home. What's it like?'

Along with the others, she listened avidly to Lorna's description of large, well-appointed rooms, the building's gracious façade, and the patients enjoying a lively game of croquet on the front lawn. Fancy having a chap from a background like that! Deborah was dying to ask if Lorna expected to end up married to George, but it might be a bit of a cheek seeing as she hadn't known her all that long. But should Sally or Betty ask the question...

But, instead, what Sally asked was, 'How did you get on with George's parents?' The way she leaned forward as she asked showed what an important question it was.

'With Sir Jolyon, fine,' said Lorna. 'That was never really in doubt. But with Lady Broughton...'

Betty's blue eyes filled with sympathy. 'Was it tricky?'

'You could say that.' Lorna frowned slightly. Was she considering whether to make light of the matter? If so, she decided against it, because her next words were, 'It was pretty awful, actually. She didn't approve of me last year when we were engaged, and clearly she hasn't changed her mind.'

'Oh, Lorna,' said Betty. 'What a blow.'

'I thought I was prepared for it,' said Lorna, 'but you can't really prepare yourself for that.'

'Did she make it obvious?' Louise asked.

'Don't get me wrong,' said Lorna. 'She was civility itself in a cool sort of way, but there was this one time when it was just the two of us, and she left me in no doubt as to what she thinks of me.'

'What did she say?' Sally asked.

'She started by praising George to the skies, then she made it abundantly clear that she's aware of the wish my father had last year for me to marry into a family with a title, and she rounded it all off by saying that I haven't got what it takes.'

'You mean, because of your father wanting a title last year?' Deborah asked.

'That – and my background in trade,' said Lorna.

'Well, honestly!' Louise exclaimed. 'How old-fashioned. That's positively Victorian.'

'Oh, it was more than that,' Lorna replied. 'She pointed out – quite rightly, as it happens – that I wasn't born to the job of lady of the manor.'

'That doesn't mean you aren't perfectly capable of doing it,' Betty said loyally.

'When you look at all the different sorts of jobs women are now doing in wartime,' said Sally, 'not to mention the voluntary work we all do, it's barmy to suggest that only women with certain blood running through their veins are able to run a stately home.'

'Thanks – all of you.' Lorna's smile showed her gratitude for the support. 'But that's enough of Lady Broughton for the time being. I just have to accept that she'll never think well of me, and that's all there is to it.'

With the kindly tact that Deborah knew of old, Sally moved the conversation along, and they ended up talking about the infants' hospital Lorna had helped set up.

'The WVS women are amazing.' Louise's words summed up the feeling in the room. 'There's nothing they can't achieve.'

Pride made Deborah sit up straight. She loved her WVS work. Her old job at the mortuary had been important at the time – essential, really, because everybody had fully believed

Jerry was going to drop gas-bombs – but waiting night after night for something that had never happened had taken its toll. Now she felt fully engaged, efficient and adaptable, and she enjoyed the companionship.

Betty got to her feet. 'I must be making tracks.'

'We're not on fire-watching duty tonight,' said Sally. 'You haven't got to go and get ready.'

'No, but Samuel is on ARP duty,' Betty replied, 'and I'd like to get home before he goes so we can spend some time together.'

'I need to get changed soon,' said Deborah. 'I'm on WVS duty tonight.'

What with the thought of the Atkinsons' love for one another, and Lorna's situation with George, Deborah couldn't help wondering, as she went upstairs to get changed, if she would ever hook up with someone. Lorna, Betty and Sally were all spoken for, though Louise had never mentioned a fellow, even though she was older than the rest of them. Deborah's mum would say Louise was in danger of being left on the shelf.

Lots of the girls at the Town Hall had sweethearts or fiancés, and sometimes Deborah felt left out. What if it never happened to her?

She put on her olive-green uniform and stuck her head round the sitting room door to say goodbye before she set off for MacFadyen's. Looking at the duty lists on the noticeboard, she found that she was down for mobile canteen duty that night. First, the big water-tank inside the van had to be filled, which took ages, and they also made meat-paste and fish-paste sandwiches to be distributed at their first stop.

The mobile canteens went out day and night, providing sustenance for rescue and demolition crews, bomb disposal men, gravediggers and, of course, the general public.

'Time to go,' said Mrs Ashley, a sturdy individual with an efficient manner.

Deborah pulled herself up into the cab and shunted along

the bench seat, followed by Miss Garfield, a lanky, determined spinster who had been a nursing auxiliary in the last war. Mrs Ashley was the driver. Deborah was impressed because this was a large van, and Mrs Ashley had learned to drive specifically to be able to take it out.

Their first stop was at a St John Ambulance station. First aid posts had been manned round the clock ever since war broke out, the posts varying in size according to how big the local population was.

Working side by side with Mrs Ashley and Miss Garfield, Deborah provided hot drinks and sandwiches for the first-aiders before setting off again. It was as they drove away that the siren sounded. It didn't matter how many times Deborah heard it. That eerie noise always sent a chill down her spine.

'We'll drive to the closest ARP station,' said Mrs Ashley firmly. As the driver, she was in charge. 'They'll tell us if we're needed anywhere.'

They were indeed needed. With enemy planes flying overhead, being chased by the white beams of the searchlights, and with the gun batteries trying to bring them down, Mrs Ashley fixed her gaze resolutely on the road ahead. She leaned forward over the steering wheel, peering into the darkness that was made up of night-time and smoke.

'We'll stop here and have a look-see,' she said after a few minutes. 'Then I'll drive us closer, if I can.'

They descended from the van into a haze of smoke and dust. The smell of charred wood hung heavily in the air. Deborah was the first to turn the corner, and heat smacked her in the face.

There were two pairs of semi-detached houses up ahead. One pair was on fire. Of the other pair, the one closest to the fire had been half swiped away by the bomb blast.

Mrs Ashley spoke to an ARP warden, then she addressed Deborah and Miss Garfield.

'I'll bring the van as far as the corner, then we can open the canteen and get fettling. As well as what's happened here, there's a surface shelter two streets away that has taken a hit. The folk from there will be glad of a cup of tea before they head to the nearest rest centre.'

'And these firemen will need sustenance presently,' Miss Garfield added.

'A heavy rescue team is due to arrive any minute now,' said Mrs Ashley. 'Apparently, there's an old chap trapped in the wreckage of that semi.'

Deborah turned and looked. 'The house beside the fire? The one that's half gone?'

Mrs Ashley nodded, looking grim. 'He's buried in there, evidently. The ARP warden said the only way in is going to involve removing the fireplace from the adjoining house and breaking through the party wall.'

'That makes it even more important that they put out the fire next door,' said Deborah. 'They mustn't let it spread to the damaged house.'

The firelight showed her the tense, anxious, yet determined faces of the men around her.

'Let's hope they can manage,' said Mrs Ashley. 'The heavy rescue men are the experts when it comes to this sort of thing. Meanwhile, we have our job to get on with. Chop-chop, ladies.'

For the next ninety minutes, Deborah and her companions provided scores of cups of tea and meat-paste sandwiches, occasionally breaking off to run for cover when prolonged whistling sounds warned of strings of incendiaries plunging to earth. An old woman provided them with a rug to drape over the urns to help keep the water hot, and a group of women approached carrying stools and folding chairs for anyone who needed to take the weight off their feet.

Every now and again, news came via an ARP warden of the progress of the rescue.

'It's taking a long time,' said Deborah.

'You can't rush something like that,' was the reply.

'I know.' She wished she hadn't said anything.

Shortly afterwards, the ARP warden once more came to the canteen. He spoke to Mrs Ashley, who beckoned to Deborah with a jerk of her chin.

'He's asking for you,' said Mrs Ashley.

'What for?'

'Something they need you to do.'

Deborah went with the warden towards the damaged buildings, relieved to see that the fire had now been extinguished, though the air was still full of smoke and pockets of heat.

'Why am I needed?' she asked.

Instead of answering her question, the warden said, 'They've removed the fireplace from the first house, shored up the chimney and dug their way through the wall to the second house, where the old fellow is.'

'That's good,' said Deborah, feeling relieved on the old man's behalf. 'The rescue must be nearly over.'

'One of the heavy rescue men has spoken to Mr Freeman – that's who's trapped. The thing is, he's quite badly injured. His legs are crushed.'

Deborah winced. 'How dreadful. But they'll have him out soon, won't they?'

'It's going to take them at least a couple more hours,' the warden told her. 'They've got to put up joists before they can even think of moving him, you see. That's where you come in. There's currently a small enough hole that a slip of a thing like you can squeeze through.'

'To do what?' Deborah asked, her breath catching in her throat.

'Don't worry. The doctor will tell you what to do.'

As Deborah stopped dead in shock, the warden strode on ahead. Then he turned and looked back at her.

'Come on!'

The next few minutes passed in a blur of panic. The doctor couldn't get through the hole and Mr Freeman was in great pain and couldn't wait while it was made larger, so Deborah would have to feed herself through from one house to the next and give the trapped man an injection of morphine.

'Don't look so scared,' said one of the heavy rescue men. 'It's not the first time we've had to ask someone to do this sort of thing.'

'As soon as you've done it, you need to slide back out again,' said another heavy rescue man. 'It isn't safe through there.'

Deborah barely listened. She was too busy being appalled at the idea of administering an injection.

'Show me once more,' she said to the doctor. Her brain felt as if it was spinning. She drew a breath. She would *not* think about herself. She would concentrate on Mr Freeman.

Before she knew it, she was squeezing and crawling through a tight passage between the two houses, terrified of getting stuck and convinced she couldn't breathe. Mr Freeman was lying, covered in dust and fastened in position by debris, immediately on the other side. Deborah wriggled her way close to him.

'Mr Freeman?' Her heart thudded. What was she supposed to say? 'I'm here to help.'

For a long moment he didn't respond. Then, to her infinite relief, he nodded.

'I'm going to give you an injection,' Deborah said, fighting to keep her voice steady. 'It'll take the pain away.'

With a surprisingly steady hand, she administered the injection, hoping with all her heart that she had done it correctly. She felt bad about leaving the old man where he was when all her instincts were urging her to stay and offer moral support, but she'd been given her orders and she had to follow them.

She opened her mouth to utter a few words of comfort to

Mr Freeman, and inadvertently breathed in dirt. She coughed and tried to take shallow breaths.

'It won't be long now,' she said to the elderly man. 'The rescue men know what they're doing.'

She wriggled backward, which took a lot longer than moving forward, or seemed to.

After all her nerves and fears, once she was outside and on her feet again she felt a surge of well-being. She'd done it!

'Well done!' said a voice.

'Good show!' said another.

Then a strong pair of hands gently moved her out of the way so the rescue could continue.

When she went outside, there was a small, bustling crowd.

Mrs Ashley immediately appeared by her side. 'Did you do it? Good girl! Congratulations. That will have made all the difference to the trapped gentleman.'

Someone said, 'Jolly good,' though others were busy with their own duties and barely glanced at her. Deborah caught a glimpse of someone she recognised – a young man – though she couldn't think where from. Did he work at the Town Hall? He was covered in grime and was clearly part of the heavy rescue squad.

A voice yelled, 'Watch out! The fire next door isn't out after all. The wind is blowing sparks across.'

The man Deborah had sort of recognised grabbed a bucket, as did another chap – Deborah seemed to know him as well. They both chucked water behind her, only the first man didn't aim properly. Missing his target, he drenched her instead.

Her mouth dropped open in a great gasp of shock. For one moment, everything around her stilled – and then the laughing started.

'Oh, I say – I'm sorry...'

That was when she knew who he was: the fellow from the cottages near Chorlton Green, the one who had mistaken her for a man when she'd been wearing Betty's dungarees. His square face was grimy, making his eyes appear darker.

'*You!*' she exclaimed, her muscles going tight with annoyance.

His companion – and yes, he too had been there on the day Deborah had been mistaken for a man – could hardly speak for laughing.

'Well done, old son!' he exclaimed in between spurts of unashamed delight. 'You've just extinguished the WVS lady!'

CHAPTER SIXTEEN

The Saturday after she returned from Platt House, it was Lorna's day for opening the depot. A fortnight ago, she had travelled to Yorkshire with such high hopes for the time she was to spend in George's company; and then last weekend she had come home again, having spent less than twenty-four hours with him. That had been a bitter disappointment, and hoping every day of her visit that he would come back, only for it not to happen, hadn't helped.

She had made light of it, though, when she had spoken to him on the telephone. This was wartime and his job came first. It was important that he knew she understood that. But it had still been a horrible let-down at the time.

After she had tackled the daily sacks, Lorna spent at least an hour fiddling with a substantial tangle of rope, string and twine, until she finally managed to create three separate piles. Then she took delivery of some broken bicycles, dented petrol cans and watering cans with holes, after which one of the groups of Boy Scouts arrived with their weekly collection, eager to have everything weighed and recorded.

'Could you take this box of old electric lightbulbs over to

MacFadyen's for me, please?' Lorna asked. 'The WVS ladies will take them to pieces.'

The box was clearly labelled for the attention of Mrs Lockwood, the WVS salvage officer. Had relations between that formidable lady and Sally been amicable, Sally would undoubtedly have offered Mrs Lockwood and her helpers the use of a room inside the depot, but as things stood, she very much preferred to keep Mrs Lockwood at bay.

At the end of the day, Lorna locked up the depot and headed home to Star House, where the front door opened before she could reach it. Mrs Beaumont stood on the step.

'There's somebody here to see you,' the landlady said, taking Lorna's things and giving her a little push in the direction of the sitting room.

Lorna opened the door.

'*George!*'

His name burst from her lips in a cry of surprise and joy. The sight of his tall, confident figure, his narrow face and those intelligent grey-blue eyes made her pulse race. Emotion swept through her and tears sprang to her eyes. Always handsome, he looked especially dashing today, in an evening suit, the jacket's lapels faced with black satin, the straight-cut trousers with no turn-ups as per wartime rules and regs about not using fabric unnecessarily.

Grasping her hands, he lifted them to his lips and planted kisses on her knuckles, his eyes never leaving hers.

'Why didn't you tell me you were coming?' she cried.

'I didn't know for certain I'd be able to,' he replied. 'After what happened at Platt House, I didn't want there to be any more disappointments.'

Lorna moved into his arms and rested her cheek against his chest. 'I've missed you so much.'

'I've missed you too. How quickly can you get changed so I can take you out for the evening? Dinner and dancing.'

Lorna flew upstairs. Sally and Louise, who had been keeping out of the way, now appeared and followed her to her bedroom to help her dress.

'This is so romantic,' said Sally, 'George arriving here out of the blue, all decked out in his best bib and tucker.'

'He's very handsome,' said Louise approvingly.

'He's not bad, is he?' Lorna answered.

'You shan't mind being seen on his arm, then?' Louise asked, her lips twitching.

'Well, you have to be grateful for what you can get in wartime, don't you?' Lorna answered with a cheeky grin, and the others laughed.

'Have you got any dresses he hasn't seen before?' Sally asked.

'I brought a couple back with me from Lancaster,' said Lorna. 'I took them with me all the way to Platt House, but of course George wasn't there to admire them.'

'Let's have a look,' Louise urged her. 'You're going to need something decidedly spiffy.'

As Lorna opened her wardrobe, she glanced at Louise. 'If you ever wish to borrow anything of mine, you're very welcome. I know how lucky I am to have such a stash.'

She took out the two gowns. One was a long dress in dove grey with elbow-length sleeves; the other was sea-green with a fitted bodice that was ruched from the low neckline down to the hip, below which a floaty skirt flared gently to the floor.

Sally laughed. 'I'm tempted to say, "Wear one and put the other in a bag to change into halfway through the evening." They're both gorgeous.'

'They are,' Louise agreed, her brown eyes warm with admiration. 'You can't go wrong with either.'

'What do you suggest we do, then?' Lorna asked with a grin. 'Toss for it?'

After a little discussion, the sea-green dress with the long-line ruched bodice was selected. Lorna had quick wash and applied a touch of make-up, then Louise put up her hair for her. Lorna stepped carefully into the dress and Sally fastened it. Lorna clipped on a pair of sparkly earrings and dipped her head so Louise could fasten her necklace.

Stepping back, Sally eyed Lorna from a short distance and sighed. 'George is going to be so proud of you.'

Sally and Louise went downstairs first, and they must have dragged George into the hallway because there he was at the foot of the stairs, gazing up at her. Lorna's pulse quickened. This was going to be the perfect evening.

Feeling like a queen, she descended the stairs, and stopped on the last one. She was tall but George was taller. Stopping here put them at eye-level. George's usually serious eyes were bright with admiration.

Lorna leaned forward and kissed him softly on the mouth, resting her forehead against his afterwards for a moment as she breathed in his familiar scent – soap, tobacco and sandalwood cologne.

'That's quite enough canoodling, thank you,' Mrs Beaumont said briskly, though not unkindly.

Lorna instantly thought of patients and nurses canoodling in the shrubbery. George must have pictured it too, because he gave her a broad grin, which knocked years off his sometimes-stern features.

'I ordered a taxi,' he said. 'It's waiting.'

'Oho,' Lorna teased. 'You took it as read that I'd go out with you, then?'

'Actually, I invited Mrs Beaumont first, but she turned me down in favour of her knitting circle,' George retorted, and Mrs Beaumont swatted his arm, pleased.

Louise had already opened the front door.

'Your carriage awaits,' she announced.

Surrounded by their friends' wishes for a wonderful

evening, Lorna and George left the house and he helped her into the taxi.

'The Claremont Hotel, please,' he instructed the driver.

'Right you are, sir.' The driver started the meter and drove off.

'Are you staying there again?' Lorna asked.

'Like old times,' he replied, 'only better.'

He held Lorna's hand all the way there, only letting go when the taxi pulled up and he opened his door to get out. He walked round to open Lorna's door, a small attention she loved. Then he leaned in to pay the driver.

He offered his arm to her, and they went up the steps together. The doorman opened the door for them, smiling a welcome and touching the brim of his hat.

'I remember coming here in the hope of bumping into you accidentally on purpose,' Lorna recalled.

'I'm glad you did,' said George. 'I was desperate to see you again.'

He had booked a table for them in the handsome dining room on the first floor. They went up the curving staircase and the smartly dressed maître d' showed them to their table, in the centre of which was a crystal vase of red roses. Lorna glanced around swiftly.

'Did you arrange for these?' she asked George. 'We're the only ones with roses.'

'Dash it. You've rumbled me.'

'George, they're exquisite. Thank you.'

'You deserve them.'

From the menu they both chose a cabbage, apple and pear salad to begin, then Lorna decided to order leek-and-tomato bake, while George opted for the meat curry. He selected a wine from the list.

'I hope this will go some of the way towards making up for my absence last week,' he said, lifting his glass in a toast to her.

'That couldn't be helped,' she replied, more than happy to enjoy the moment and put the previous experience well and truly behind her. 'Your work comes first. I understand that. In wartime, everybody's work comes first. That's something we'll look back on with pride in years to come.'

'Something else I shall look back on with pride is your conduct in the Christmas Blitz – no, don't try to wave it aside. It's important to me that I say this. You were the best kind of brave, putting the safety of other people before your own and doing whatever each situation called for. You were remarkable, Lorna. You made me see you through fresh eyes and I realised that I simply had to get to know you again. I haven't the words to describe how much I longed for you to agree to it. It was like seeing you for the very first time all over again. You took my breath away that first time in London last year, and you took my breath away again in the middle of all that horror and destruction and danger at Christmas.'

Lorna felt fluttery and her heart beat faster. 'I'm so glad we met again and that we gave ourselves this second chance.'

'We said in the spring that we'd take things slowly this time round,' said George. 'We didn't set an actual time limit on it, and I don't know if you feel we've had long enough to be certain of our relationship, but I most certainly do. And so...'

He rose from his seat and Lorna caught her breath as he sank to one knee beside her. He produced a ring-box from his pocket. He flipped it open and held it up so she could see the emerald nestling within.

'Lorna West-Sadler, you are without doubt the best girl in the whole world. You're clever and kind and brave. You're every bit as beautiful on the inside as you are on the outside. Would you please do me the very great honour of becoming my wife?'

'George...' Lorna whispered. A breathy sound that was half laughter and half joy came from her lips. 'Yes – *yes*.'

Tears trickled down her cheeks as, to the sound of applause

from the other diners, George tenderly took her hand and placed the sparkling ring on her finger.

The taxi dropped George and Lorna on Beech Road, outside the salvage depot. Lorna hurried across the yard in a cloud of happiness. Behind her, George laughed and followed. She led him up through the building to the foot of the ladder that went up to the skylight.

'Sally!' she called. 'Betty!' She waited a moment, then called again.

Betty's face appeared above her. 'Lorna? What are you doing here?'

'Come down and I'll tell you. Bring Sally!'

Betty looked over her shoulder and said something. Then Sally's face appeared.

'Are you all right, Lorna?'

'Come down here for a minute,' Lorna answered. 'I'm not dressed for shinning up ladders and crawling through little windows.'

She stepped back from the ladder, reaching to take George's hand, as her friends descended. When they had both come down, Lorna, still holding on to George with her right hand, thrust out her left hand for inspection. It was all she could do to stop herself from bouncing up and down on her toes in excitement.

There was a collective intake of breath, then her friends squealed simultaneously.

'Lorna! Let me see,' cried Sally.

'It's beautiful,' Betty declared. 'Is it an emerald?'

'To go with Lorna's lovely green eyes,' George answered.

'Congratulations, both of you,' said Betty.

'Actually,' Sally said with a twinkle, 'I read in a women's magazine – *Vera's Voice*, I think it was – that you don't congratulate the girl. You just congratulate the man for being lucky enough to have got her to say yes.'

'In that case,' said George, 'you should congratulate me a dozen times over.'

Lorna laughed. 'You see. He already knows all the right things to say.'

'It's wonderful of you to come here and tell us,' said Betty.

'You're the first people to know,' said Lorna. 'Well, apart from the other diners who were listening in.'

'Thank you,' said Sally. 'What an honour.'

'I did suggest that maybe we ought to tell our families first,' George said, smiling broadly, 'and Lorna said, "Sally and Betty *are* family," so we came here.'

Lorna had to let go of George's hand as she found herself enveloped in a joint hug from her friends. She hugged them back. They both understood the heartbreak she had endured after her relationship with George had ended first time round and they had supported her as she faced her new life. Now it felt entirely right and natural that her dear chums should be the first ones to share the happy news.

On Sunday, straight after church, Lorna headed into town to the Claremont. She couldn't wait to be with George again – her fiancé! He had been her fiancé before, but this time it felt different. It had been all romance and excitement last time, but now their relationship was underpinned by steadiness and resolve. They knew one another now in a way they previously hadn't, and they were sure of themselves and each other. Lorna harboured no doubts about their future together.

She had chosen to wear a cream-and-bronze striped dress with padded shoulders and patch pockets, together with a linen jacket and a pretty straw hat with a cream band, an attractive, summery look that matched her happiness. She wanted to look lovely for George so he would feel proud of her, but she'd never forgotten Betty telling her she ought to dress for herself, and she was pleased with how she looked.

George was waiting for her in the foyer. He came forward to take her hands in his as he brushed her cheek with a kiss.

'Are you ready to make your telephone call?' he asked, looking into her eyes.

She nodded. Excitement bubbled up inside her.

The Claremont had a telephone booth for the convenience of its guests, discreetly tucked away round a corner off the foyer. George escorted Lorna to it and shut the door behind her. She sat down on the padded chair and picked up the receiver. After speaking to the operator, she waited for the connection, and then her father's voice barked down the line, clearly irritated at being disturbed on a Sunday morning. Typical Daddy, feeling shirty and then insisting upon answering the telephone in order to prolong the vexation.

'Daddy, it's me.'

His annoyance gave way to paternal concern. 'Is everything all right?'

'More than all right. Is Mummy there? Can you call her to the telephone so I can tell you both together? I've got news.'

She held the receiver away from her ear as her father bellowed for her mother. Then came some muted sounds that suggested a scuffle between her parents as they jockeyed for the best position for listening. Lorna pictured them, her dark-eyed, heavy-set father and her slender mother.

'Your mother's here,' said Daddy. 'Go ahead.'

'I've got wonderful news,' said Lorna, 'and I hope you're going to be thrilled. George has asked me to marry him, and I've said yes.'

She held her breath. Please don't let Daddy make some crass reference to their previous engagement.

But Daddy came up trumps. 'That's splendid. Topping, as

we used to say in my day. Well done, both of you. Your mother and I have had our hopes ever since George came here for that weekend.'

Finally, Mummy got a word in. 'Yes, darling, it's marvellous. I'm so very pleased. Seeing the pair of you together that weekend, it was clear that you're meant to be together.'

Lorna could feel happy tears rising. 'Thank you. He really is the right man for me. It was true last time, only everything got messed up, but it's even more true now.'

'Just don't let things get messed up again,' said Daddy.

'*Hector!*' Mummy reprimanded him.

But frankly, if that was the worst thing Daddy said, Lorna knew she'd got off lightly. And anyway, he was only saying what the world in general was bound to say. She wasn't going to let it bother her.

'It's all right, Mummy. I don't mind. I promise you that nothing is going to go wrong this time.'

'I'll start making plans,' said Mummy. 'You must come up here as soon as you can, so we can talk about it.'

'George and I haven't even talked about it yet,' said Lorna, delighted that her mother was already getting into the swing.

'We can put on a wedding every bit as lavish as George's family could,' said Daddy. 'That's all he needs to know about it.'

'I have to go now,' said Lorna. 'Thank you both for being happy for us.'

'Of course we're happy,' said Mummy.

Lorna said her goodbyes and hung up. She sat there for a moment, the blood singing in her veins. Then the door opened behind her, and she looked round to find George peering at her enquiringly.

'Is it safe to assume from your dreamy expression that your parents approve?'

'They're *thrilled*,' Lorna told him. As she left the booth, she stepped aside to make way for him to go inside. 'Your turn.'

'I've already spoken to my parents,' said George. 'I had to telephone them separately, of course. My father's in London, as he almost always is these days.'

'Were they pleased? What did they say?'

'My father said all the things you'd expect. He hopes we'll be very happy, and so forth.'

'And your mother?' Lorna held her breath. This was the one that mattered.

'She sends you her best wishes.'

Lorna thought of the etiquette that said that only the groom was to be congratulated. Had Lady Broughton congratulated George? It was a question she didn't dare to ask.

How Lorna hated having to remove her beautiful emerald engagement ring on Monday morning, but it wouldn't be a good idea to wear it for work, even though she wore thick gloves to handle the salvage. With a soft sigh, she replaced the ring in its box and snapped the lid shut.

She and George had spent all day yesterday together, discussing what they wanted for their wedding. Lorna had no idea what George's family would be hoping for or expecting, but she knew that what they had decided upon was emphatically not going to fit in with what her own parents would wish for. That was a huge shame, but it couldn't be helped. Lorna had been badly bruised last year by the treatment she'd received in the press and that had coloured her attitude now.

'Are you positive this is what you want?' George had asked, his eyes tender with concern. 'I'm happy to agree to anything – but I need to be sure that it's what you truly wish for in your heart of hearts.'

Lorna had taken a moment to examine her feelings before she nodded. 'It isn't what I'd have wanted first time round – and my parents would never have allowed me to have it, I can tell you that – but this time, things are different and this is right for us. As long as it suits you?' she asked anxiously.

'More than,' George assured her. 'All that matters to me is that you're happy.'

'Me?' she had said with a laugh. 'I'm floating on air.'

She hadn't arrived home until late last night because of lingering with George until the last possible moment.

Now she was looking forward to telling Sally and Betty about her wedding plans while they were all at work together. Then she would tell the others at Star House this evening.

Later that morning, Lorna, Betty and Sally grouped round the staffroom table overlooking the yard to have their tea break.

'*Finally!*' Betty smiled widely at Lorna, her dimple showing as she added, 'Tell us *every*thing.' She laughed happily and her peaches-and-cream complexion glowed. 'I made the two of you live through every single moment of my wedding preparations, so this is your chance to get your own back.'

'We haven't chosen a date yet,' said Lorna, 'because we need to confer with our families, though we don't want to wait too long. But we have made a definite decision on the type of wedding.'

Sally leaned forward. 'Come on, then. Don't keep us in suspense.'

Betty looked misty-eyed. 'With the families you and George come from, I'm imagining yards of lace, and a diamond tiara that belonged to George's great-great-grandmother, and probably a cathedral.'

Lorna laughed. 'Have you been talking to my parents? They'd like nothing better.' Then she sobered. 'Actually, that isn't what George and I want at all. We've decided to marry in a registry office.'

'Like so many wartime couples,' said Sally.

'Not just because it's wartime,' said Lorna, 'although obviously there is the patriotic thing about having a simple ceremony. But the real reason is because of what happened last year.' She looked earnestly at her friends, willing them to understand. 'George and I met and quickly got engaged and everything was romantic and wonderful, then things began to go wrong. George's mother was never keen on me, and gossip went round London about my father wanting to marry me off to a title. Finally, George ended the engagement. He would gladly have done the gentlemanly thing and pretended that it had been my decision, so I could save face, but then Daddy insisted on bringing that frightful breach-of-promise suit against him.' Old feelings rose up inside her, forcing her to stop.

'And after that the newspapers were beastly to you,' said Sally.

'Only because the judge was.' Lorna tried to make light of it, as if it hadn't been dreadfully hurtful. 'He said it was unpatriotic of me to bring what he called a frivolous case to court in wartime.'

'But it wasn't you,' said Betty. 'It was your father.'

'On paper, breach-of-promise cases are always brought by the jilted girl,' Lorna explained, 'no matter who actually instigates it. The judge made it sound as if I was the one and only person in the whole country not doing my bit for the war effort.'

'And all of that nastiness has made you want a registry office wedding?' asked Betty.

'Well – yes,' Lorna said frankly. 'I want – we both want to get married quietly in a registry office with no fuss; and we'll save the glittering high-society reception until after the war is over.'

'But that will be several years off,' said Betty.

Lorna smiled at her. 'Exactly. By that time, we'll have been happily married for however long and we'll have proved to all and sundry that our marriage is based on solid foundations. There will be nothing for people to gossip about, and our first engagement will be old hat. That's how I want things to be.'

Sally nodded thoughtfully. 'I can understand that.'

'So can I,' said Betty.

'Thank you,' said Lorna. 'It's important to me that you can see this the same way as I do.'

'Have you told your mother yet?' Betty asked.

'I'm going to write to her and Daddy this evening and explain what George and I have agreed on, and why we want it. They'll be upset, but, after everything our family went through last year with the press, I hope they'll understand.'

'There was one good thing about the press,' said Sally. 'If they hadn't hounded you and made your life miserable, your father would never have needed to send you to hide away in Manchester working in a salvage depot.'

Lorna shook her head, remembering. 'I wasn't pleased at the time, but I'm glad now.'

'We know you weren't pleased,' Betty said with a chuckle. 'We remember it well.'

'When are you next seeing George?' Sally asked.

'This weekend.'

'So soon?' Sally asked. 'Lucky old you.'

'Yes, I am lucky,' Lorna agreed, feeling awful in that moment for her friend, with all she had been through. 'He has to come north to attend a meeting, and he's told me that if I can get to Chester on Saturday we can spend the day together. It isn't much but, at the same time, it's everything.'

'Yes, it is,' Sally said seriously. 'Make the most of it.'

Lorna spent the next few days doing precisely that. She wrote to her parents to let them know her and George's decision and, while she awaited her mother's response, she indulged in numerous conversations with the Star House girls about what she should wear for her registry office wedding.

'I know what you ought to do,' Deborah declared with a twinkle in her bright-blue eyes. 'You should try on some of your clothes for us.'

'She might not want to wear something from her wardrobe upstairs,' Mrs Beaumont pointed out. 'I'm sure she must have lots of lovely things up in Lancaster.'

'Or she might want to buy something,' Louise added.

'I just meant,' said Deborah, 'that if she tries on a selection of things for us to see, then we could talk about what style or what length might look best.'

'Basically, you want me to play in the dressing-up box,' said Lorna.

'It'll be like when Mrs Beaumont brought home all those wedding dresses from the theatre wardrobe for Betty to try on,' said Sally. 'That was great fun.'

Lorna loved the idea. 'Let's do it, then – if the rest of you don't mind.'

'Why should we mind?' Mrs Beaumont asked. 'You'll be my second Star House bride.'

'Shall you see Stella, Lottie and Mary at work tomorrow?' Lorna asked Louise. 'Ask them along – and Betty must come too, of course. The more the merrier.'

And indeed it turned out to be a decidedly merry occasion. Lorna tried on various things, and everybody put in their two penn'orth. Stella adored the elegance of the midnight-blue two-piece evening suit, which had a long, flared skirt and a hip-length jacket, fitted so that it went in at the waist and out at the bust, making Lorna's bosom more shapely.

Deborah thought the colour of her dusty-pink dress was perfect.

'It makes your hair look even darker,' she said, 'and all those sunray-pleats are gorgeous.'

Mary and Sally were both in favour of a flared skirt and Mrs Beaumont said that accessories were every bit as important as the dress or suit.

Lorna relished every moment and couldn't wait to see George so she could tell him what a lark it had been. Joy coursed through her veins. How lucky she was to be marrying the handsome, clever, thoughtful man she loved with all her heart.

George met Lorna off the train at Chester and they walked hand in hand into town, enjoying looking at the distinctive black-and-white timbered buildings that the city was famous for. It was a fine day, and they walked down to the riverside.

George laughed when she told him about the trying-on session.

'Did it help you decide what to wear?' he asked.

'Not really,' Lorna admitted. 'It was just fun dressing up and hearing everyone's opinions and ideas. The girls were keen to see me in evening gowns, but obviously I'm not going to turn up at the registry office in one of those. I think the real choice is between a day dress and a suit.'

'You'll look beautiful whatever you wear.'

'Flatterer.'

'The simple truth,' said George. 'I'm glad all I have to do is put on a suit and pop a carnation in my buttonhole. Have you told your parents our plans yet?'

'Yes, and I've heard back from Mummy. They're both deeply disappointed, which I knew they would be. For probably the first time ever, Mummy's letter included the words, *Daddy says to say...* so that shows how disappointed he is.'

'And what did he say?' George asked.

Lorna sighed. 'That it wasn't what he had envisaged, for my wedding. I'm sorry to let them down, of course, but after everything that happened last year we have to do this our way.' She stopped walking and turned to face him. 'We aren't being selfish, are we?'

'If protecting you from the glare of unwanted attention, not to mention downright intrusion, is selfish,' George replied, 'then I'm proud to call myself the most selfish man in the world.'

That made Lorna feel cherished and looked after. It also made her feel respected.

But all those feelings crumbled to dust on the Monday when the newspapers were published.

The newspaper was always pushed through the letter box while Mrs Beaumont was busy in the kitchen preparing breakfast, and the girls politely left it for her to read after they had gone to work. Those who wished to read it did so when they got home.

In the middle of the morning, Mrs Beaumont appeared in the depot yard, looking upset. The girls hurried to her.

'What is it?' Sally asked.

The landlady held out the folded newspaper. 'I'm so sorry to be the bearer of bad news, but I thought you ought to see this right away, Lorna.'

Chilly fingers ran down Lorna's spine. Her hand trembled as she took the newspaper.

A moment later her mouth filled with the sour taste of dread.

'Oh *no*,' she gasped. 'How did they get wind of our engagement? And look what they're calling me: *the breach-of-promise bride*. How could they do this to me? How could they do it to me *again*?'

CHAPTER SEVENTEEN

The beginning of September brought news of the capture off Iceland of a German U-boat by the Royal Navy, and the continuing struggles between the Russians and the Germans.

It also brought Sally's thoughts and feelings about her lost baby very much to the fore. In happier circumstances, the new month would have been a milestone along the road to holding her precious child in her arms, but instead it was now a source of sorrow and pain, a poignant reminder of all she had lost. Every time she went out shopping or on the bus to Withington to see Mum and Dad, the streets seemed to be populated by young women with bulging stomachs, and that hurt too.

'I'm glad for the mothers-to-be,' she told Mum, 'and I hope everything goes well for them.'

'But it makes you feel bad for yourself,' said Mum, finishing the thought for her. 'Believe me, I've had more than my share of those feelings.'

The two of them had been brought closer by the loss of Sally's baby and the confidences that had followed. Accustomed to a rather edgy relationship with her normally critical mother,

Sally was deeply appreciative of this new rapport – but, oh my, what a way to achieve it!

She kept her thoughts to herself at Star House. She wanted to concentrate on supporting Lorna. After the way Lorna, an inexperienced driver, had bravely taken her to hospital in the middle of an air raid, and not just any air raid but the third worst one Manchester had suffered, providing a shoulder for her now felt like a small way of repaying her.

'Evidently we were seen together that day in Chester,' said Lorna. 'The only good thing is that the journalist – or should I call him a shark? – who saw us didn't have a photographer with him.'

In the absence of a fresh photograph, the newspaper had trotted out a picture of Lorna that had been taken last year on the day of the breach-of-promise case. It couldn't be called a good picture. The quality was grainy and, instead of catching Lorna facing the camera, it showed her sideways on, with a hand held up in an effort to protect herself.

'At least your face doesn't really show,' Betty had said.

'But the image of me trying to shield my face makes me look as if I have something to hide,' Lorna had replied. 'They haven't even made it clear that it's an old picture. Anybody seeing it for the first time will probably leap to the conclusion that I think my engagement is shabby.'

'It's a dirty rotten shame,' Betty had declared fervently. Bless her, she could always be relied upon to show loyalty, could Betty.

'Listen,' Sally said to Lorna. 'I can't offer to let you use the office telephone during our hours of work, but do feel free to use it in the evenings – as long as George places the call to you, not the other way round, so that he pays for the call. The two of you have a lot to discuss and it'll be easier for you if you use the depot telephone rather than going to a public telephone box.'

'Thanks,' said Lorna. 'You're a brick.'

'I want to help,' Sally told her. 'I just wish I could do more. So does Betty.'

She and Betty kept a close eye on Lorna at work. After a day or two, Lorna had news to share with them.

'I've written to my parents to tell them, and George is going to tell his family, so now I can tell you.' She huffed out a jagged sigh. Her green eyes looked strained.

'Please don't say you've called off the wedding,' breathed Betty.

'Not the wedding, no. Just the registry office. Now that I'm the "breach-of-promise bride", a registry office wedding might seem to be a hole-and-corner affair. Just imagine what those beasts at the newspapers would make of that.'

'Don't let them stop you having the wedding you want,' Sally said, vexed.

'That's the point,' said Lorna. 'I don't want a registry office do any longer.'

'Then what are you going to do?' Betty asked, looking troubled. 'Wait until after the war? That could be an awfully long time. Just look at the last one...'

'And why should you have to wait anyway?' Sally added.

All at once, Lorna smiled and her eyes, which had been wary since the newspapers had reported her engagement, softened and glowed.

'We're not going to wait,' she said happily. 'I've decided to have the big wedding my parents have always dreamed of, and the press be damned.'

'Are you sure this is what you want?' Sally asked anxiously.

'It wasn't what I wanted to start with,' said Lorna, 'but things have changed and it's definitely what I want now. We chose to have a registry office do as a way of keeping our wedding private, but the newspapers have kissed that goodbye for us. So, I've decided to give my mother the wedding she's always wanted – the wedding I've always pictured, for that matter.'

'The wedding you'd automatically have had if the press hadn't hounded you?' asked Sally.

'Exactly,' said Lorna. Turning to Betty, she grasped her by both hands. 'What was it you wanted for me? Yards of lace and a diamond tiara? Well, your wish might be about to come true!'

Sally wrote *All my love, always* and then had to stop before she signed her name, because tears had filled her eyes. She missed her beloved Andrew more than she could say. She carried a picture of him in her mind, his warm brown eyes, straight nose and narrow, firm jawline. She also carried special knowledge of him in her heart, his steadiness of character, his sense of humour and his loving nature.

For him to be absent when she was profoundly sad following her miscarriage added to her sorrow, but every time she thought along those lines she told herself not to be so self-centred. She was far from being the only wife who would have benefited from having her husband's loving support. Women were having to cope with everything, from the family home being blown up, and the children being miles away in places of safety, and long hours of war work, to coping with bereavements that might well involve a visit to the mortuary for identification purposes, and organising funerals and jumping through all the administrative hoops associated with a death.

Women were doing all those things. She, Sally Henshaw, was just another woman getting by as best she could. It was all anybody could do.

Sally signed her name at the bottom of her letter and added a row of kisses. For the first time in their marriage, she was keeping a secret from Andrew, and that was desperately hard for her. Before they were married, she had told him she was more than just his future wife.

'I'm your friend,' she had told him, 'your best friend. You can talk to me about anything.'

Andrew had trusted her with the knowledge of the secret war work he used to do before he joined up, work that had put him under a tremendous emotional strain. Being able to share that with Sally had helped him to cope with it.

Yet now here she was, writing yet another cheerful letter scattered with snippets of news about life in Chorlton, and about Lorna and George's decision to have a big wedding, and the white clover and wild marjoram she had seen when she and Betty had gone for a walk on the meadows last weekend – and she hadn't written a single word about her lingering sorrow for their lost child and their altered future. Instead, she had been a good little wife obeying the generally accepted rule that letters to the troops should be chipper and reassuring.

She could see the point of this. More than that, she agreed with it. There was nothing to be gained by causing Andrew worry or unhappiness. That was the very last thing she wanted. But it still hurt to feel she was withholding the truth.

It wasn't just Andrew she was keeping her continuing sorrow from. She had to keep it tucked away the entire time except in front of her mother. It was especially necessary at Star House, where the other three girls were all single. Perhaps if all four of them had been married it might have been different, but you couldn't possibly talk about a miscarriage in front of a spinster, and never mind that Lorna and Louise had both been by her side on that fateful night. Sally felt obscurely guilty for having put them in the position of witnessing that. As unmarried girls, they shouldn't even know that miscarriages existed.

What marvels the two of them had been. It had been something of a baptism of fire for Louise as a new resident of Star House. Sally took a moment to think about Louise, the new girl. She liked her. There was something poised and self-contained about her, but not in a stand-offish sort of way. Sally suspected she was the sort who didn't make friends willy-nilly, but took her time to decide.

There was something else about her, too, that Sally found intriguing. A while back, before the tragedy of losing her baby, Lorna had told her that Louise intended at some point to leave the munitions factory in favour of a job that would carry her not just through the remainder of the war but also into the world of peacetime.

'I hope you don't mind, but Lorna mentioned your plans to me,' Sally said when she and Louise were digging up potatoes in the garden one warm, golden evening. 'I hope you don't think we were talking about you behind your back, because we weren't. Well, we were, but not in a nasty way.'

Louise paused in her digging to give Sally a grin. 'And now you want to ask me about it, but you're not being nosy. Well, you are, but not in a nasty way.' She laughed. 'Don't worry. I know what you mean. Ask away. It isn't a secret, and I can understand your being interested.'

'You don't see yourself going back to your old job after the war?' Sally asked.

'Uh-uh.' Louise shook her head.

'Lorna said you used to work in a dress shop.'

'I did. A very posh one. Plenty of girls would give their eye-teeth to have a job in a place of that calibre, but not me. It was my mother's idea of a suitable job, not mine. I was never given a choice. What I want is a position that's a challenge, something that makes me glad to get out of bed in the morning because I'll be doing something interesting and useful.'

Sally nodded. She could understand that. 'That's how I feel about the salvage depot.'

'Good,' said Louise. 'I'm glad you're happy there. You're lucky.' She paused before adding, 'If it doesn't sound like a mad thing to say, I think that by looking for this other job – that I haven't found yet, by the way – I'll be being true to myself.'

'It doesn't sound mad at all,' said Sally. 'The war has changed things. It's given girls and women masses of new responsibilities, but it's also provided opportunities that we've never had before and that would never have happened otherwise. If being in the dress shop wasn't right for you, and you now have the chance to find something that is, then... well, it has to be good for you, doesn't it? Not just in terms of earning money or enjoying what you do, but in the way you feel about yourself and your life.'

Louise looked at her. 'Yes,' she agreed quietly. 'I'm glad you understand.'

Sally thought about it afterwards. Louise's words – 'I'll be being true to myself' – resonated deep inside her. She could see the importance of it for Louise. More than that, she could also see the importance of it for herself and Andrew.

It was time to stop writing the superficial, safe letters. Right back in the early days of their relationship, she had been the one to recognise the importance of honest and open discussion.

She remembered telling Andrew, 'You can talk to me about anything, and I'll love you even more deeply because of it, because it will bring us closer.'

She had talked about seeing marriage as a partnership and wanting a husband who could appreciate the value of sharing life's problems.

And yet here she was, keeping the most important thoughts of her life from Andrew. It wasn't right. Never mind the 'rule' about sending cheerful letters to servicemen, letters that would keep them from worrying about what was happening at home at the same time as giving them something to fight for. That might be the correct thing to do as a general rule, but it wasn't right for

Sally and Andrew, not now, not after they had suffered this heartbreaking loss.

It was time to be true to herself, time to be true to her marriage and the importance that she and Andrew placed on being honest with one another.

She saw her mother that evening and told her what she proposed to do.

Mum's hazel eyes widened in horror. 'Don't! You can't! You don't talk about women's matters with a man. It isn't right.'

'Miscarriage isn't just a matter for women, Mum,' said Sally.

'Oh yes, it is!'

'What about all the fathers? How can you sweep them and their feelings under the carpet?'

'Because that's the right place for them. Having a baby is nothing to do with men – and you know exactly what I mean, my girl, so don't look at me like that. It's why men are kept out of the way when the baby is being born. It's *nothing* to do with them. And for you to suggest that losing a baby is a big thing for the father – well, it isn't like that. I'm not saying that a father doesn't care. Of course he does. He cares that his wife has had a painful loss.'

'But that's as far as it goes?' Sally asked.

'Yes,' Mum said stoutly. 'Since you ask, yes. There are some things that are best kept private, and that includes between man and wife.'

Sally felt a wave of compassion for her parents. How hard it must have been for Mum to have coped with her string of miscarriages on her own. And poor Dad too. What had he felt? Had he been allowed to feel anything? Had the two of them ever talked about what had happened to them? Or did they truly see the losses as something that had happened solely to Mum?

Well, it wasn't going to be that way with her and Andrew, Sally vowed to herself. They were from the next generation – in fact, they were from the next generation but one, when you took Mum and Dad's ages into account.

Above all, they were from the wartime generation and their ideas were different.

When Sally arrived home from Withington, she stayed up half the night writing a long letter to Andrew, pouring her heart onto the paper along with her tears.

The next morning, she got up early to take her letter to the pillarbox. She held it up in front of the slit near the top of the box. Was Mum right? Was she making a terrible mistake in sending this? Acting inappropriately? Acting unkindly by sending something that would fill her husband not just with sorrow but also with the despair of knowing he could do nothing to support her?

But no. Something deep inside her told her this was the right thing to do. Maybe it wouldn't be right for another couple, but it was right and important and natural for her and Andrew, and she needed to do it.

She popped the letter into the box and heard it land on the pile inside. She gave herself a moment to feel regret, to wish the action undone, but no such thoughts or feelings took hold of her – not then, and not as she waited for Andrew's reply, which came more quickly than she had dared to hope for.

My dearest Sally,

I hardly know how to write this letter and how to express the jumble of thoughts I have been carrying around with me all this time.

I have been very worried about you. All I wanted after I heard the tragic news about our poor baby was to be there at home with you to take care of you and hold you close while we mourned together. You are right to speak of the future we have lost. I too had pictured it and I imagined you telling our son or daughter all about me and encouraging them to look forward to the day when I finally come home. I even imagined being greeted by a little Henshaw waving a small flag – you know, the sort you stick into a sandcastle. I pictured carrying the child aloft on my shoulders when we went onto the meadows on a family picnic in the sunshine – and I hoped with all my heart that this blasted war would be over while our precious child was still small enough to be carried like that.

So many hopes and dreams – and all of them now gone for good. I know it is the same for you, my darling, but we have to be strong, stronger than ever.

For a while I was fighting for my wife and child, but now I am fighting ~~just~~ for my wife. I have crossed out 'just' because there is no 'just' about you or my deep love for you, Sally. Now I fight for a different future for the two of us.

Whatever happens, whether we are blessed with a family or we are not, our future is to be together and to make a loving and worthwhile life for ourselves. Having you as my wife is all I need.

With all my love,

Andrew x

Sally brought a trembling hand to her cheek as her emotions built up and threatened to overwhelm her. Sharing her thoughts and feelings with Andrew had proved to be exactly the right thing to do. She experienced a surge of raw grief for what the two of them had lost. She breathed her way through it until she came out the other side. Normally she felt weak and tearful when she emerged from a wave of grief. She was tearful this time, too, and she felt wobbly, but not weak, because now, and for as long as it took, she would no longer be mourning in isolation. She and Andrew would grieve together, even though they were miles apart.

As painful as it would be, there was also the certainty of strength and support. Whatever they had to face, they would face it together.

CHAPTER EIGHTEEN

Lorna's Saturday at the depot had come round again. She hoped it would be a busy day, as Saturdays so often were, with the Boy Scouts bringing in their latest salvage collections to be weighed and office workers arriving with the week's scraps from their wastepaper baskets. The more visitors the better, as far as Lorna was concerned. It would take her mind off her personal life.

As happy and excited as she was to be marrying George, she couldn't stop thinking about how their plans had been upended by the press. She had even had a dream about it. The only good thing was that the journalist who had spotted her and George in one another's company, with her sporting an engagement ring, had done so when they were in Chester, so the fact that Lorna was living and working in Manchester was still a secret from the newspapers and the world in general. In her experience, being in the public eye was utterly horrible. Last year the papers had denounced her as shallow and unpatriotic, and now she was the breach-of-promise bride. It made her shudder every time she thought of it.

'I feel as if, no matter what we do, it's going to be the wrong thing,' she had told her mother over the telephone. 'A registry office wedding would give the impression that we're ashamed and a church wedding with as many trimmings as wartime allows might be called gaudy.'

'You're not going off the idea of the church wedding, are you?' Mummy had asked anxiously.

Lorna was quick to reassure her. 'No, not at all. I think I must have journalists on the brain at the moment. George and I both think marrying in church is the right thing to do and we're looking forward to it immensely. I just pray the newspapers leave us alone.'

Right now that seemed like a forlorn hope, but, since there was nothing Lorna could do to change it, she would have to do her best to push it out of her mind. Shaking her head, she huffed out a vexed little sigh. That was easier said than done.

She spent much of that Saturday morning sorting through the contents of the daily salvage sacks and weighing the salvage brought in by two Scout troops. There was hot competition between all the local Scouts, Guides and schools as to who could collect the most.

Sally had encouraged Lorna and Betty to have a few facts at their fingertips so they would always be ready to tell the children how their collected salvage might be used.

'This enamel saucepan could end up being a bayonet,' Lorna told the first troop of boys, 'and this enamelled bucket could become a Tommy gun.'

'Cor,' said the boys, their eyes widening.

'These old hot-water bottles and this leaky hosepipe might end up as part of a barrage balloon or a dinghy,' she informed the second group.

'We'll fetch more for next week,' the lads promised before they went on their way.

Lorna watched them go. It was heartening that children

were so involved in the war effort, but also dreadfully sad. What a way to grow up. Boys no longer collected cigarette cards to swap in the playground. Now, they all competed to find the best piece of shrapnel.

The last of the boys disappeared through the tall gates. As Lorna made to turn away, her gaze brushed across a woman entering the yard. It was the weirdest thing, but in that split second she looked like Lady Broughton, which just showed how your eyes could play tricks on you.

Then Lorna looked properly – and it was indeed George's mother, looking elegant in a quietly expensive edge-to-edge collarless coat and a hat with an upturned brim, worn with a white fox-fur stole and white gauntlet gloves.

Lorna's skin prickled all over, not just with surprise but also with the awareness of her dungarees, headscarf and thick gloves. Talk about being caught on the hop.

She put on her best smile and walked towards her future mother-in-law, the woman who she was quite sure did not want her as a member of the family.

'Lady Broughton, this is a surprise.' Good manners dictated that she ought to have added, 'A pleasant one,' but the person who had made it clear she wasn't up to snuff didn't deserve that consideration.

'Good morning, Lorna. I apologise for disturbing you at work, but I hope this isn't an inconvenient moment.'

How Lorna wished she could get away with saying, 'Well, of course it's inconvenient. I'm busy,' but, even if she could have said such a thing, there would have been no point. Her ladyship had already seen her in her work clothes in the middle of a yard filled with salvage. And why should that be a problem, anyway? This was her war work, and she was proud to do it.

'Have you a few minutes to show me around?' Lady Broughton enquired. 'I should like to understand what it is you do here.'

'Of course.'

Lorna did as she was asked, but all the while her thoughts were running wild inside her head. Had Lady Broughton come here to persuade her not to marry George? To remind her that her father was brash and that she herself lacked the required pedigree? She couldn't come up with any other reason.

The tour didn't last very long, not least because Lorna was keen to get it over and done with.

As soon as she decently could, she asked in the most casual tone she could muster, 'Does George know you're here?'

Lady Broughton looked straight at her. 'No, he doesn't. This is between you and me.'

Oh cripes. Well, that settled it. Lady Broughton had come here to warn her off.

'I've been hearing about the work you undertook for the WVS after George was obliged to leave Platt House,' said Lady Broughton.

That was the very last thing Lorna had expected.

'I told you about it at the time,' she said.

'You told me you had helped with the pie scheme and with getting an infants' hospital ready.'

'That's right,' said Lorna, puzzled.

'And I took you at your word,' said Lady Broughton.

Lorna half-laughed in sheer surprise. 'Why shouldn't you? It was true.'

'But not the whole truth.'

For the first time since Lorna had known her, Lady Broughton's deep-blue eyes, usually so shrewd and assessing, actually softened. Lorna had no idea what to make of it.

'I've been hearing exactly what you did,' Lady Broughton continued. 'In detail,' she added.

Lorna was even more puzzled. 'So I may have missed out some of the details when I told you what I'd done. What of it?'

'Why did you miss them out?'

'Well, one doesn't wish to blow one's own trumpet,' said Lorna, feeling uncomfortable.

'I might never have found out the truth about what you did, about what the extent of your contribution really was,' said Lady Broughton. 'You didn't simply help with the pie scheme. You were a driver, even though you're inexperienced behind the wheel and were new to the locality. And as for claiming you helped get the hospital ready – it turns out that you were the person in charge. Not only that but you also set in motion the plan whereby mothers will be able to visit their sick children.'

'A lot of women were involved,' said Lorna quietly.

'You showed spirit and leadership,' Lady Broughton declared, approval showing in her eyes. 'You might have chosen to return to Platt House every evening full of tales of your exploits and successes, but you didn't, and that tells me something important. It tells me that you didn't do these things with a view to impressing me and trying to win me round. No, you simply got on with what needed to be done, without fuss. Spirit, leadership, good sense and discretion: those are the qualities you displayed.'

'Oh,' said Lorna, unable to come up with any other response. After a moment she added a belated, 'Thank you.'

'Those are the very qualities that are required of the mistress of a place such as Platt House,' Lady Broughton informed her, 'and this will be the case all the more so after the war, when there will without question be changes and fresh challenges to be faced. You have shown you can cope, and I respect that. Last year I felt positive that George had made a serious error in his choice of bride, but now I can see that it was I who was mistaken. Welcome to the family, my dear.'

'I can hardly believe it,' Lorna told the residents of Star House when she got home at the end of the day. 'George's mother has never liked me. She's always thought I wasn't good enough and, of course, the gossip about my father's determination that I was going to nab a title infuriated her. But now...' She shook her head and shrugged, letting her unspoken words hang in the air.

'That's an extraordinary about-face,' said Mrs Beaumont.

'It certainly is,' Deborah concurred, 'after what you told us she said to you.'

'But now she's accepted you.' Sally's tone held a mixture of wonder and satisfaction. 'Well done, you! You earned her good opinion without even realising you were doing it.'

'If you'd set out to do it, she'd have seen straight through you,' said Deborah and the others nodded, agreeing.

'I'm relieved that things have turned out so well,' said Mrs Beaumont, 'not least because when Lady Broughton turned up on the doorstep asking for you, my first thought was to wonder how I could possibly let you know before she got to the depot.'

That made the girls laugh, but Lorna knew exactly what her landlady meant.

'Everything turned out for the best,' she reassured Mrs Beaumont, 'though I don't mind admitting to being glad I didn't know in advance, or I'd have been terrified.'

Lady Broughton was staying that night at the Claremont, and she had invited Lorna to join her for dinner. Sally, Deborah and Louise all piled into her bedroom to help her choose what to wear.

It was Louise who suggested the midnight-blue evening suit.

'It's a beautiful costume,' she said, 'and the colour is perfect for you. You'll appear elegant but at the same time understated. I think that's just what you need when your fiancé's fearsome mother has just called a truce.'

'Louise is right,' Sally concurred.

Louise shrugged lightly. 'I'm good at judging clothes.'

'Of course,' Lorna replied, remembering. 'You used to work in that upper-crust dress shop.'

'You must have been a big help to your customers,' said Deborah.

'We didn't have customers.' Louise stuck her nose in the air. 'We had lady-patrons, I'll have you know.'

While Lorna got changed, Deborah went to the telephone box to request a taxi. It wasn't long before Lorna was on her way. She felt a little flutter of happy excitement at the thought of meeting Lady Broughton on friendly terms. It certainly made a change from dreading the encounter.

They went into the dining room together.

Lady Broughton was wearing burgundy velvet with rubies. When Lorna admired her jewellery, she said, 'These will be yours one day,' her smile showing that it was no longer painful to her to picture Lorna as the next Lady Broughton.

'I want you to know,' said Lorna, 'that I'd want to marry George no matter what his station in life. What I mean is, I was never out to get myself a title.'

'I can see that now,' Lady Broughton replied with approval in her smile.

'I appreciate your kindness in coming all the way to Manchester to speak to me,' Lorna added. It felt important to say this and there would never be a better chance. 'You've made me feel better about things – stronger. I've been so upset and worried about the press and being the breach-of-promise bride, but now I feel ready to sweep all that aside.'

'Because of receiving my blessing?'

'Yes,' Lorna said frankly. 'I always knew you didn't think I was good enough, but now that you have accepted me – well, who cares about the press, compared to that?'

'Well said, my dear girl,' Lady Broughton replied.

The two of them looked at one another and shared a smile that promised to be the first of many.

. . .

The following Friday evening after work, Lorna caught the train from Manchester Victoria up to Lancaster. Her parents couldn't have been more thrilled to see her.

'Or possibly they couldn't be more thrilled at the prospect of us having a church wedding instead of a quickie in the registry office,' Lorna said laughingly to George later on that evening.

He was in Lancaster as well for the weekend. His train had been due in two hours later than Lorna's, though it had been closer to three hours by the time it actually pulled into the station. Lorna had driven to the station to collect him. She had no fears these days about being behind the wheel. Driving was a skill to be proud of and it made her feel useful and accomplished as well as modern.

George had brought with him a small valise for the weekend and also a packed suitcase, which Mummy had arranged for him to deliver to a hotel the next morning. By leaving the suitcase at that address for three weeks, he could officially claim to be a resident of Lancaster, which would make the wedding arrangements more straightforward, especially as they were keen to get married as soon as they could.

'What's going to happen to your job at the salvage depot, Lorna?' her father asked as the four of them enjoyed an after-supper cigarette together before bed.

'Yes,' Mummy added. 'You can't just up sticks and move on from war work. It's not allowed. Shall you be able to get permission?'

'Sally says she'll look into it for me,' Lorna answered. 'I don't know what I'll do if I'm not allowed to move to London.' She felt a tug of anxiety as she shared a glance with George.

George's grey-blue eyes were tender as he said, 'We'll have

to wait and see. I'd hate us to have to live apart, but duty comes first.'

'Should I see if I can pull some strings?' Daddy asked.

'No,' Lorna and George said in one voice.

'Thank you, sir,' George added, 'but no. We want to do this by the book.'

'Oh well, the offer's there,' said Daddy.

Lorna had no idea how much, if any, influence Daddy might have over what was a matter for Manchester Corporation, but it was typical of him to flex his businessman muscles.

'And now we should think about retiring for the night,' said Mummy. 'Lots to get through tomorrow.'

When Lorna went up to bed, Mummy came to her room and sat on the mattress.

'I'm delighted that everything has worked out for you and George in the end,' she said. 'It's true that Daddy wanted a title for you, but no title would have been worth it without the happiness.'

'We're far happier second time round,' Lorna told her, reaching for her hand.

Mummy nodded. 'I can see that.' Leaning forward, she kissed Lorna. 'Good night, darling. We've got lots to do tomorrow if you're going to get married in three weeks.'

After her mother had softly closed the door behind her, Lorna snuggled beneath the covers. Three weeks! Mummy had already provisionally booked the church for them, and tomorrow she and George had to make the arrangements with the registrar, but not until after George had dropped off his suitcase at the hotel, giving him a local address. It was a funny rule. It made weddings easier to organise if the happy couple lived in the same locality, but it must be causing no end of bother and problems now that couples were separated by the war.

Still, Lorna thought with a shiver of delight, it would make a good story to tell their children one day.

. . .

'You must have whatever sort of dress you want,' Daddy said after Lorna and George returned from their meeting with the registrar. 'Money no object. We want those gossips in London to see how wrong they were.'

'With respect, sir,' said George, 'I have no intention of taking the gossips into account when organising my wedding.'

Lorna smiled. 'You can forget "money no object" too, Daddy. It isn't like that with wedding dresses these days. Girls borrow them, or they get married in something smart they can wear for best afterwards, or they wear their uniform.'

Daddy's thick eyebrows pulled together above his dark eyes. 'You are *not* getting married in your WVS uniform.'

'I wasn't thinking of that,' Lorna said in the most serious voice she could manage. 'I meant my salvage depot dungarees.'

'Very funny,' said her father.

'I didn't think men were supposed to be interested in wedding dresses,' she replied.

'I am,' Daddy said in a grumbly voice, 'when my daughter is the one wearing it.'

'I've got some dresses upstairs for you to try on,' said Mummy. 'They've been offered by the daughters of various friends. You might recognise one or two of them, because we were at the weddings. Maybe one of them will catch your eye.' She turned to George. 'You'll have to make yourself scarce for the afternoon. You aren't allowed to see the gown.'

'I'll keep George busy,' said Daddy.

His health had improved no end since Lorna's last visit and he was no longer relying on his walking-stick.

'I worry that he might be pushing himself too hard,' Mummy had confided when Lorna had asked for details, 'but that's your father for you.' She sighed. 'He hated being incapacitated and now he wants the world to see that he is every bit as strong and active as he ever was.'

When she followed her mother upstairs to view the dresses that awaited her, Lorna couldn't help thinking of the evening at Star House when Betty had tried on all the dresses Mrs Beaumont had borrowed from her friend, the wardrobe mistress. That had been such fun. Having Betty, Sally, Lorna, Mrs Beaumont and Mrs Henshaw all focusing on the dresses had made a real occasion out of it. This time, it was just Lorna and her mother. It wasn't going to be a lark, but it was going to be special and intimate, a private occasion to be cherished.

The most modern of the dresses was made of winter-white rayon-crape. It had a shaped seam beneath the bust and short sleeves that puffed at the shoulders. Lorna knew the instant she saw it that it wasn't the one for her, but she tried it on all the same, wanting to show appreciation for the trouble her mother had gone to.

'A seam under the bust is all very well,' she said, looking at her reflection, 'but it presupposes you have a bust to show off.'

'This one might be better for you,' said Mummy. 'It's made from long panels with no waist-seam. It was Jacintha Berryman's dress and she's as tall as you are.'

The gown was indeed elegant and a good fit, but it didn't make Lorna feel special, not even when Mummy carefully placed the headdress of wax orange blossom with a veil of embroidered tulle on her head.

The next dress had a slash of a neckline and a skirt that fell straight down at the front, while at the back it had a short train that pooled prettily on the floor.

'It's lovely on you,' said Mummy, taking a step back and eyeing her critically with her head tilted to one side, 'but I can tell you aren't keen.'

'It's beautiful,' Lorna said, 'but it feels more like a glamorous evening gown than a wedding dress.' She turned her gaze anxiously on her mother. 'Am I being picky?'

'Not at all,' Mummy answered at once. 'It's your wedding dress and it has to be perfect, war or no war. Besides,' she added with a twinkle in her greeny-hazel eyes, 'I've been dying to see you in all these different dresses. You've no idea how exciting it is to be the mother of the bride. I was dreading you choosing the very first one and not bothering with the others. It's wonderful to see you in all these gowns. You're such a beautiful girl and I'm proud of you.'

Touched, Lorna gave her a hug. 'I'm glad I've got you for my mother of the bride and I'm glad you're getting the white wedding you wanted so much.'

'I'd have gone along with the registry office plan if you'd wanted me to,' said Mummy. 'It would have been a disappointment, but I'd have respected your wishes. You've grown up a lot since last year, Lorna.'

'In a good way, I hope,' said Lorna.

'In the best possible way,' her mother replied warmly. 'Now turn round and let me unfasten the buttons.'

There were three more wedding dresses. Although Lorna enjoyed trying them on, none of them cried out to her. Strangely, this wasn't disappointing. On the contrary, she felt she had reached a new, more mature understanding with her mother, and that mattered much more.

Later, she explained it to George during a few private minutes in the garden.

'I think the war has brought Mummy out from under Daddy's shadow. It's done the same for me. Our wedding is going to bring Mummy and me close together in a new way, and it feels even more special after the way your mother has accepted me too.'

With a laugh, George chucked his cigarette onto the path

and ground it beneath the sole of his shoe. Then he drew her to him.

'There's something you're forgetting.'

'What's that?' she asked.

'I'm delighted that you're feeling closer to your mother and mine, Miss West-Sadler, but kindly leave some room in there for me.'

'I think I might just about manage that,' Lorna said. To prove it, she snuggled closer to him for a kiss.

Lorna arrived back at Star House late on Sunday evening. She opened the front door softly and slipped inside, batting her way past the door-curtain. Before she could feel for the switch, the hallway light came on as Sally and Deborah emerged from the sitting room to greet her.

'Let me help you off with your things,' said Sally.

'Was the journey tiring?' Deborah asked, picking up Lorna's valise and placing it beside the foot of the stairs.

'I suppose so – for other passengers,' said Lorna, thinking about it for the first time. 'Not for me.' Her face broke into a wide smile. 'I was too excited to notice.'

'Come and sit down and tell us all about it,' said Sally.

In the sitting room, Louise had wool draped round her spread hands and Mrs Beaumont was deftly creating a ball from it as Louise moved her hands to and fro, keeping pace with the landlady's winding. Without stopping, they both looked up and smiled.

'You haven't all waited up for me, have you?' Lorna asked, touched.

'Did you think we'd all toddle off to bed without waiting to hear the latest about the wedding?' Deborah asked.

'Have you set the date?' Mrs Beaumont wanted to know.

'October the eleventh – three weeks yesterday.' Lorna released a happy sigh. 'It's happening. It's really happening.'

'And so quickly,' said Louise.

'No one is hanging about these days,' said Sally.

'It isn't taking place as quickly as some weddings,' said Lorna. 'Don't forget George and I got back together before Easter. There are plenty of couples who meet and marry in far less time.'

'So your mother has got three weeks to make everything perfect for you,' said Mrs Beaumont.

'And for herself,' said Lorna. 'I want it to be perfect for her too. This is her one and only chance to be the mother of the bride and I want her to enjoy every moment.'

'Won't it be tricky,' Deborah asked, 'with you being here in Manchester while all the preparations are going ahead in Lancaster? Won't you feel you're missing out?'

'It would be nice to be closer to what's going on, obviously,' said Lorna, 'but this is where my war work is. My mother and I understand one another and I know she'll do everything she can to produce the wedding that George and I want.' She laughed. 'She'll have all the work, and we'll turn up on the day and have all the pleasure.'

'What about the cake?' Mrs Beaumont asked.

'Which one?' Lorna asked mischievously. 'The lavishly decorated, four-tier cardboard cake that my father has ordered—'

'Four tiers!' the others exclaimed almost in one voice.

'—or the edible cake?'

'Well, I did mean to ask about the real cake,' said Mrs Beaumont, 'but now I want to hear all about the four-tier one.'

'Your father doesn't do anything by halves, does he?' Sally remarked.

'As far as Daddy is concerned, there never was a social occasion that couldn't be improved upon by spending yet more money on it.' Lorna was unembarrassed. 'And as he said, I'm marrying into an ancient family, so we have to have something spectacular for the wedding photographs.'

'Four tiers,' said Louise and they all laughed in delight, the warmth of their feelings filling the room.

'With a V for victory on the top of each layer,' said Lorna, and the warm feeling deepened to encompass patriotism, resolve and deep concern for all the men away fighting.

'A towering cardboard cake with Vs for victory,' Mrs Beaumont said approvingly. 'It sounds *perfect*.'

CHAPTER NINETEEN

At the salvage depot on Monday morning, Sally smiled to herself as Lorna happily described her wedding arrangements all over again for Betty's benefit while the three of them sorted the daily sacks together. Even though Sally missed Andrew every day, it did her heart good to see Lorna in such high spirits and to know that she and George could look forward to a future together.

'Four tiers!' Betty exclaimed. '*Four?*'

Sally laughed. 'That's exactly the same tone of voice we all used last night.'

After Lorna had shared her information, Betty asked the all-important question.

'What about the dress?'

Lorna groaned softly. 'My mother had borrowed several for me to try on, but none of them was right for me. Don't get me wrong. They were lovely, but—'

'—none of them was your dream dress,' Betty finished. 'I know what you mean. Just think how many I had to try on.'

'Let's not worry about that now,' said Lorna. 'I want to ask the two of you if you'll be my bridesmaids – well, matrons of honour, really, seeing as you're both married.'

Betty squealed and Sally caught her breath in delight.

'Oh, *thank* you,' said Betty. 'I'd love to. I was Sally's bridesmaid last year and now I'm going to be your matron of honour.'

'Samuel will be invited to the wedding as well,' said Lorna.

Betty glowed. 'That makes it even better.' She looked at Sally. 'Isn't it wonderful?'

Sally hid her dismay behind a smile. 'Of course it is. I'm honoured to be asked.'

'Do I hear a "but" in there?' Lorna asked.

Sally felt her shoulders slump a fraction. 'I'm so sorry, but I don't think I can accept. You must, of course, Betty, but I'm not sure I can.'

'Why not?' Betty asked.

'Because of the depot,' Sally explained. 'None of us would be here to open up.'

'So what?' Betty asked. 'We shut up shop for the day when I got married and you two were my bridesmaids.'

Sally pressed her lips together. 'I know, but I got special permission for that. Mr Pratt and Mr Merivale at the Town Hall made it clear that it was a one-off.'

'That's a blow,' Lorna said quietly.

Sally's sensible nature came to the fore. 'It's a shame, but it can't be helped.'

'Perhaps we ought to toss for it,' Betty offered.

'That's sweet of you,' said Sally, 'but no. That Saturday is my day to be here to open up. No arguments – and no glum faces, you two. I'll be thinking of you all day and I'll be there with you in spirit. Oh yes, and I'll expect you to bring me back a piece of the wedding cake – the *real* one, mind, not the cardboard one!'

Sally put on a brave face for the rest of the day, although her disappointment at not being a matron of honour intensified after a telephone call from Mr Merivale at the Town Hall. He and Mr Pratt had made their decision concerning Lorna's future.

After hanging up, Sally went to give her chum the good news.

'You're going to be allowed to leave the depot.'

Betty squealed and gave Lorna a hug. 'That's wonderful!'

'You sound keen to see the back of me,' Lorna teased.

'In the nicest possible way,' Betty replied, her happy smile making her dimple appear.

'You have to write me a letter,' Sally told Lorna, 'stating your wish to resign and the date of the wedding. I'll send it on to the Town Hall.'

Lorna couldn't stop smiling. 'Thanks for sorting it out for me, Sally.'

'I didn't do anything,' Sally answered. 'I just asked the question for you. I'm glad you got the answer you were hoping for.'

'Oh, I got that with bells on,' Lorna exclaimed. She caught hold of Sally's hand. 'If you could be one of my attendants, everything would be perfect.'

Sally sighed. 'You know what they say. "If wishes were horses…" I'd love to be a matron of honour – and I'd love the war to be over – and above all else, I'd love Andrew to come home…' She allowed herself a little shrug. 'Things are the way they are.'

Oh, but if only…

Tea that evening at Star House was fish with vegetables and mashed potatoes followed by a layered pudding of dates and apples. While the girls tucked in, Mrs Beaumont sat with them, smoking. The main topic of conversation was Lorna's wedding.

'My mother says it's probably a good thing that the war has imposed limits on weddings,' said Lorna. 'Otherwise, my father would have used it as a reason to invite all his business cronies, most of whom I've never even met.'

'Fancy turning your daughter's wedding into some sort of business do,' said Deborah.

Mrs Beaumont blew out a stream of smoke. 'Weddings don't mean the same to men as they do to women.'

'Mummy has put her foot down and told him it's only to be family and close friends,' said Lorna. 'But I have made one exception. I said I'd like to invite the three businessmen Daddy was with when he drank the tainted whisky – and their wives, of course.'

'That's a kind gesture,' said Mrs Beaumont.

Sally caught Lorna's eye and gave her a look of understanding. Aside from George and Lorna, she was the only person who knew of George's involvement in the breaking-up of an illegal alcohol ring here in Manchester. Inviting the men who had been in Lancaster with Mr West-Sadler on that fateful night, two of whom had likewise been temporarily paralysed, was a private nod to an important piece of George's secret war work.

It wasn't long before the conversation turned to the subject of bridesmaids.

'I asked Sally and Betty to be my joint matrons of honour,' said Lorna. She looked at Deborah and Louise. 'I hope you two don't mind not being asked to be bridesmaids.'

'Of course not,' said Louise. 'You've known Sally and Betty much longer. I'm very much the newcomer here.'

'And you have to think of the wedding numbers,' Deborah added.

'Betty has said yes, which I'm delighted about,' said Lorna, 'but unfortunately Sally had to decline.'

That meant Sally had to explain all over again.

'That needn't be a problem,' said Louise. 'I'm not working at the munitions that day, so I could open up for you – assuming

I'd be allowed to, that is. I could pop along between now and then for a lesson in how to operate the weighing machine. You did say that Saturdays are when children like to come to the depot to have their salvage weighed.'

'Would you really do that?' Lorna asked, looking hopefully at Sally.

Sally felt a flicker of excitement. 'As Louise says, it's a question of being allowed to. I'd have to ask.'

'I'll see if I can have that morning off so that I can be at the depot as well,' Deborah offered. 'When you ask Mr Pratt and Mr Merivale for permission, tell them that another Town Hall employee has offered to step in and that she and a munitions worker have volunteered to undergo a spot of training in advance. How does that sound?'

'It sounds to me,' said Mrs Beaumont, 'as if Sally is going to be a matron of honour.'

Back in the spring, Deborah had borrowed some wedding dresses from the girls at the Town Hall on Betty's behalf. Now here she was doing the same thing all over again for Lorna. Her fellow clerks were only too pleased to help out and the canteen seemed to be filled with wedding chatter.

'My mum says it's a matter of pride to have a wedding that's as close as possible to the ones we had before the war and all the shortages,' said Miss Brelland.

'It's a shame they outlawed the making of confetti,' said Miss Greening, a bubbly girl from Housing. 'I can see why they did, obviously, but it's still a shame.'

'My nan had a gorgeous rose bush in her garden,' said Miss Jameson from Welfare. 'The girl next door to her was getting married and her little sisters decided there could be no more romantic kind of confetti than real rose petals.'

'No...' breathed her audience, seeing where this was heading.

'Yes,' Miss Jameson replied. 'The little devils sneaked into my nan's garden and stripped her rose bush bare. The bride was mortified.'

'What did your nan do?' Deborah asked, well and truly caught up in the story.

'What could she do? She let the bride have them. It would have been churlish not to. It wasn't as though she could have glued them back on, and it wasn't the bride's fault.'

'She was nicer about it than I would have been,' said Miss Brelland. 'What is your friend doing for confetti?' she asked Deborah. 'We could make sure she has a few handfuls of hole-punch circles, if you like.'

Ever since the war began, the girls at the Town Hall had been saving all the tiny circles of paper that were left over when sheets of paper were hole-punched in the top corner to be fastened together with treasury-tags.

'Would that be all right?' Deborah asked eagerly. 'I didn't like to ask, because she doesn't work here.'

'We'll always help any bride,' said Miss Jameson.

'Thanks,' Deborah said, pleased.

They all looked round at the sound of excited squeals from across the busy room. Deborah caught a glimpse of a girl eagerly thrusting out her left hand for her dinner companions to admire.

'That's Miss Stacy from Welfare,' said Miss Greening. She smiled at Deborah. 'Your chum will have to go halves on the confetti.'

Miss Brelland leaned forward and the others around the table did too, so as to share whatever confidence she was about to impart.

'I'm always glad for another girl when she gets engaged, I

honestly am, but it sometimes makes me wonder if it'll ever happen to me.'

'There just aren't enough men these days,' Miss Jameson said with a sigh. 'They're all away fighting.'

'The ones in reserved occupations are still here,' Deborah pointed out.

'Like your brother you mean,' said Miss Brelland. 'But he's miles away.'

'And he's married,' Miss Greening added.

Miss Brelland chuckled. 'You should get him to send a list of all the eligible chaps he used to work with on the Manchester Ship Canal.'

Deborah laughed as well. 'That might not be such a bad idea. I wouldn't mind meeting a nice chap myself, but, knowing my luck, something awful would be bound to happen.'

'What d'you mean?' Miss Jameson asked her.

Deborah began to tell the story of how she'd been helping to improve the cottages in Chorlton so that their tenants could move back in. It hadn't been funny at the time, but she was ready to laugh about it now. Before she reached the interesting bit – being mistaken for a man – she was interrupted by Miss Brelland wanting a description of the young men putting together the blackout frames.

'I've no idea what they looked like,' said Deborah.

'Yes, you have. You must have.'

Deborah found that she hadn't particularly noticed what the other chap had looked like, the one who hadn't made the awful blunder, though she could remember the one who made the mistake. That must be because he had embarrassed her so deeply. No wonder she could recall him.

'I didn't really look at one of them, but the one I'm going to tell you about, he had dark hair and dark eyes.'

'Ooh, I do like dark eyes,' murmured Miss Greening.

'There you are,' Miss Brelland said with a note of triumph.

'I told you you'd noticed. It's important to describe the hero of the story.'

'If you let me finish,' Deborah replied, 'you'll see that a hero is the very last thing he was.' She went on to finish her anecdote, hamming it up for effect.

'He took you for a *man*?'

'He *never*!'

'I bet it put you off dungarees for life.'

'At least he was a stranger, and you'll never see him again,' said Miss Greening.

'If only it were that simple,' Deborah answered, and went on to talk about the rescue she had taken part in when she had crawled through from one house to the next to inject the trapped gentleman, and how the same young man had doused her with cold water afterwards. As before, she played it up, making it sound funny, and was rewarded by laughter from the others.

'And it was the same man?' Miss Jameson asked.

'Well, you know what they say,' Miss Brelland said with a chuckle. 'These things happen in threes. If you see him again, you'd better watch out.'

'Believe me,' Deborah answered with conviction, 'if I ever see him again – which I never will – but if I did, I'd run a mile in the opposite direction.'

The number of air raids had tailed off significantly over the summer, which Sally's dad said was because Herr Hitler had turned his attention on Russia. Sally thought back to last year and the Battle of Britain. That had been when she and Andrew had met. The onslaught had been nightly then, and that level of attack had continued for over a year, leaving everybody feeling exhausted but still full of resolve.

This year she'd had her own personal battles to contend

with. Waving Andrew off; getting used to the great gap in her life caused by his absence. The physical trauma and profound emotional distress of losing their baby. The chilling thought that she might never be blessed with another.

One good thing had emerged from it all. Her decision to write that honest and heartfelt letter to Andrew had undoubtedly been the right one. It had opened the door to a stream of loving and deeply meaningful correspondence between them, and this had sustained her. Strange though it sounded, even though this was a time of separation she had never felt closer to him.

She also knew the value of concentrating on the good things, and this included Lorna's wedding. It was wonderful to know she was going to be a matron of honour alongside Betty. Years ago, back when they were little girls, she and Deborah had promised to be one another's bridesmaids, and Deborah had been one of hers along with Betty.

'Now I'm going to be a matron of honour for the second time,' she teased Deborah, 'but I'm still waiting for you to tie the knot.'

'Don't look at me,' said Deborah. 'I haven't got any plans in that direction. I like my life just the way it is, living at Star House, working for the Food Office and doing my WVS duty. No disrespect to Mum and Dad, but I love living in Star House.'

'And I love having you here.' Sally gave her a hug. The presence of her lifelong friend under the same roof was another good thing to be appreciated in her life.

As was her post at the salvage depot. Others might wonder why it meant so much to her on a personal level, but she had always been one to immerse herself in her work and look for ways to improve her own performance. Being made the manager of the depot had been a tremendous feather in her cap.

Working with her chums was another thing to be grateful for. They all loved discussing the forthcoming wedding.

'It's a shame that none of the dresses Deborah brought home from the Town Hall was suitable,' Sally remarked as the three of them took a break from rolling old tyres across the yard to put them under shelter.

Betty perked up. 'I've got some news about a possible dress.'

'What does it look like?' Lorna asked at once.

'Well, it's not a dress *exactly*—'

'Wait!' said Sally, hearing the telephone bell in the office. 'Not another word until I get back.'

She hurried inside and sat behind her desk to lift the receiver. She spoke to the operator and waited a moment for the connection.

'Go ahead, please,' said the operator.

'Chorlton-cum-Hardy Salvage Depot,' Sally said clearly.

'Sally – is that you? George Broughton here.'

'George!' Sally said in surprise.

'I apologise for telephoning during work hours, but may I speak to Lorna, please? It's important.'

'Of course,' said Sally. 'I'll fetch her.' She placed the receiver on the desk and opened the window to call to Lorna. 'It's for you. It's George.'

When Lorna hurried into the office, Sally left her to it – but she hadn't gone more than a few steps along the passage before she halted at the sound of Lorna's exclamation of distress.

CHAPTER TWENTY

Lorna spent the first day or two in a state of disbelief. They'd had to postpone their wedding.

The War Office was sending George away on business – had already sent him, in fact. Within a matter of hours of making that telephone call to the depot, he had been on his way to America. America! Everybody knew how perilous the Atlantic crossing was. That was why the merchant navy travelled in convoys escorted by the Royal Navy. Those damned U-boats were everywhere, intent upon sinking the merchant ships bringing essential supplies to Britain and the naval vessels protecting them.

What George's mission was in America, Lorna had no idea. It was only because of the wedding that he had been permitted to contact her at all.

Lorna and George's mother exchanged letters, sharing their concern for his safety, though without making a song and dance out of it. That wouldn't have been right. It was important not to make a fuss. Lorna had never been more grateful for the way her relationship with Lady Broughton had moved onto a new footing.

The other girls and Mrs Beaumont were all concerned too, of course, which made Lorna realise something she had not been aware of before. It led her to tap softly on Sally's bedroom door in search of a quick word.

'Come in,' Sally called, looking round to see who it was.

'I've come to say something,' Lorna told her. 'It might stir up unhappiness for you, and I'm sorry if it does, but it's important to say it.'

'What is it?' Sally asked, a note of confusion in her tone.

'It's all the concern that I've been shown over having to postpone the wedding and about George crossing the Atlantic.' It was pure emotion that had brought Lorna up here to her friend's side. Now she had to find the right words. 'I appreciate the kindness, of course, but I haven't wallowed in it. I don't want others worrying about me when it's George who matters now – George's safety.'

'Go on,' Sally said quietly when she paused.

'It has made me realise that when something bad happens to you, you find yourself having to be strong for other people so that they don't feel bad, which sounds as if it's the wrong way round, but I think that's the way it often happens.' She looked earnestly at her friend. 'And it's made me realise that you must have had to do the same thing after... after the baby. We were all so sorry about what happened, and you – well, you quietly got on with things and didn't make a fuss. You tried to lessen our worry. I can see that now. You were being strong for us.'

Sally's tawny-hazel eyes shone with tears. 'It's just like you say. When something bad happens, it's no use crumbling; and, yes, there is this need to make it easier for others because you can see how upset they are on your behalf.'

Lorna hugged her. 'I'm sorry if I didn't give you as much support as I could have done.'

Sally returned the hug briefly, then stepped away, dashing a tear from her cheek. She hauled in a deep breath.

'Having a miscarriage isn't something you talk about, not to anybody, and certainly not to your unmarried friends, but I want you to know that I have received a great deal of support and understanding from my mother and from Andrew. I don't know what I'd have done without them.'

'I'm more glad than I can say to hear that,' said Lorna.

'And I always knew how much you and the others cared.' Sally took Lorna's hand in both of her own. 'Please don't think you have to be strong on my account. If you need to weep and wail because you're scared silly about George, then feel free. I mean it. You never have to put on a brave face with me.'

October saw the tall stems of goldenrod appear in the corners of gardens, along with low-growing asters and the pom-pom heads of dahlias in a mixture of rich jewel colours. The leaves on the trees and shrubs started turning to warm orange, burnished gold and deep red, the autumn tints glowing in the sunshine.

To add to Lorna's worries for George, the newspapers had cottoned on to the information that the wedding had been put off.

Lorna was hopping mad.

'A journalist found out the original date from the list on the church noticeboard. Honestly, did they visit every single church in the county until they found the right one? Then, of course, our wedding had to be crossed off. According to Mummy, reporters have tried to corner the vicar, but he refused to say anything; and they've asked all sorts of people – in shops, at the WVS, even at a fundraising event for the Red Cross.'

'Has anybody told them anything?' Mrs Beaumont asked.

'Nothing of use to the papers,' Lorna had to admit. 'Because it's to do with the War Office, I had to swear Mummy and Daddy to secrecy about George going to America, and they haven't told a soul.'

'That's something,' said Louise.

'It is and it isn't,' said Lorna. 'It's good that the real reason is under wraps – but just look at what they're saying in print.'

It was just awful.

Breach-of-Promise Bride Jilted For Second Time

Wedding Woes For Breach-of-Promise Bride

Breach-of-Promise Bride Fails to Get Her Man – Again

And even:

Breach-of-Promise Bride Fails to Bag a Title – Again

Lorna's throat ached fiercely, and she had to shut her eyes for a moment.

'It's humiliating,' she said between her teeth. 'Last year's headlines were bad enough, but these—'

'They shouldn't be allowed to get away with it,' said Deborah, and the others echoed her sentiment.

'Can't you complain?' Sally asked.

'Oh, they'd love that,' Lorna answered bitterly. 'It would give them a reason to keep the story rumbling on. Besides, what would a complaint actually say? "The wedding hasn't been cancelled, just postponed. Please enquire at the War Office for details." No one can utter a word.'

'I'm so sorry that you're being put through this,' Sally said sympathetically. 'It's the very last thing you need when you're worried about George.'

Lorna lifted her chin. 'That's the point, isn't it? As hard as it might be, I have to ignore the press. George's safe return is all that matters now.'

. . .

It was the day before what should have been Lorna and George's wedding day. In happier circumstances, she would have travelled up to Lancaster yesterday and Sally and Betty would have followed her this evening after work, leaving Deborah and Louise to open the depot tomorrow.

Lorna's heart was heavy. She didn't want to be shallow, but it was dreadfully disappointing to picture what might have been. Realising that her shoulders had slumped, she stood up straight. Of course George's well-being was all that mattered, and of course his safety was her top priority, way ahead of anything else – but it was disappointing all the same.

At her request, she, Sally and Betty no longer had a shared dinner break at the depot. After all, it wasn't as though they had a wedding to talk about at the moment. It made it feel a little easier for Lorna to have things on a slightly more formal footing.

Today – on what was meant to have been her wedding day eve – she was the last of them to go for her midday break. Not liking where her thoughts were taking her, she bolted down her sandwiches and her cup of tea and returned to the yard, where she came across Betty and Sally huddled together talking in low voices.

They looked up as she approached.

'Now there's a pair of guilty faces if ever I saw one,' said Lorna. 'What were you whispering about?'

'There's something I've been wanting to tell you,' said Betty, 'and, today being the day it is, this might be a good time – or it might be the worst possible time.'

'Don't stop there,' said Lorna.

Betty glanced at Sally, who nodded.

'You probably don't remember,' Betty went on, 'but when the telephone call came from George to say he had to go away, I was about to tell you something.'

'I don't recall,' said Lorna. 'Come on, Betty, you have to tell me now.' Realising she might have sounded sharp, she smiled at her chum.

'You've heard me mention the Kendalls?'

'The elderly couple you and Samuel help. You do their shopping for them and things like that.'

Betty nodded. 'I told Mrs Kendall about you not finding a wedding dress you liked and she showed me a length of fabric. It's the most beautiful material I've ever seen. It's satin in a soft cream shade shot through with tiny gold threads.' She looked anxiously at Lorna.

'It does sound lovely,' Sally added.

Betty continued, 'Mrs Kendall said that if you would like to have it, then you're welcome to it and you could have it made up into whatever style suits you best.'

'How very generous of her,' said Lorna, touched. 'I'd pay her for the material, of course.'

Betty shook her head emphatically. 'She thought you might offer to do that and she said to say that she doesn't want your money. Years ago, Mrs Kendall used to be in service. That was how she met Mr Kendall, because he was in service with the same family. They fell in love and the family granted them permission to marry.'

'Permission?' Sally repeated.

'That was the way it was in those days,' said Betty. 'Mrs Kendall stayed in service until her own children came along. She had a son and a daughter. The daughter's name was Tilly, short for Matilda. Years later, when Tilly was going to get married, the family presented her with this fabric for her dress, but Tilly was killed in an accident not long afterwards and the material has been locked inside Mrs Kendall's trunk ever since.'

'Poor Tilly,' said Lorna, 'and poor Mrs Kendall. I can understand why she doesn't want any money for the fabric. What a tragic story. Please will you tell her that I'd be honoured to come and see the material and hear all about Tilly, if she'd like to talk about her. And please will you also say that I'll make a donation to the Red Cross in Tilly's memory, whether I take the fabric or not.'

On the morning of the day when Lorna was due to go round to meet Mrs Kendall, Betty arrived at the depot looking very cheerful.

'You're all smiles,' Sally commented, also smiling.

'All dimples, you mean,' Lorna added.

'I've had good news,' said Betty. 'There was a letter waiting for me when I got home last night, from the Radiance people. Apparently, the advertisement they used featuring the picture of me has been a success, and they have decided to go ahead with the second advert.'

'That's wonderful,' Sally exclaimed. 'Congratulations.'

'It shows how right they were to pick you in the first place,' said Lorna.

'I won't get any more money for it,' said Betty, 'but they're going to send me some jars of Radiance as a thank-you.' She laughed. 'The letter said it's important for the Radiance girl to use their product.'

'I wonder if they'll want to use you again for another of their advertisements,' said Sally.

'I hope so,' said Lorna. 'It was quite a lark that day, wasn't it? Do you remember how the photographer and Mrs Inglis kept arguing over which bits of salvage to include in the picture?'

That made Betty laugh. 'I swear they were more bothered about the blessed salvage than they were about me.'

'Of course they weren't,' said Sally. 'It was just the image they wanted to project. That was why they wanted you in your work togs. Advertisements today aren't just about the product. They're about the war effort – like that Oxo advertisement about saving your vegetable water for making soup with Oxo.'

Lorna nodded. 'I saw an advert the other day for indigestion lozenges.'

'How can they possibly help the war effort?' Betty asked, amused.

'Because if you suffer from indigestion, it means you don't benefit from the goodness in your food, and therefore having indigestion lozenges to hand will ensure that your food coupons don't go to waste.'

The girls groaned at that, but it gave them a chuckle as well. The mood was buoyant in the depot that day, not least because Betty was going to take Lorna to meet Mrs Kendall that evening.

'Mrs Kendall asked if you would like to come as well, Sally,' Betty offered. 'Please say yes. She doesn't get out much because of her rheumatics and she loves company.'

Sally looked at Lorna, who nodded.

'In that case, I'd love to,' said Sally. 'Thanks.'

'I can't wait to see the material,' said Lorna. 'You made it sound so beautiful, Betty. It's quite overwhelming to think that Mrs Kendall is prepared to pass it on.'

'It's an honour for you,' said Sally.

Lorna was well aware of that. She had already decided privately that, as well as making a donation to the Red Cross in memory of poor Tilly Kendall, she would also buy flowers for Mrs Kendall and write her a warm letter of appreciation.

At the end of the day, the girls hurried to lock up and go home for tea, after which Lorna and Sally wrapped up warmly and set off to walk to the bookshop to fetch Betty. Mr and Mrs Kendall lived over the road from the bookshop in a small but spotless upstairs flat. Mrs Kendall was a dainty creature who had clearly been pretty when she was young. She still had bright, kind eyes and a warm smile, and was obviously delighted, as Betty had said, to have visitors.

'This is so very kind of you, Mrs Kendall,' said Lorna. 'I'd love to see your special fabric – if you're still sure.'

Mrs Kendall's pale-blue eyes clouded over for a moment, then she smiled with a hint of sadness. 'It's time,' she said. 'I've kept it all these years because I couldn't bear to let it go, but after Betty here told me about how you can't find the right dress, I asked myself what was the point of keeping such a beautiful piece of fabric tucked away in a trunk. Such a waste!'

'Not a waste at all,' Lorna said gently. 'It was part of your sorrow at losing your daughter. That was such a terrible thing to happen. I'm very sorry.'

'Thank you, my dear.' The old lady's eyes glittered. 'She was such a dear girl. When she died, it was as if the light had gone out of our lives.' Then Mrs Kendall roused herself. 'But this is meant to be a happy occasion. Betty, be a dear and fetch the fabric, will you, please?'

With a smile, Betty rose to her feet and left the cosy little parlour. A few moments later she returned, carrying across her forearms a length of folded fabric that frankly made Lorna's heart sink. Cream satin shot through with tiny gold threads? This looked like nothing more than an old sheet!

'Your face,' said Mrs Kendall. 'Don't worry, my dear. That's just the material I use for keeping the wedding material in, to protect it, you understand.'

With Sally's help, Betty unfolded the protective cotton. Once the material inside was revealed, Lorna breathed out a sigh of pure happiness. This was indeed the fabric that dreams were made of. She reached out to touch it with reverent fingertips. It was every bit as special as Betty had made it sound.

To her surprise, Lorna found tears pricking the backs of her eyes. 'Are you sure?' she asked Mrs Kendall. 'I really will understand if it's too much for you to part with it.'

'And that tells me that you are the right girl to give it to,' Mrs Kendall replied emotionally. 'I've clung to it for all these years, unable to let it go, and what good has it done me? It's more than time for me to say goodbye to it, and to give another girl the chance to wear it and look beautiful in it. Betty talks about you a lot, so I know what a good person you are. I'm happy to pass my Tilly's wedding dress material on to you.'

October dragged on, surely the longest month there had ever been. Although Lorna loved the glorious fabric offered by Mrs Kendall, and had gratefully accepted it, she refused to have it made up into a wedding dress.

'I know it sounds superstitious,' she told her friends, 'but I don't want to jinx George's safe return. My mother is keen for me to send the material up to Lancaster so that a local seamstress can set to work on it, but that would involve a certain amount of to-ing and fro-ing for measuring and fittings and so on, and all that would feel like a jinx as well.'

'What have you said to your mother?' Louise asked.

'I don't want to worry her or upset her, so I've said that I need to hang on to what holiday leave I've still got.'

The next thing she knew, she received a letter from her mother to announce that she had made arrangements for the dress to be made at Mademoiselle Antoinette's in St Ann's Square in the middle of Manchester.

When Lorna read out the letter at breakfast, Deborah's bright-blue eyes widened.

'That's the most exclusive dressmaking place for miles around,' she said in awe.

Sally chuckled. 'So exclusive that they call themselves a salon.'

'Fancy having your wedding dress made there,' said Mrs Beaumont, impressed. 'You are a lucky girl.'

'Not that you're ready to have the dress made yet,' Louise

added quickly. 'We all understand that. But when you are ready – oh my!'

Lorna knew she ought to be grateful, but it was impossible to concentrate on the wedding when she had no idea when George was going to come home. She thought all the time about the terrible dangers faced by the men in the Atlantic convoys.

Then, at the very end of the month, a cablegram arrived.

BACK IN TWO WEEKS STOP SEE YOU AT THE ALTAR STOP
GEORGE

CHAPTER TWENTY-ONE

It was all hands to the pump to get the wedding organised. George had given her two weeks and so Lorna was determined to marry on that very day, the fifteenth.

'It will mean having a special licence,' said Sally, 'because of not giving three weeks' notice.'

Lorna shrugged. 'That's easy to organise. Everyone is getting special licences these days. Our wedding will be the odd one out because of being a whole two weeks away. Heaps of couples are marrying on much less notice than that.'

'You'll need to be in contact with your mother a great deal,' said Sally, 'so if you want to use the office telephone after hours, you're welcome to.'

'Are you sure?' Lorna asked, concerned. 'I don't want to get you into trouble. I think we both know what Mr Pratt and Mr Merivale would say if they knew.'

'These are special circumstances,' said Sally. 'As long as your mother places the call and pays for it, that's fine by me. And it's only for the next two weeks.'

Lorna couldn't prevent a smile stretching practically from

ear to ear. 'Two weeks! In two weeks, I'll be a married woman. Mrs George Broughton.' Happy tears spilled onto her cheeks.

Sally gently brushed them away, her hazel eyes filled with fondness. 'You've waited a long time for it, one way and another. I'm glad everything has turned out for the best in the end. You deserve it – you *both* deserve it.'

'Thank you,' said Lorna. 'I'll write to Mummy and give her this telephone number. We'll arrange all the calls in advance so you'll always know when the telephone is going to be used, and we'll keep the number of calls to a minimum,' she added.

Sally was being a good egg about the use of the telephone and the last thing Lorna wanted was for her kindness to rebound on her later.

'Don't forget to write your letter of resignation,' said Sally.

'As if she'd forget that!' Betty said with a chuckle.

Lorna knew that all that was required of the letter was to provide her wedding date and request permission to resign, but it felt important to include some extra heartfelt sentences.

... I would also like to take this opportunity to say what a pleasure it has been to work for Mrs Henshaw, from whom I have learned a great deal. As well as being an expert on the subject of salvage, she is a highly organised depot manager and the way she has built up links with the local community sets a good example to everyone.

A couple of evenings later, after work, Lorna said goodbye to Sally and Betty and saw them on their way, then returned to the office to sit by the telephone to await the first of what she thought of as her wedding calls.

'Darling, I'm so very sorry,' said Mummy as soon as the operator had left them to talk, 'but I have bad news.'

Lorna's heart plummeted. 'What is it?'

'The church. We can't have it. It's fully booked all that day – but you can have it the following Saturday. That's only one more week to wait, which isn't very much, is it? I've booked the church provisionally. That'll be fine, won't it?'

Lorna gave herself a few moments to come to terms with the disappointment. Foolish as it now seemed, it had never occurred to her that there would be any problems like this.

'Lorna, are you still there?'

'I'm here, Mummy.'

'Well? Shall I tell the vicar that the following Saturday will do?'

She ought to say yes. Of course she should. But somehow, she just couldn't.

'The last thing I want is to be difficult, but it's important to me to marry on the fifteenth. It ties in with the wording of the cablegram from George. I know that shouldn't matter, but it does. It matters to me. It's all part of how he was sent away and our first wedding had to be put off. Knowing that he is on his way home, and that he's looking forward to this new wedding every bit as much as I am, makes it very important that we stick to the two weeks he mentioned in the cablegram. It's – it's something to tell our children about.' She pressed her lips together, willing her mother to understand.

After a short silence, Mummy said, 'In that case, I'll try the nearby churches.'

'Thank you,' breathed Lorna, so softly that she wasn't sure if the words would travel down the line.

'This is your wedding day,' said her mother, 'and I want it to be perfect for you. If you want your wedding to take place on the fifteenth, then that's when it shall be.'

Lorna laughed. 'You sound like Daddy. That's the sort of thing he'd say.'

'Maybe I've learned a thing or two from him over the years,' Mummy answered drily.

. . .

'What a shame that you can't have your own church that day,' Betty said the next morning, as she and Lorna sorted the daily sacks together while Sally attended to some paperwork in the office. 'It won't be the same getting married in a church you aren't familiar with.'

'If it's a choice between having the fifteenth and using our local church, then I'm afraid the date feels more important to me,' said Lorna. 'The wording of that cablegram means I want to get married on that day and no other. Does that sound shallow?'

'Nope. It sounds romantic.'

'Thanks for saying that.'

'It's true,' said Betty. 'It's all part of how much a wedding day matters. I got married in the same church as my mum did, and that was very special. Sad, but special. For you, the date has taken on this huge significance. I can understand that. You'll be able to keep George's cablegram from America in with your wedding telegrams and it'll be part of the story of your wedding. Things like that matter.'

Lorna nodded. 'Like at your wedding when we had the photograph taken of the three of us girls with Mrs Beaumont.'

Betty's dimple made its usual appearance when she smiled reminiscently. 'She loved that picture, didn't she? I was so glad we did it.'

'You're right,' said Lorna. 'When there's a wedding, the details matter. They all twine together to make the day perfect.'

'And one of your perfect things is the date,' said Betty.

'And another will be the dress,' said Lorna. 'I have to go to Mademoiselle Antoinette's to look at designs and think about what I want. They have a designer and she needs to see me and take my measurements and look at the fabric, so she can put together some ideas.' She stopped working so she could look at Betty. 'I wondered if you would like to come with me – you and Mrs Kendall.'

Betty caught her breath. 'Oh, I'd love to. I'm honoured to be asked.'

'What about Mrs Kendall? Do you think she'd like to? I wouldn't want to upset her by bringing back unhappy memories of Tilly.'

'I could have a quiet word with her and see what she says,' Betty suggested. 'Instead of you asking her, I mean. It might be easier for her if I do it.'

Lorna nodded. 'Good idea. I hope she says yes, but I'll understand if it's too much for her.'

'I'll make sure she knows that,' said Betty. Then her eyes twinkled, and her dimple popped like crazy. 'I'm going on a trip to Mademoiselle Antoinette's. I can hardly believe it. I never imagined I'd ever go to a posh place like that.'

'We'll have a wonderful time,' said Lorna.

Betty chuckled. 'You make it sound like a day trip to the seaside.'

'I'm going to ask Sally to come along as well,' said Lorna. 'I need both my matrons of honour with me.'

'You hear of girls having dresses made out of parachute silk,' said Betty, 'but you're going to have real satin. It's going to be gorgeous. You'll look stunning. George will burst with pride.'

'I can't wait to see what Mademoiselle Antoinette's designer suggests,' said Lorna, 'and obviously I want to have the most glorious dress imaginable. But the honest truth is that I'd happily get married in my dungarees and headscarf if it would bring George home safe and sound. That's really all that matters.'

Lorna sat in Sally's office at the end of the working day, tapping her fingernails on the desk as she waited for the telephone to ring. When it did so, she answered it immediately and accepted the call, though she announced herself in the professional way Sally expected, just in case it turned out to be somebody else.

'Chorlton-cum-Hardy Salvage Depot.'

'Lorna, it's your mother. Who else were you expecting at this time of day?'

'No one, Mummy. It's good to hear your voice. How are you and Daddy?'

'Tearing our hair out over a venue for the wedding, since you ask. It's been very frustrating. I'm so sorry, Lorna. Between us, we've visited every single church for miles around and the answer is the same at every one of them. They are all booked up on the day you want.'

'Oh no,' Lorna breathed.

'I'm not going to ask you if you'll change the date, because I know how much it means to you. But if we can't find a church that's available...' She let the sentence trail away. Was she waiting for Lorna to cave in over the date?

Lorna pushed aside her disappointment. There was nothing to be gained by feeling glum. 'In that case, I'll have to ask Lady Broughton if we can hold the wedding in their local church. I hope that's all right with you, Mummy. I know you and Daddy would far rather that we got married in or near Lancaster.'

Hearing her mother draw a breath, she crossed her fingers that she wasn't going to cut up rough. But Mummy took it squarely on the chin.

'It's fine, Lorna. In wartime we all do what we have to. I know you've set your heart on that date for a special reason and I do understand, really I do. Don't worry, darling. I'll square it with your father.'

'Thanks, Mummy. You're an angel. I'll let you know what Lady Broughton says.'

In a wry tone, her mother added, 'I'm sure your father will be pleased to think of you marrying in the church where one day you'll be the lady of the manor.'

'As long as you don't mind, Mummy, that's what matters.'

At the end of the call, Lorna locked up and walked home, thinking hard. Had the time come to give up on her precious idea of marrying on the exact day implied by George's cablegram? She didn't want to insist on something at the expense of other things that mattered, but on the other hand, as Mummy had rightly pointed out, she had set her heart on marrying on the fifteenth for a special reason.

At Star House, she gave everyone her news and was comforted by their exclamations of disappointment on her behalf. They were also rather thrilled at the thought of her marrying in the church adjoining the ancestral home of George's family.

'That sounds a very swish thing to do,' said Deborah.

'Did you see the church while you were there?' asked Louise.

'Yes,' Lorna told her. 'There's an ancient stone font dating back several hundred years and the pews are so old that they creak every time someone moves.'

'That's one way of making sure no one fidgets,' Mrs Beaumont remarked.

'When are you going to talk to George's mother about it?' Sally asked. 'Are you going to write to her and give her the office number?'

'No, I'll call her from a telephone box,' Lorna replied. She didn't want Sally to feel she was being put on the spot. 'It'll be quicker. We need to get this sorted out. I can't do it this evening because I've got to get ready for WVS duty in a little while. I'll ring her tomorrow after the appointment at Mademoiselle Antoinette's.'

The mention of that name conjured up smiles all round. Everyone was excited about Lorna having her dress made at such an illustrious place. Because of Lorna's working hours, and the need to keep the depot open all day, an arrangement had been made for her and her companions to go into town after work. Mademoiselle Antoinette's was going to stay open specially for her to have a private appointment.

Mrs Kendall was delighted to have been invited to go with them. Rather than going on the bus, which Lorna would very likely have done if it had just been the three girls going, she ordered a taxi, wanting the elderly Mrs Kendall to travel in comfort and feel she was being spoilt.

'This is very kind of you,' said Mrs Kendall when they were all settled in the taxi. She was wrapped up in a frankly ancient overcoat that made Lorna strongly suspect that she and Mr Kendall didn't have a lot of money.

'I'm pleased you were free to come with us,' Lorna assured her, suddenly aware of sounding exactly like her mother, with the right words for every social occasion. 'I hope you're going to approve of the style the designer suggests.'

The taxi dropped them outside St Ann's Square and Lorna paid and tipped the driver before offering her arm to Mrs Kendall. With Betty carrying the glorious material carefully wrapped up inside its cotton protector, the little group walked along the square, with its handsome buildings several storeys high and St Ann's Church at the end. They took their time, partly because of the blackout and also because Mrs Kendall wasn't exactly nimble.

'We're looking for a little cul-de-sac called Caroline Street,' said Lorna, shining her tissue-dimmed torch on the pavement in front of them. 'Mind your step, Mrs Kendall.'

They entered Caroline Street and found Mademoiselle Antoinette's, which proved to have a bow-window at the front.

'It must look very pretty when it isn't covered in anti-blast tape and blackout curtains,' Sally remarked.

'You've no idea what a treat it is for me to be here,' said Mrs Kendall. 'Years ago, when I was in service, Mademoiselle Antoinette's was where the ladies of the family came to have their dresses and other garments made. And now here I am, about to walk inside.'

Betty opened the door and they all walked into a dark interior.

'If you'll please stand still, ladies, while I shut the door behind you,' said a woman's modulated voice, 'I can switch on the light.'

They all blinked as the light came on. The woman who had spoken was a beautifully turned-out lady in a demure dress the dark colour of which showed she was here to serve them and the cut of which spoke volumes for the skill of Mademoiselle Antoinette's seamstresses.

'Good evening. I am Miss Sheridan. And this is the West-Sadler party...?'

Lorna stepped forward. 'I'm Lorna West-Sadler. Thank you for opening for us this evening.'

'We always do what we can to accommodate ladies who are engaged in war work. Would you like to follow me?'

Miss Sheridan took them into what looked not unlike a tasteful sitting room. A dainty oval table that was polished to a warm, honey-coloured shine stood between a chair and a settee, both upholstered in green velvet. There were other matching chairs, which presumably had been brought in to accommodate the size of the party.

When the visitors were comfortable, Miss Sheridan offered them tea. Lorna might have declined, but, heck, this was all part of the build-up to her wedding, so why not? Besides, it made it more of an outing for dear Mrs Kendall.

'Is that the cloth?' Miss Sheridan enquired. 'Perhaps I could take it along to our designer for her to have a look at so she can formulate some ideas before she comes in here to speak to you. Our Miss Weston has worked here at Mademoiselle Antoinette's for many years and no one knows fabrics as well as she does.'

The bundle of material was whisked away. Miss Sheridan played the hostess and poured the tea, as well as offering shortbread biscuits shaped like seashells. Presently a door on the far side of the room opened and another woman entered. If Lorna had expected Miss Weston to look like a model straight from the Paris catwalk, she was disappointed. Miss Weston was a neatly dressed lady of what Mummy referred to as upper-middle age.

After the introductions had been performed, Miss Weston invited Lorna to go with her to be measured. Lorna would have been happy to be measured in front of her companions, but clearly things were done a certain way here. As well as submitting to the tape-measure, Lorna had to stand there while Miss Weston and another woman eyed her up and down and walked all around her, taking her in from top to toe.

'Like they were choosing a racehorse,' she planned to tell her chums on the way home. 'They didn't actually force open my mouth and examine my teeth, but they might as well have done.'

After that Lorna was escorted back to the sitting room. The others looked up with such expectation in their faces as she walked in that she simply had to laugh.

'Sorry,' she said. 'Did you imagine I'd come back wearing a fabulous wedding dress?'

Presently Miss Weston entered the room. She had a large sketchbook with her and, with just a few dashes of her pencil, she created graceful images of the style she recommended.

'Long sleeves because of the time of year. Lightly padded shoulders, of course. A floor-length gown, with its own train. No seam at the waist, though I do suggest some gathers to either side of the ribcage. That will give you a little more shape.'

'I'm all in favour of anything that makes me look less straight up and down,' Lorna said frankly.

'As to the neckline,' went on Miss Weston, 'do you have any preferences? I suggest something simple and unfussy. You are, if

I may say so, a beautiful young lady, and you'll be wearing a stunning fabric. Neither you nor the cloth requires anything ornate.'

Betty was gazing at Miss Weston's sketches. 'Lorna, you're going to look exquisite.'

'Yes, you are, dear,' Mrs Kendall added.

Lorna gave the elderly lady a swift glance in case she was feeling emotional because of her lost daughter, who never had the chance to have this lovely material made into a wedding dress that would make her feel like a princess. But, to Lorna's relief, Mrs Kendall seemed to be enjoying the occasion.

'You're very fortunate, Miss West-Sadler,' went on Miss Weston. 'You've been given not just a beautiful material that will flow nicely, but also a generous quantity. Are you having attendants? There will be enough cloth for them to have stoles to match your dress, if you think you'd like that. I suggest lining them with cream velvet.'

'That sounds perfect,' said Lorna. She looked at her friends. 'Yes?'

'Yes, please!' Betty said at once.

'It would be a lovely finishing touch,' said Sally.

'Then please can we have stoles for my two matrons of honour?' Lorna asked Miss Weston. She glanced at Mrs Kendall for a moment before turning back to the designer. 'Actually, might there be sufficient fabric to make three stoles? There is a very special guest I'm going to invite to my wedding, and I'd like her to have a stole as well.'

CHAPTER TWENTY-TWO

'Are you quite sure you're all right about using the public telephone to call Lady Broughton this evening?' Sally asked while she and Lorna tied up bundles of paper ready to be sent off to the paper-mill. 'This chill hasn't let up all day.'

Lorna smiled. 'Are you worried about me freezing to death in the queue for the telephone box?'

'I just want you to know that you can use the office telephone, if it helps.'

'Thanks, but no,' Lorna answered. 'I'd have to write and ask her to ring me here and I don't want to use up the extra time that would take. This church question needs to be sorted out quickly. I shan't be happy until it is. And also, while I appreciate enormously how kind you've been about giving me access to the office telephone so far, I don't want to take advantage. I know you've pushed your authority by helping me, and I don't want to put you in a difficult position.'

'Thanks for understanding,' said Sally. 'When Mr Merivale and Mr Pratt gave me full authority over the depot, I don't suppose they imagined me letting a chum use the telephone on wedding business – though I'd defend my decision if push came to shove. Organising a wedding in wartime is no mean feat, and it's not as though the depot is paying for the calls.'

They carried on with the job. When all the paper was ready, Sally disappeared into the office to compile some statistics and Lorna got on with sorting through a box of small bits and pieces of metal, checking that it didn't include ointment tubes or shaving-cream tubes, because those contained tin and lead, which would get lost in the smelting process if they were put in with everything else.

She had almost finished when Betty appeared.

'Mr Millington has arrived to look at the jewellery.'

'I'll be there in a mo,' said Lorna.

She hurried to finish her task. Mr Millington owned a respected jewellery shop on Barlow Moor Road and Sally invited him along to the depot every so often to sort through the jewellery that had been offered up as salvage. People in general made huge personal sacrifices to do everything they could to support the war effort and for many women that included parting with their jewellery. Every now and again Mr Millington would find a ring or a brooch of serious value and then Sally would make an effort to trace the lady who had donated it – no easy task, as most jewellery arrived as part of a job lot. But if she could find the original owner, then she would offer to return the valuable piece; but so far the women in this position had been happy to have the jewellery sold and the funds donated to the war effort or a wartime charity, such as the Red Cross.

All three girls loved it when Mr Millington came to examine the jewellery because it gave them a chance to linger over the pretty pieces themselves, comparing and admiring the various styles.

Today there proved to be nothing of special value. Mr Millington departed, waving aside Sally's thanks.

'Always a pleasure,' he said. 'Good afternoon, ladies.'

As the working day drew to a close, Sally sent Lorna off early.

'Are you sure?' Lorna asked her.

'Don't be daft,' Sally answered lightly. 'Betty and I can easily manage. Go and get your church sorted out, missy.'

Lorna darted upstairs and changed out of her dungarees and old jumper into a blouse, cashmere jumper and wool skirt. She put on her overcoat and settled her hat in place, checking it in the tiny mirror, before she drew on her gloves.

Carrying her gas-mask box and handbag, she went downstairs. Sally had been correct about this being a cold day. There was a real nip in the air, and it was only going to get sharper as day turned to night.

It wasn't far to the nearest telephone box. A middle-aged woman was already inside, speaking urgently into the receiver, but there was no queue waiting outside. In spite of her warm, high-quality clothes, Lorna got chilly as she waited. She had sometimes seen impatient people rapping on the panes of glass to make the person inside the box get a move on, but she would never do anything so rude or unfeeling.

At last the woman hung up. She shoved the door open and hurried away, looking upset.

Lorna stepped inside, holding her bag under her arm while she removed the coins from her purse. Soon she was speaking to Lady Broughton.

'This is an unexpected pleasure,' said her ladyship. 'At least, I hope it's a pleasure. I hope there isn't a problem.'

'Well, since you ask...' Lorna replied with a smile in her voice, and went on to explain about the churches local to her parents' home.

'What a nuisance for you,' said Lady Broughton. 'You must be very disappointed. What shall you do instead?'

'I was hoping that we could get married in your local church,' said Lorna.

'And you'd feel comfortable doing that?' asked Lady Broughton. 'I'll take that as a compliment to our much-improved relationship.' Her voice rang with satisfaction, but then her tone changed. 'As much as I would like to agree, I'm afraid there is a problem.'

'Don't tell me the church is already fully booked,' said Lorna.

'I have no idea,' Lady Broughton replied. 'The trouble is that your parents aren't the only ones whose local church has been visited by a nosy reporter. We've had one hanging around here as well, no doubt hoping to see the details of your wedding on the board.'

'Oh *no*,' breathed Lorna.

'Not to worry,' was the bracing reply. 'I soon saw him off. Well, not me personally. You know how the local children enjoy searching the grounds for German spies? Well, I may have mentioned the stranger with the notebook who'd been hanging around the church.'

'And the children went after him?' Lorna didn't know whether to be delighted or astounded.

'They most certainly did – in a highly organised way, too, which did them credit. He ended up banging on the police station door in search of refuge.'

Lorna laughed. 'I wish I'd been there to see it.'

'So, he's gone from the neighbourhood – for good, I sincerely hope, though there's nothing to say another might not turn up to try his luck,' said Lady Broughton. 'Frankly, Lorna, I can think of nothing better than for you and George to celebrate your wedding here, but you could well find it reported in the newspapers.' After a moment she added, 'Actually, I can think of something better: you and George having a simply wonderful wedding somewhere that the so-called gentlemen of the press and their photographers wouldn't dream of looking.'

Lorna walked away from the telephone box, torn between anger at the press and disappointment that her new plan had fallen to pieces. She had to swipe away a tear, and that left her feeling annoyed with herself for being weak. When she was halfway back to Star House, she abruptly turned on her heel and marched back to the telephone box. There was nobody inside it, so she was soon speaking to her mother.

'Darling!' said Mummy. 'Are you telephoning because you've spoken to Lady Broughton?'

'Yes, and it's bad news, I'm afraid,' said Lorna.

'Don't tell me their church is booked up as well?'

'No, it's worse than that,' said Lorna. 'They've had a journalist sniffing round. And you know how it goes. Where one reporter pops up, another soon follows, so it wouldn't be wise to hold the wedding there.'

'What a blow. I'm sorry to hear it. You sound rather down in the dumps.'

'That's because I am,' Lorna admitted. 'We can't get married near where you live and we can't get married in George's church, and I can't think what to do next. I've really rung up to have a good old moan.'

'That's a waste of a telephone call,' Mummy said matter-of-factly, 'and all the more so if there's a queue forming, which there will be in a minute even if there isn't one now. Listen to me, darling. It seems to me perfectly obvious what you have to do.'

'What's that?' Lorna asked.

'When I got married, my mother and grandmother made all the arrangements, and I was hardly asked for my opinion. If you had got married before the war, your wedding would, at least in part, have been a way for your father to show off to his business colleagues. But things have worked out differently for you because of this war. I want you to have whatever kind of wedding you want, Lorna. Yes, it's a shame it can't be up here or in Yorkshire, but you, as a war worker, have another option: the place where you live and work. Lots of girls are doing that these days.'

Lorna caught her breath as her mother's words sank in.

'You love living in Star House, don't you? And you love your job and the girls you work with? Have the wedding there. You've been attending the local church, haven't you?'

'Yes,' Lorna told her. 'I go with Mrs Beaumont and the others.'

'There you are, then,' said Mummy, as if it was self-evident. 'Hang up the telephone and get along there right away – what's it called?'

'St Clement's,' said Lorna, picturing holding her wedding there. It had never occurred to her before but, now that Mummy had suggested it, it seemed obvious.

'Go to St Clement's immediately and call at the rectory or the vicarage or whatever it is and see if your special Saturday is free for a wedding.'

'Mummy, that's a *wonderful* idea. Thank you. Oh, I hope that day is free.'

'Well, what are you waiting for? Cut along there and ask.'

A little more than half an hour later, Lorna was once more heading for the telephone box. The daytime chill had intensified as the evening drew in. She could tell that from the way other pedestrians were hurrying along, warmly wrapped up in thick coats and scarves, with hats pulled down and, in one or two cases, collars pulled up. But Lorna didn't feel the cold. She was too excited.

Would there be a queue for the telephone? She might explode if she couldn't speak to her mother soon and share her good news. Her good news? No, her *wonderful* news.

The telephone box was occupied and there was one person waiting, a young woman who turned as Lorna approached and gave her a polite smile before turning away again as if she needed to watch the speaker closely for fear he might finish his call and walk away without her noticing. Not that there was any chance of someone exiting a telephone box without being seen. The doors were too heavy for that.

The person in the box, a man in a flat cap and thick-soled boots, emerged and strode away, leaving the girl to enter. Lorna crossed her fingers that this wouldn't be a long call.

A few minutes later, it was her turn. With joy fluttering in her every nerve end, she waited to hear her mother's voice.

'Mummy, it's me again.'

'Any news?' her mother asked at once, the anxious tone telling Lorna that she had been on tenterhooks ever since their previous conversation.

'Yes! We've got the church for the fifteenth. Isn't that champion?'

'Darling, it's splendid. Couldn't be better.'

Lorna laughed. It was either laugh or cry, so she laughed. 'I've been to St Clement's so many times, not just to Sunday service, but also to the church hall next door for jumble sales and amateur concerts and talks given by various civil defence bods – and now I'll be going there to make arrangements for my wedding. I knew it was the right choice the moment you suggested it, but it's only just sinking in how perfect it is. Thank you.'

'You must send me the church's address for the invitations,' her mother directed, 'and let me know the name of the local florist too so that Daddy can open an account with them.'

'I hope you'll be able to spare a day to come down so we can choose the flowers together,' said Lorna.

'Of course I will, darling. I want to be as involved as possible.'

Lorna felt a pang of guilt. 'Are you positive that you don't mind that I shan't be getting married from home?'

'Positive,' Mummy replied, sounding it. 'Just because it isn't what I'd always envisaged doesn't mean I'm not going to throw myself into it, so please don't ask that question again.'

'I won't,' Lorna promised.

'What about the reception?' was the next question. 'I know I keep saying it's important that you have what you want, but I must tell you that Daddy isn't going to be best pleased if you opt for the church hall. You know what he's like. He feels that things are only worth having if they cost a lot—yes, Hector, we are talking about you,' she added in an aside.

Lorna smiled. 'Please tell him that, if he's kind enough to pay through the nose, I'd like the Claremont Hotel.'

'Where you and I went just before Christmas – immediately before that appalling Blitz.'

'That's right. It's a special place for George and me,' said Lorna. 'Tell Daddy I'll love him for ever if we can hold our wedding reception there. It would make our day perfect.'

A tiny shiver of delight passed through Lorna as she realised how dear certain places in Manchester had become to her.

'I'll get in touch with them,' said Mummy, 'or your father might like to do it himself. One last thing, for now at least. Is there anyone else you'd like to invite? We still have space on the guest list. I imagine you'd like to have your landlady there. You seem fond of her.'

'I am – very fond,' Lorna confirmed.

'And then you'd have room for two more,' said Mummy. 'Think about it and let me know as soon as you can for the invitations.'

Lorna didn't need to think about it. She instantly knew she would love to invite Louise and Deborah – but they were meant to be opening the depot that day in order to free up Sally for her role in the ceremony. The best thing would be to keep quiet about it for now while she thought it through.

After all, it wasn't as though there would be nothing else to talk about at Star House. Lorna smiled happily as she hurried home, eager to share all her news.

Sally was home from work by this time and Betty had come with her.

'I can't stop long,' Betty explained, 'but I couldn't wait for tomorrow to hear about your wedding plans. Are we all going on a trip to Yorkshire?'

'Come and sit beside the fire and warm up while you tell us,' said Sally. 'It's jolly parky out there.'

That made Lorna laugh. 'I have my own inner glow to keep me warm, thanks all the same.'

'That sounds like there's good news,' said Betty.

'There is,' Lorna confirmed, 'though not the good news you're expecting. Not what I was expecting either, for that matter.'

'Sounds intriguing,' Sally commented, her smile showing she had picked up on Lorna's mood. 'Shall I go and see if Mrs Beaumont can leave the stove for long enough to come and listen?'

'Yes, please,' said Lorna. 'Where are the others?'

'Louise is at work,' said Sally, 'and Deborah went upstairs a few minutes ago. Should I give her a shout?'

'Do,' said Lorna.

Mrs Beaumont and Deborah joined them, and everyone sat gazing expectantly at Lorna. She looked around at them, savouring the moment.

'There's so much to say that I'm not sure where to start.'

'Tell us the story in order,' Deborah suggested, eagerness

shining in her bright-blue eyes. 'First of all, did Lady Broughton say yes? I assume she must have done, or you wouldn't look all excited.'

'She would have been only too delighted for us to hold the wedding there,' Lorna began.

Mrs Beaumont frowned. 'Oh dear. "Would have"? That doesn't sound good.'

'A newspaper reporter was hanging around making a pest of himself,' Lorna answered, 'so it's for the best if we steer clear.'

The others exclaimed in disappointment and frustration.

'No – wait,' said Lorna. 'This has a happy ending. It's all sorted out. I've found a church for us.'

'Where?' Sally asked. 'Where else is there?'

'Five minutes from here,' Lorna announced. 'St Clement's.' Hardly allowing any time for a very different set of exclamations, she went on joyfully, 'It was my mother's idea, and she was quite right. I live here, I work here, so why not get married here?'

'Put that way, it sounds perfect,' said Mrs Beaumont, and the girls chimed in with their agreement.

'So, it's full steam ahead for the fifteenth,' said Deborah. 'I'm thrilled for you.'

'We all are,' Betty declared. She stood up. 'I'm sorry to have to break things up, but I need to get home to do Samuel's tea.'

'Of course,' said Lorna. 'Thanks for being here to share my news.'

'My pleasure,' Betty said before she hurried on her way.

'And I have to get back to the kitchen,' said Mrs Beaumont. 'We've got macaroni cheese this evening.'

Deborah disappeared back upstairs, leaving Lorna and Sally on their own.

'I'm glad we've got a minute to ourselves,' said Lorna. 'I've had an idea and need to know what you think of it.'

'There you go again, being intriguing,' Sally replied, smiling.

'With holding the wedding here,' said Lorna, 'I'm going to invite Mrs Beaumont.'

Sally beamed. 'She'll love that.'

'And I'd also like Louise and Deborah to be there.'

'That's a kind thought,' said Sally. 'They'll be pleased as Punch.' Then she remembered. 'Oh, but—'

'This is why I wanted to talk to you,' Lorna said quickly. 'For them to come to the wedding and the reception, we need someone else to open the depot for us. I wondered about asking Mrs Lockwood.'

Sally looked dismayed.

'Listen,' said Lorna. 'I know she's made things hard for you in the past, but your Town Hall bosses took away her authority over the depot and placed you in charge. That isn't going to change just because she does this favour.'

'You haven't already asked her, have you?'

'Of course not. I wouldn't go behind your back,' said Lorna. 'If anybody asks her, it has to be you because you're the depot manager. I'm not going to force the issue if you're unhappy about it,' she added. 'That's why I wanted to speak to you in private. If you feel strongly about not asking Mrs Lockwood, then I respect that – and understand it. Deborah and Louise will never know this subject ever came up.'

Sally gave a sigh, but it wasn't a sorrowful or resigned one. Lorna hadn't realised that sighs could sound determined but, evidently, they could.

'I wouldn't dream of standing in the way of Deborah and Louise attending your wedding,' Sally said in her usual sensible manner. 'If this will enable them to do it, then let's go and ask Mrs Lockwood if she'll help out.'

. . .

Lorna and Sally went round to Mrs Lockwood's house the following evening straight after closing the depot. Lorna knew where the Lockwoods lived because she had been their lodger when she had first come to Manchester. They lived in a spacious semi-detached Victorian villa on Edge Lane, with a bay-window beside the front door and another bay-window up above.

Mrs Jenks answered the door. She was the daily help, a middle-aged woman with scraped-back hair. She was a no-nonsense type, but she had shown kindness and understanding when Lorna had suffered a wobbly moment on her very first day here. Lorna was pleased to see her again.

'Evening, Mrs Jenks,' she said. 'Is Mrs Lockwood at home? We need to see her. I promise not to hold up the evening meal.'

'It's nice to see you again, miss,' said Mrs Jenks. She stood aside to permit them to enter the hall. 'I'll tell Madam you're here.'

The hall boasted textured wallpaper, a table on which the dinner-gong stood and a barometer on the wall. Lorna made a point of watching Sally's face as she spotted the pair of umbrella stands from which poked out, as well as just one solitary umbrella, a variety of long sturdy sticks and gardening implements.

'If Jerry is misguided enough to come marching up Edge Lane,' Lorna whispered, 'that's how Mr and Mrs Lockwood intend to engage the enemy.'

'Good for them,' Sally whispered back.

'That's what I thought when I first came here,' Lorna answered.

'In you come,' said Mrs Jenks from the sitting room doorway.

They went in. Mrs Lockwood had risen to greet them. She was dressed in a tweed skirt and thick, cable-knit cardigan that was buttoned to the throat and over the collar of which she wore her pearls. Lorna had seen her out of WVS uniform many times, but presumably Sally hadn't before.

'Good evening, Mrs Henshaw, Miss *West*-Sadler.'

There was a bit of an edge to that 'West'. When Lorna had lived here, her real name had been a secret, and she had been known as plain Miss Sadler. The Lockwoods had been duped along with everyone else. Now that Lorna had reappeared in her house, Mrs Lockwood clearly wasn't above making a little dig.

'Please sit down,' she added in the same sort of tone a headmistress might use, and the girls sat side by side on the sofa.

'Please excuse us for barging in like this,' Lorna said in her brightest voice as if this was a social call. 'I know how busy you are with all your commitments.'

'Are you attempting to butter me up?' Mrs Lockwood enquired.

'Not at all,' Lorna replied smoothly. 'I know you'd never fall for such a thing. I'm simply accompanying Mrs Henshaw, who has something to ask you.'

'Indeed?' Mrs Lockwood raised her eyebrows expectantly in Sally's direction.

Sally straightened her shoulders. 'Yes. I wonder if you would open the depot for me on the fifteenth. It's a Saturday.'

'You are asking *me* to open the depot?'

'Yes, please, and to man it for the day.' To her credit, Sally sounded completely impartial and businesslike.

Lorna judged this to be the moment for her to jump in. 'It's to help me out, really, Mrs Lockwood. The fifteenth is my wedding day and I'll be getting married here in Chorlton, where the press won't find me.'

'Ah yes, the press,' Mrs Lockwood remarked. 'I've seen what they've been calling you. Most distasteful.'

'You see, I'd like both Mrs Henshaw and Mrs Atkinson to

be my matrons of honour, and that means...' Lorna smiled winningly.

'There's nobody else to open the depot,' Mrs Lockwood finished. A shrewd look came into her grey eyes.

'As the WVS salvage officer,' said Sally in the same formal voice, asserting herself in a quiet yet authoritative way, 'you are the obvious person to ask.' They had agreed that it would be simpler to leave Deborah and Louise out of the explanation.

'That's very true,' Mrs Lockwood agreed. 'I'm pleased to hear you acknowledge it, Mrs Henshaw, and I shall be pleased to assist you in this matter.'

CHAPTER TWENTY-THREE

The final days before the wedding flew by. It was difficult for Lorna to keep her mind on the job when she was at the depot.

'There's still so much to do for the wedding that I don't know how I'm going to fit work in,' she declared, not entirely joking.

'You could ask Sally for a day or a couple of days off,' Betty suggested, glancing at Sally.

'You could,' Sally replied, deadpan, 'but not unless you're prepared to curtail your honeymoon. I'll tell you what you could do. Finish early a couple of times.'

'Bunk off, you mean?' Lorna asked.

Sally shrugged. 'If you or Betty needed to go to the dentist or the doctor, leaving early wouldn't be a problem. You wouldn't have any leave docked for it.'

'Are you sure?' Lorna asked. 'You've bent enough rules for me already – and you've agreed to let your arch-enemy take over your beloved depot for the day.'

'I must be going soft,' Sally said with a grin.

Betty gave Lorna a nudge. 'Quick! Say yes before she

changes her mind. You know what a slave-driver she can be when she gets going.'

'Actually, it would be a big help if I could slope off early,' Lorna admitted. 'My mother arrives this afternoon for a couple of days. I thought we'd have to dash to the florist's in my dinner break, but now we can take more time over it. And I can change the evening appointment at the Claremont so we can go at the end of the afternoon to sort out the details for the reception. But I'll still need an after-hours appointment at Mademoiselle Antoinette's for the final fitting so you two can come as well.' She gave Sally a hug. 'Thanks for everything. You've been an absolute brick.'

'Especially about letting Mrs Lockwood open the depot,' Betty added.

'It's worth it so that Deborah and Louise can come to the wedding,' said Sally.

'They're tickled pink,' said Lorna.

The inclusion of the two girls and Mrs Beaumont on the guest list had certainly increased the sense of excitement that pervaded Star House, making Lorna even more certain that inviting them had been the right thing to do.

'I can't wait to see Mummy again,' she said. 'If I leave here early, I can meet her off the train and go with her to the Claremont. She's staying there anyway. Daddy has already booked a section of the dining room for the reception, as well as the ballroom. Mr Lever, the manager of the Claremont, is going to get a dance band for us. In fact, he might already have booked one.'

'What's left for you and your mother to do?' Sally asked.

'The menu, for a start; a list of tunes for the band. I don't know if they'll have a singer, but that will make a difference to what they play. Flowers. Things like that.'

'I'll want to hear every single detail tomorrow,' said Betty. 'And I want the details to have details.'

'You won't be able to stop me talking about it,' joked Lorna.

Excitement kept bubbling up inside her on and off all day until at last it was time for her to get changed and head off to town. She met her mother at Victoria station. To be sure of not missing her, she stood beside the ticket collector at the entrance to the platform.

'Lorna, I wasn't expecting you to be here,' said Mummy.

'I'm on wedding business,' Lorna replied, kissing her. 'Sally let me slip out early.'

Soon, they were at the Claremont, where her mother's suitcase was taken up to her room for her and she freshened up.

'I hope Mr Lever is going to be available,' Lorna said, suddenly feeling uncertain. 'We weren't meant to be seeing him this afternoon.'

'With the amount of money your father is spending,' Mummy said wryly, 'I'm sure he'll make himself available.'

He did, too, and with such aplomb that it was impossible to say if it was in any degree inconvenient for him.

'Chef has suggested the following menu choices, if you would like to select from them,' he said, offering the list.

'Creamed salmon?' Mummy asked, looking at the suggestions.

'The salmon is tinned,' said Mr Lever. 'Served with a risotto of rice and vegetables.'

'What are "*sausages en surprise*"?' Lorna asked.

'Grilled sausages, skinned, then gilded with beaten egg and baked. Chef recommends serving them with sweetcorn pudding, courtesy of the food shipment from our American friends. The tinned sweetcorn is mixed with egg and mock cream, then baked.'

Mummy set the lists aside. 'We'll think about these ideas after this meeting.'

'Of course, Mrs West-Sadler. I understand you are providing your own wedding cake.'

'Cakes, plural,' said Mummy. 'The real one and the cardboard one.'

'We shall be happy to provide a suitable table to show off the cardboard cake.'

'Make sure it's a substantial one,' quipped Lorna. 'Four tiers.'

'Indeed?' Mr Lever was too professional to react with anything more than the politest of smiles. 'That will add to the festivities.'

'Now then, can we talk about the band and the decorations for the ballroom?' asked Mummy.

'We have an archway of red, white and blue rosettes for the entrance to the ballroom.'

'Very appropriate,' said Mummy.

'We have a set of silver and white table ornaments that we usually bring out for the dining room at Christmas. They would make attractive decorations for the tables in the ballroom.'

'Have you any bunting?' Lorna asked. 'Patriotic bunting.'

'We have bunting of all the flags of the Empire, Miss West-Sadler.'

'I'd like to have that, please,' said Lorna, looking at her mother for approval. 'That for the walls, and the silver and white pieces for the tables.'

'And the flowers?' asked Mr Lever, making a note in a black notebook.

'We're meeting with my daughter's local florist tomorrow,' said Mummy, 'so will you please wait until you hear from her?'

'Naturally. I have secured the services of a dance band for you, and here is the list of tunes they have suggested. The bandleader can act as the master of ceremonies if required. And they work with a rather good singer, if you would like a vocalist.'

While her mother and Mr Lever talked, Lorna thought about all the arrangements. Her parents were going to such a lot of trouble for her. Expense too – not that that would matter to

Daddy. The more he spent, the better, as far as he was concerned. But for her to have all of this at a time of shortages suddenly brought to mind all the nasty things the judge had said about her last year, about how she had no business bringing George to court at a time of national crisis.

'I regard Miss West-Sadler's breach-of-promise case as flippant, frivolous and profoundly disrespectful to every right-minded and patriotic person who takes the war seriously. Case dismissed.'

Those had been the judge's final words and, by crikey, how the newspapers had lapped them up. They had made her suffer ever since.

Now she and George were going to have a lovely, private wedding, followed by a meal that the clever chef would turn into something very special. After that there would be the dance and the 'cutting' of the four-tier cake for the photographer. The dance was only going to be a teatime thing, but most girls, if they had a dance at all, had it in the church hall with a gramophone or a piano, and she was going to have her own band in one of the best ballrooms Manchester had to offer, complete with pretty decorations and bunting.

All at once, it was too much.

But not if…

Lorna sat forward. 'Mr Lever, is there time to organise another dance in the evening after the reception? A fundraising dance. The ballroom will already be decorated and I'm sure my father will be happy to pay for the band to stay on.' She looked at her mother. 'Please say you agree, Mummy. I'm so very lucky to have all this organised for me and I appreciate it no end. I want others to benefit from it too. I want the war effort to benefit. I bet you anything the local WVS would be happy to muck in and have a fundraiser that night after the wedding reception and dance. Wouldn't that be the best possible end to the day?'

. . .

The following afternoon in the depot, Lorna left her mother with Sally and Betty while she dashed upstairs to get changed. She deliberately hadn't said anything to her chums about the proposed evening dance to raise money; she was leaving that to Mummy. Once she was in her own clothes she went back downstairs, to receive the exclamations of delight from Sally and Betty.

'That's such a generous thing to do,' said Sally.

'It's easy to be generous when you're spending someone else's money,' Lorna said lightly.

'My husband was only too pleased when I told him last night on the telephone,' Mummy confirmed to the two girls. 'It makes perfect sense when you think about it. The ballroom will already be decorated, and the band will be on the premises, so why not have an evening occasion as well?'

'Our wedding guests can stay on for the evening bash if they want to,' Lorna added. She looked at her mother. 'Shall we make tracks?'

'Yes. I'm looking forward to this,' said Mummy. 'I'll enjoy helping you choose the flowers.'

After saying their farewells, they set off. Both of them were warmly wrapped against the cold, Lorna in her plum-coloured coat with wide lapels and deep turned-back cuffs with topstitching, and her mother in a wool overcoat with a wide fur collar. They walked up to Wilbraham Road, where the florist, Miss Rodgers, was expecting them.

'Some flowers will be easier to supply than others,' she told them. 'Flowers that are out of season are still to be had, but not with the same guarantee of availability that I could have offered you before the war.'

'I'd prefer something that's in season, anyway,' said Lorna, 'though I imagine that's not very much in November.'

Miss Rodgers smiled. 'There are chrysanthemums in a variety of colours and with a choice of small or larger flowerheads. Or you may prefer something with berries, such as wintersweet, which has clusters of red berries but without the prickles you get with holly.'

Lorna looked at her mother. 'What would you say to greenery and berries rather than flowers?'

'I'd be concerned about a berry getting squashed and leaving a stain on your dress,' said her mother.

'Then what about myrtle?' suggested Miss Rodgers. 'Instead of berries, you'd have a mist of white flowers with dainty tufts on them that would give an unusual hazy effect.'

'Oh, I like the sound of that,' Lorna said at once. 'It sounds so pretty.'

Miss Rodgers smiled at her. 'It is. It's also completely in keeping with the season. Myrtle has dark-green leaves, and might I suggest adding some stems of eucalyptus? The leaves are a subtle rather bluey-grey-green that will add a note of interest.' In answer to Mummy's nod of approval, she added, 'I have to admit I stole the idea from a friend who is a florist over to the north of Manchester. Mrs Hanberger always suggests eucalyptus as the finishing touch for the winter bouquet.'

'And now you do too,' Lorna added, smiling in return. 'Please say thank you to her for me next time you see her.'

'I'll do that,' Miss Rodgers replied. 'She'll be delighted.'

They went on to discuss and count buttonholes for the men and corsages for the ladies.

'The Claremont will be getting in touch with you to sort out floral decorations,' Mummy told Miss Rodgers.

'I'll look forward to it,' the florist said.

'And now we really ought to be going,' said Mummy. 'We have another appointment later on for the final dress fitting.'

'It's a very exciting time,' said Miss Rodgers. 'I wish you well, Miss West-Sadler.'

'Thank you,' Lorna said, shaking her hand.

She and her mother walked to Star House. Mrs Beaumont had invited Mummy to join the girls for tea.

'I'm glad the flowers have been chosen,' Lorna said with a happy little sigh. 'Now there's just the dress to make sure of.'

'I'm sure Mademoiselle Antoinette's will have created perfection itself,' said her mother. 'It's what they're famous for, and have been for years.'

'The whole day is going to be exactly what I'd hoped for,' said Lorna. 'Well, as long as the wedding isn't interrupted by an air raid.'

'Have you had many raids recently?' Mummy asked, linking arms with her.

'Actually, no, since you mention it. We had a couple right at the start of the month, but none since then. And the frequency of the raids was lessening before that. The last time we had a really bad one was round about the middle of October, when Oldham was targeted. I don't recall exactly how many fatalities there were, but it was closer to thirty than twenty; and quite a few people were seriously injured as well.'

'We'll have to hope that your wedding day escapes unscathed,' said Mummy.

They arrived back at Star House and Mummy produced a gift of a tub of Bournville, a jar of Marmite and a packet of Foster Clark's Fruit Jelly Crystals for Mrs Beaumont, and a selection of film magazines for the girls. Then they all sat down to a meal of tasty vegetable ragout with jacket potatoes and winter cabbage, followed by jam pudding.

'I shall have to watch how much I eat,' Lorna joked, 'or I might not fit into my dress!'

Sally and Betty had asked her a day or two ago if she wanted to attend the final fitting with just her mother, but she had asked them both to come along to share the excitement.

'And do please ask Mrs Kendall as well,' Lorna had urged

Betty. 'I wouldn't have had the gorgeous material if she hadn't been so generous, and I'd like her to be there too.'

Her mother ordered a pair of taxis and the five of them travelled in comfort to St Ann's Square. Mummy took Mrs Kendall's arm to assist her in making her way to Caroline Street. Presently, they were all inside the famous salon.

'If you will kindly accompany me, Miss West-Sadler,' said Miss Sheridan in her well-modulated voice, 'you can change into your wedding dress and then come back and show your guests. While they wait, your matrons of honour and Mrs Kendall may like to try on the stoles we have made for them.'

Lorna allowed herself to be spirited away.

'To all intents and purposes, your wedding gown is finished,' Miss Sheridan told her, 'but we need this final fitting before the seams are finalised.'

Lorna's pulse skittered as she undressed. As she was helped into her dress, she felt all trembly. Three women fluttered around her, fastening buttons and settling the skirt. Then they stepped away from her. Their heads were tilted sideways, making them look critical, but they were also smiling.

'What do you think?' Miss Sheridan asked.

Lorna gazed at her reflection in the mirror. There were other mirrors to the sides and behind her so she could see herself from all angles. She hardly knew which reflection to examine first.

The dress was everything she had hoped for – more than she'd hoped for. The beautiful fabric skimmed her figure, while the skirt had a subtle flare, with more fabric behind than in front so that she had a train. The gold threads twinkled delicately in the cream satin, and the promised gathers at the sides of the bodice gave an illusion of shape that she didn't really possess.

Miss Sheridan gave her a hanky, which made Lorna realise she had tears on her cheeks.

'It's beautiful,' she whispered. 'Thank you so much.'

'Come and stand over here near the back of the room,' said Miss Sheridan, 'and walk towards the mirror. This is what you'll look like on the day – though, of course, you'll have your veil and bouquet as well then.'

Lorna did as she was told, her breath catching in her throat as she watched herself.

'Would you care to show your guests?' Miss Sheridan asked.

They returned to where the others were sitting waiting. Miss Sheridan got her to stand back from the door, then opened it with a flourish so she could make a grand entrance. Her mother, Sally and Betty jumped to their feet. Sally and Betty had both removed their coats and wore the velvet-lined stoles that matched the wedding dress. Mrs Kendall wore her stole round the shoulders of her coat.

'Lorna!' Mummy exclaimed and then seemed lost for words.

'Will I do?' Lorna asked, feeling more tears rising. She spent a short while lapping up all the comments and compliments Sally and Betty showered on her, then she took Mrs Kendall's hands gently in hers. 'Thank you for letting me have this divine material. I know seeing me like this must bring back lots of memories and sorrow for you. It was brave of you to pass on the fabric to another bride.'

Mrs Kendall looked up at her. 'My dear, it wasn't brave at all. It was more than time. Nothing will ever bring Tilly back and, yes, it hurts a little to see another girl in her special fabric – but it does my heart good too. You can pay me back by having a long and happy marriage.'

'I can promise you that,' said Lorna.

CHAPTER TWENTY-FOUR
SATURDAY, 15 NOVEMBER

'Lorna, you *can't!*' Deborah exclaimed. 'The groom isn't allowed to see the bride before the wedding. It's bad luck.'

Lorna paused in the act of putting on her plum-coloured wool coat. She looked at the faces of the other Star House billetees and Betty. They were all completely taken aback.

'I think George and I have already used up our quota of bad luck,' she said. 'He was due to arrive in Manchester last night and I want to see him. I need to see him. It feels as if we've been apart for ever. If the first time I see him is when I enter the church and he turns round to look at me, I'll be so overwhelmed that in all probability I'll burst into tears and howl the place down, which wouldn't be the most auspicious start to the wedding.'

'Couldn't you just telephone him at the Claremont?' Sally suggested.

'No,' Lorna answered firmly. 'I want to *see* him. The taxi is waiting outside. I'll be back in plenty of time, I promise.' As an afterthought she said, 'My mother will be here soon. Look after her for me.'

She almost skipped out of the house and down the path.

She smiled all the way to the Claremont, her heart pitter-pattering in excitement. George had no idea she was on her way to see him. Her smile widened. It wouldn't be the first time she had turned up unexpectedly at the Claremont.

In the handsome foyer, she asked the receptionist to inform Mr George Broughton that he had a visitor.

The receptionist reached for the in-house telephone. 'What name should I give?'

'Just say it's a visitor.'

A couple of minutes later, George appeared on the curving staircase. Lorna saw him before he saw her and she took a moment to drink in the sight of his lean good looks, her heart filling with gratitude that he had come back to her.

His eyes met hers and his face lit up. Lorna hurried across the foyer and into his arms. They held one another tightly until George, clasping her hand to him as if he never wanted to let it go, led her to one of the discreet little alcoves on the far side of the foyer.

A shimmer of delight passed through her as he helped her off with her coat. They sat down and gazed at one another.

'I'm sure my mother would insist that we shouldn't see one another before the wedding,' said George, 'but right now I can't say I care about that particular tradition.' He leaned forward to brush her mouth with a kiss. 'I've missed you so very much.'

'I've missed you too. It's such a relief that you've come home safely. I can't begin to imagine what the Atlantic crossings were like.'

'There were some hairy moments, I don't mind admitting,' George told her seriously. 'I already admired the men of the merchant navy and the Royal Navy, but I respect them even more now.'

'Am I allowed to ask if whatever task took you to America was a success?'

'It will be some time before the visit bears fruit, if indeed it does,' said George. 'But that's enough of that. This is our wedding day – at last. I gather from my parents that things haven't gone entirely smoothly this past two weeks.'

'Who cares?' Lorna answered breezily. 'It's all arranged now, which is the only thing that matters.'

'Were your parents disappointed not to be able to hold the wedding in Lancaster?'

'Yes, they were,' said Lorna, 'but they understood why it was important to have it on this particular date. Plenty of war workers are getting married near to where they're billeted, so it's not as though you and I are doing anything odd. Chorlton is a special place for me now.'

'For me as well,' said George, 'because it's the place that has kept you safe from the newspaper reporters. After everything they've put you through, that's something to be grateful for.'

Lorna sat back in her chair and gazed at him. 'You're here. You're really here and we're together. I feel as if I've waited for this for a lifetime.'

'I feel the same.'

'You don't mind that I organised the wedding for the moment you got back?' Lorna asked.

George laughed as he shook his head. 'Not in the slightest. It's the best way I can think of to welcome me home.'

'I had to come here and see you this morning,' Lorna added. 'I couldn't wait another moment.'

'I'm glad you did. I've had a quick look in the ballroom and they're busy preparing it.'

Lorna was about to say she'd love to see what was going on, but she didn't really have the time. What time she did have, she wanted to spend here with George in private.

'I'm trying to concentrate on every single moment,' she said, 'so I remember the whole day in glorious detail. Not just the wedding and the reception but getting ready too, and the anticipation.'

George smiled at her. 'Speaking of getting ready...'

'Yes, I really should be getting back, or they'll wonder what's become of me. Mummy will send out a search party to find me.'

'We'd better say our goodbyes, then,' said George.

An important detail occurred to Lorna. 'One last thing.' She put on a serious voice. 'I had to sort out the special licence myself, so you'd better pay me back. If you want to marry me, George Broughton, you can jolly well pay for the privilege.'

'It will be the greatest pleasure imaginable,' George said with a smile.

'Oh, Lorna, you look *beautiful*,' her mother whispered. 'I think I might cry.'

Lorna gazed at her reflection in the full-length mirror Mrs Beaumont had provided for her bedroom on this most special of days. The gown made by the expert seamstresses at Mademoiselle Antoinette's was a dream. With it, Lorna wore her mother's veil, which had previously been worn by her granny and both her great-aunts, and provided a sense of family and continuity.

'Look at her,' Betty said sentimentally. 'She can't tear her eyes away from her reflection.'

Lorna glanced at her through the mirror. 'Can you blame me?'

Mummy sent the other girls downstairs so that Lorna could make a grand entrance for her father's benefit.

'By the stars, Lorna,' he said, his voice gruff with emotion, 'you look like a queen.'

'Not a queen,' she replied with a smile. 'Just a future baronet's lady.'

After her mother, Mrs Beaumont and the bridesmaids were ferried off to St Clement's, Lorna and her father were left in

Star House to wait their own turn. It was a chilly but dry and brilliantly clear day.

'I'm glad you sent me here to do my war work,' said Lorna.

'You weren't pleased with me at the time,' Daddy reminded her.

Lorna smiled. 'No, I wasn't. I thought you'd send me to a fancy hotel in the West Country, but I'm glad you didn't. This has been the making of me – and it's reunited me with George.' She looked frankly at her father. 'You must be pleased about that.'

'Because of the title? Well, I shan't deny it,' he replied with equal frankness. 'But I'll tell you this, Lorna. George is a good man and he's the right man for you. That's something that has been brought home to me since the two of you started things off again with one another, and I'll be happy to hand you into his care.'

Lorna closed her eyes for a moment in pure gratitude before she kissed his cheek. 'Thank you, Daddy. That means everything to me.'

Her father glanced out of the front window. 'There's the motor.' He offered her his arm. 'Let's go and get you married.'

Lorna's heart pitter-pattered with joy all the way to St Clement's. When the motor pulled up outside the church, Sally and Betty came hurrying to greet her. Sally held the bridal bouquet while Daddy helped her from the vehicle.

Together, the four of them walked up the path to the church porch, where Daddy stood to one side as Betty and Sally arranged Lorna's train and fluffed out her veil while the organ played softly inside.

'You look beautiful,' Sally whispered.

'So do you,' Lorna said, 'and so do you, Betty.'

Sally laughed. 'We all look beautiful, so that's a good start.'

Lorna looked admiringly at her two matrons of honour. Sally was dressed in the forget-me-not-blue costume that had been both her wedding dress and the outfit she had worn at Easter as Betty's attendant. Betty wore the royal-blue dress Lorna had given her. Both girls were in the lovely stoles made at Mademoiselle Antoinette's, with the satin on show and the lining made of cream velvet. They carried bouquets that were smaller versions of Lorna's.

But it wasn't just how they looked that Lorna was aware of. She also felt deep appreciation for the friendship she shared with them, and all the kindness, understanding and support she had received. It was odd now to think that she'd hadn't been keen on them when she'd first met them. Now, they weren't just her friends. They were friends she would have for the rest of her life.

An RAF officer, who was one of the guests on George's side, popped his head round the door.

'Looking utterly enchanting, if I may make so bold,' he said to Lorna. 'All set?'

Sally and Betty were about to lower Lorna's veil over her face when Daddy stepped forward.

'That's my job,' he said in a voice that held a croak of emotion.

For half a second, Lorna wondered if she should wave him away and ask the girls to do it, for fear of Daddy making a hash of it. Then she realised that it didn't matter if he didn't arrange her veil to perfection. What mattered was that he wanted to perform this final service for her before he officially gave her into George's keeping for the rest of her life. If she walked up the aisle looking slightly skew-whiff, it really wouldn't matter.

'Skew-whiff', however, clearly wasn't a word that was in Sally and Betty's vocabulary. They each made a deft change to the veil and Lorna knew that, while Daddy had had the satisfaction of preparing her to walk down the aisle, she would do so looking as perfect as Mummy could possibly wish.

'Ready?' the RAF officer enquired as Sally and Betty took their places behind Lorna.

'Ready,' Daddy replied with a crisp nod.

He offered his arm to Lorna, giving her a special smile. The organist ceased playing and, in front of Lorna and her father, the double doors opened, causing Lorna's heart to leap into her throat. The organist played the introduction to 'Here Comes the Bride' and the guests all rose to their feet.

Daddy gave the hand tucked in the crook of his arm a little squeeze and the two of them began their walk down the aisle. Lorna had intended to look right and left, smiling at her guests, but the instant George, standing at the front, turned round and looked at her, she couldn't take her eyes off him, her handsome husband-to-be. Even from here, and with her veil creating a misty soft focus, she could see the intense expression in his eyes and the way his sharp-cheekboned, rather stern face softened with a look of pure love as he returned her gaze.

It was a good thing she was linked with Daddy and he was proceeding at a steady pace. Otherwise, Lorna might have dashed straight for the altar.

When she reached George, she was trembling with happiness and excitement. Her father lifted her veil and murmured, 'My darling girl.' Lorna handed her bouquet to Betty and turned to her almost-husband, feeling she could drown in his look of adoration.

She listened carefully as the vicar introduced the occasion. When she and George were called upon to recite their vows, Lorna injected sincerity and love into the familiar words, wanting George to be in no doubt that she meant them with all her heart.

When the time came for the exchanging of rings, Lorna's eyes filled with tears as George slid the gold band onto her finger. Then she placed his ring on his finger. Plenty of men didn't see the need for a wedding ring, but George wasn't one of them. He had said, 'I want the world to know I'm married to you.'

The vicar concluded the service, pronouncing them man and wife before telling George, 'You may kiss the bride.'

Stepping closer, George placed his hands at her waist and Lorna put hers on his arms. He bent his head to cover her mouth with his. As every single one of her nerve ends quivered with joy, Lorna was vaguely aware of a deep, collective sigh of satisfaction from all their guests and well-wishers.

George lifted his mouth from hers and murmured, 'It's time to sign the register, Mrs Broughton.'

A LETTER FROM SUSANNA

Dear Reader,

I want to say a huge thank-you for choosing to read *A Wedding for the Home Front Girls*. If you did enjoy it, and want to keep up to date with all my latest releases, just sign up at the following link. Your email address will never be shared and you can unsubscribe at any time.

www.bookouture.com/susanna-bavin

Writing this wedding story has brought back happy memories of weddings I have attended. The first one I went to was when my cousin Elizabeth married Ray. I remember six of us cramming into Auntie Colette's car for the journey – Colette, Gran, my parents, my brother and me. At the end of the day, Gran was deeply touched when Elizabeth presented her with her wedding bouquet. Years later, I gave mine to Auntie Colette.

I'd also like to use this letter to say a big hello to all my readers on Kindle Unlimited. It's wonderful to know that the Home Front Girls series is so popular. Another title of mine that appears on KU is *The Deserter's Daughter*, a standalone saga set in the 1920s, not long after the end of the First World War. In it, a secret is revealed and the lives of gentle Carrie and her snooty half-sister Evadne are changed for ever. I hope you like the sound of it and will choose to read it.

If you enjoyed *A Wedding for the Home Front Girls*, I would be very grateful if you could write a review. If you have reviewed previous titles in this series – thank you! I always love to hear what my readers think, and it makes such a difference helping new readers to discover one of my books for the first time.

I love hearing from my readers – you can get in touch through social media or my website.

Much love

Susanna xx

www.susannabavin.co.uk

facebook.com/MaisieThomasAuthor
x.com/SusannaBavin

ACKNOWLEDGEMENTS

Many thanks to my new editor, Jess Whitlum-Cooper. It was a pleasure to work on this book with you, Jess. Here's to the next one! Thanks also to my agent, Camilla Shestopal, for all her support.

I'm grateful to the team at Bookouture, who work hard to promote my books and who have built up a large audience for them on Kindle Unlimited.

Thanks to Jen Gilroy and Jane Cable, who were there behind the scenes when I needed them; to Sue Hanberger, my eucalyptus lady; and to all the reviewers and book bloggers who have supported my Home Front Girls series from the start, including Karen Mace, Julie Barham, Nicola Smith, Zoe Morton, Yvonne Gill, Beverley Hopper, Meena Kumari and Helen Hopwood.

PUBLISHING TEAM

Turning a manuscript into a book requires the efforts of many people. The publishing team at Bookouture would like to acknowledge everyone who contributed to this publication.

Commercial
Lauren Morrissette
Hannah Richmond
Imogen Allport

Contracts
Peta Nightingale

Cover design
Nick Castle

Data and analysis
Mark Alder
Mohamed Bussuri

Editorial
Jess Whitlum-Cooper
Imogen Allport

Copyeditor
Jacqui Lewis

Proofreader
Anne O'Brien

Marketing
Alex Crow
Melanie Price
Occy Carr
Cíara Rosney
Martyna Młynarska

Operations and distribution
Marina Valles
Stephanie Straub
Joe Morris

Production
Hannah Snetsinger
Mandy Kullar
Ria Clare
Nadia Michael

Publicity
Kim Nash
Noelle Holten
Jess Readett
Sarah Hardy

www.ingramcontent.com/pod-product-compliance
Ingram Content Group UK Ltd.
Pitfield, Milton Keynes, MK11 3LW, UK
UKHW031613230425
5599UKWH00003B/362